REBUILDING Joy

《 ·—— 》

Renovations ☀ 2

REGINA RUDD MERRICK

REBUILDING JOY

ISBN 978-1-7350223-1-4

Cover design by Roseanna White Designs

Formatting by The Mosaic Collection

WELCOME TO MOSAIC

We are sisters, a beautiful mosaic united by the love of God through the blood of Christ.

Each month The Mosaic Collection releases one faith-based novel or anthology exploring our theme, Family by His Design, and sharing stories that feature diverse, God-designed families. All are contemporary stories ranging from mystery and women's fiction to comedic and literary fiction. We hope you'll join our Mosaic family as we explore together what truly defines a family.

If you're like us, loneliness and suffering have touched your life in ways you never imagined; but Dear One, while you may feel alone in your suffering—whatever it is—you are never alone!

Subscribe to *Grace & Glory*, the official newsletter of The Mosaic Collection, to receive monthly encouragement from Mosaic authors, as well as timely updates about events, new releases, and giveaways.

Learn more about The Mosaic Collection at www.mosaiccollectionbooks.com and join our Reader Community, too, at www.facebook.com/groups/TheMosaicCollection

THE MOSAIC COLLECTION

Learn more at www.mosaiccollectionbooks.com/mosaic-books

*To my daughters, Ellen Merrick and Emily Merrick-Jay.
You've brought me joy unmeasured, and joy is a decision we
have to make every day, because it's only through Jesus that we
can experience true, everlasting joy.*

Count it all joy, my brothers, when you meet trials of various kinds, for you know that the testing of your faith produces steadfastness. And let steadfastness have its full effect, that you may be perfect and complete, lacking in nothing.
James 1: 2-4 (ESV)

1

MAY

The sounds of the café receded into the background as a tide of feelings washed over her.

I can do this.

Darcy Emerson Sloan closed her eyes and forced the knot in her chest to subside. Tears were near the surface, but she refused to let her mom know how inadequate she felt to take on the responsibility of the café.

Especially today.

By herself.

Alone.

As the owner-manager.

Mom deserved a break. She'd opened the café when Dad died, using his life insurance money to build a business that made her a successful businesswoman. She and Darcy would much rather have had Dad, but it had been a good life for them.

And now it was Darcy's turn to be in charge.

When Mom married Steve Reno a year ago, after being a widow for fifteen years, she had started talking to Darcy about the possibility of her taking over the business. She'd been proud of the work her daughter had done while she and Steve were on their extended honeymoon trip to Alaska. It was a gift—a gift from her Mom and her late father. For her, she reasoned, the café had seen her through tough times and taken her mind off the indescribable pain of losing a husband unexpectedly.

But I'm not Mom.

"Sweetie?" Roxy Reno, her mom, touched Darcy's arm. "Are you okay?"

She opened her eyes and smiled, coming back to the present. It was a little wobbly, she was sure, but it was there.

I always smile.

"I'm okay, Mom." No one had to know that under the guise of "I'm good, how 'bout you?" Darcy was hurting. That her feelings of inadequacy were rooted deep, through no fault of anyone. It was just her and the stuff life had thrown at her. "Biscuits are in the oven, bacon is cooking, and eggs are broken and ready."

Mom looked at her closely, realization and sadness dawning on her face. "Oh, Darcy. I'm so sorry."

Darcy had trouble meeting her eyes, and it would be time to open the café any minute now. She couldn't go out there and wait on people with tears running down her face, but she wanted to. "About what?" She lifted her chin defiantly, continuing to roll silverware into paper napkins. It was a nice, mindless task.

"I know what today is." Mom clutched her arm, forcing her to glance up. "Look at me, sweetie."

"It's fine, Mom. I'll be okay." She gave a short burst of

laughter. Bitterness came through. "Stewing about it won't change a thing, will it?"

Four years. Four years since the sergeant in a Class A uniform had knocked at her door with news no Army wife wanted to hear. When the dreaded news came that Justin wasn't coming back, she was seven months pregnant. A product of Justin's last leave and a quick trip to Hawaii for their second anniversary.

"There's stewing, and then there's grieving." Mom's eyes held the tears Darcy should be shedding, probably. But she couldn't. Not today. "It's okay to grieve."

Darcy shook her head. "Can't. Don't have time." She took a deep breath and looked her mother in the eye. "Is Mandy working today?"

Mom glanced at the clock hanging over the order window and nodded. "She'll be here at seven thirty."

"Good. Looks like good weather for fishing, so we may have a breakfast rush." If there was one thing Darcy didn't want to talk about, today of all days, it was her feelings, a black hole she had no intention of exploring. Not today.

"I can stay. I should have thought. Let me do this for you."

"Mom, I'm fine. If I'm going to be running the place, you're going to have to give me the chance to take care of things no matter what's going on. Right?" She stared her mother down, trying hard not to grit her teeth. "Wasn't that what you had to do?"

She has more tears in her eyes than I do. Aw Mom, cut it out.

"Besides, you and Steve haven't had a day to call your own in ages, and here you are, checking to make sure the biscuits are made." She grinned. "You newlyweds have to have your time alone, don't you?"

Mom smirked. "Watch it, young lady." She heaved a sigh, looking at the clock again. Their outing was business-related, as usual with Steve Reno, but he'd promised his wife a little fun along the way. "If you're sure. Steve would understand, you know."

"I know he would, and I love him for it. Really, I do. It'll be good for me to stay busy." She reached out to hug her mom and then backed off to look her in the eye. "Jimmy's here to take care of the short-order menu for breakfast, and I'll wait tables until Mandy gets here. When the next shift gets settled in, I'll start making the bread and Jimmy can help me with the lunch prep."

"Sounds like you've got it all under control." Mom's eyes were moist. "I'm proud of you, you know."

Darcy shook her head. "I'm not sure why, but it's a nice thought."

"You really don't know, do you?"

"Know what?"

"That you are a special young lady and you can do whatever you set your mind to."

From your mouth to God's ears. But then, I'd have to trust in a living God for that to work, wouldn't I?

Del Reno looked in the rearview mirror, took off his cap, and smoothed his hair back before he entered the café.

I need a haircut.

No time for that today. He was supposed to meet Nick at seven thirty, and he was running a few minutes late.

Nick's truck was already parked on the street in front of the building, so the plan was to get breakfast, consult with the

tenant—in this case, Darcy—and then get to work. He paused for a moment before entering and closed his eyes. He had imagined he could smell bacon cooking from his house just up the road, but here? Here, it was a siren call in the aromatic sense.

RenoVations and Associates Construction had been hired by the owner, Roxy Reno, to remodel the apartment above the Clementville Café for her daughter, Darcy, and the twins. The apartment atop the pre-war building—*but which war?*—was located on the single strip of businesses in the tiny town of Clementville, Kentucky. It had been empty from the time Roxy remarried last summer until last fall when Darcy and the children moved in. He frowned a bit. He'd never had a problem with the idea of Roxy living above the café, but Darcy and the kids? She was taking too many chances. The nearest neighbor was a few streets away, and she lived ten miles from the county seat in Marion and the nearest law enforcement.

Not that I have any say in the matter.

He shook his head and pulled the sparkling glass door open, setting off jangling bells. At the sound, the waitress—in this case, his cousin Mandy—was alerted.

She raised her hand in a friendly wave. "Hey, Del."

"Hey, Mandy." He grinned at his youngest cousin. She was of average height and only came up to his shoulder. "Nick here yet?"

"Yep. He stepped back to the kitchen to ask Darcy something. I'm assuming about the renovation upstairs. She's minding the ship today."

"Gotcha." He followed her to the counter, nodding as she poured him a cup of coffee.

"The usual?" His cousin raised an eyebrow and put a hand on her hip.

Del eyed her over the menu. "Are you saying I'm predictable?"

"Uh, yeah." She cocked her head to one side. "Two eggs, over easy; an order of bacon, extra-crisp; biscuits and jelly—"

"Hey, sometimes I order gravy."

"Yeah, well, only on special occasions." She continued her list. "And grits."

He twisted his lips, wondering how he could get around this lawyer-wannabe's uncomfortably accurate prediction. Truth was, he loathed his routine, and was tired of everyone thinking they knew what was going on in his head. "I might surprise you today." He perused the menu for a moment and, the decision made, laid it on the counter. "I think I'll have the pecan waffle, thank you very much."

Mandy laughed. "I'll get your order in, O Great Unpredictable One."

"Thank you." He held up his hand as she moved to walk away, remembering something. "Hey, how was your law school graduation?"

She beamed. Her eyes were sparkling with excitement, but she shrugged casually. "It was okay. The usual long-winded speeches and uncomfortable seats, but wonderful." Wrinkling her nose, she looked apologetic. "I wish I could've invited the whole family, but they only gave me ten tickets, and I wanted Grandma and Grandpa to see their youngest grandchild walk across the platform to get my diploma, and then by the time you add my brother and wife, sister and husband, and some of their kids..."

"And Clay." He quirked a brow, laughing when he saw her face tinged with red.

"And Clay." She took a deep breath and shook her head. "Now I'm studying for the bar exam in July. I waitress to stay sane."

"You'll do great." Del winked at her. "You were always the smartest one in the family, you know."

Mandy leaned over the counter and whispered. "I know, let's keep it our secret."

"What secret?" Nick Woodward scooted onto the stool next to Del. "Good luck. Since becoming a part of the Reno family, I'm learning that in Clementville, you're related to everyone in town, and everybody knows your business, as well." He laughed, clearly not worried about missing a bit of news.

"No big secret, simply confirming what we know to be true. Right, Del?" She winked at Del as he chuckled. "How 'bout some coffee, Nick?"

"Please." He thanked her as she put a mug in front of him and turned to retrieve the carafe.

Del looked around, taking note of Darcy flitting from table to table. He took a sip from his steaming cup of coffee and turned to his best friend and business partner. "How long've you been here?"

"About twenty minutes. Traffic was light between here and Kuttawa." Nick smiled up at Mandy when she filled his cup and put a menu in front of him. "Just give me what Del's having."

"Pecan waffle and syrup?"

Nick turned to Del, his jaw hanging open. "What's wrong with you? You sick or somethin'?"

"I decided I no longer want to be so predictable."

"What's wrong with predictable?" Nick frowned and then looked at Mandy directly. "I'll have waffles too, and a side of bacon."

Del raised a hand. How had he missed bacon? He'd come in dreaming about it. "I'll have bacon, too."

Mandy turned to add the item to Del's ticket and put

Nick's on the order wheel between the counter and the kitchen.

"Did you talk to Darcy about the kitchen countertops upstairs?"

"Yeah. She's good with quartz since her mom insisted on it." He lifted one side of his mouth in a grin. "The extra cost made her balk at first, but Roxy won her over. She'll come upstairs to look at samples when she can shake loose." Nick took another sip of his black coffee. "Living here has to be more convenient for her."

The business partners agreed that with two growing preschoolers, she needed the space, and the apartment had square-footage, all right.

Del shook his head. "It will be. On the other hand, I hate to think about her hauling the kids up and down those stairs."

Nick chuckled. "I don't think an elevator is in the budget."

"Probably not." Del gave Nick a sidelong glance.

"Besides, Darcy's young. Now when you get to be our age..."

Del glowered at him. "Speak for yourself, old man."

"Hey, you're older than me."

"By two months." Del took a sip and set the cup down when Darcy came up to them with the coffee pot.

"Hey, Del. Need a warm-up?"

Del saw something in her expression. Sadness? "Sure. You doin' okay today, Darcy?"

She took a deep breath like she was trying to shake something off. "Never better."

Del nodded, regarding her closely. She was avoiding him. Something was wrong.

But I have no right to ask her what it is.

Nick couldn't help but notice the change in atmosphere when Darcy, as opposed to Mandy, walked up to the counter. He shook his head. Del had it so bad, and Nick knew exactly how he felt. He'd been the same way about Del's sister, Lisa Reno, a year ago.

When he and Lisa reconnected after a few years, they'd both lived different lives. Totally different lives. Lisa had temporarily moved to Texas, where she'd had a serious relationship with a guy who, for a time, destroyed her confidence in herself. Nick had married the woman who was, then, the love of his life and lost her and their unborn child to a senseless traffic accident. It had almost destroyed him mentally and spiritually.

Lisa was the one who made him realize God might have more than one love in mind for him. He smiled every time he thought of her and their whirlwind courtship and engagement. Now if they could just speed this wedding thing along. Every week felt like a year.

"Why don't you go ahead and move into your house?" Del was pouring syrup over his pecan waffle. It smelled so good Nick was glad he'd ordered the same thing.

"I promised Lisa I wouldn't move in until I could move in with her, and that she had free rein to fix it up any way she pleased." He shrugged, snorting quietly. "Therefore, I'm still commuting from Kuttawa."

"You are way too nice to her. You know that, don't you?"

Nick laughed. "Probably." He puffed out his chest. "But then, she's worth it."

Del shook his head. "People in love are ridiculous."

"Don't knock it until you've tried it." Nick glanced from

Del to Darcy. Seemed as if his old friend Del kept an eye on the lady at all times, and Darcy was studiously indifferent.

Do Del and Darcy think nobody knows? I guess there's hope for even the most stubborn of people.

Del seemed to gather his thoughts. "Anyway, back to the apartment."

"Yeah." Nick took a bite of the luscious pecan waffle dripping in syrup, closing his eyes with pleasure. *Aw, man, these are so good.* "Besides the countertops, I want Darcy to look at the master bath before we do the rough-in plumbing."

"Ripping out the plaster was painful." Del sighed.

"I know. It was the only way to get the layout she needs." Nick stared straight ahead, thinking. "I asked Roxy if she wanted the electrical done now or in phases."

"It's going to be hard to do it in phases if she and the twins are living in it."

"I know. I have a feeling it's going to be full steam ahead, which means they'll have to move out for a few weeks."

"If Dad has anything do to with it—and you know he will—we'll be up to our necks in plaster dust by the end of the week."

Nick laughed. "So much for semi-retirement, huh?"

"The man doesn't know the meaning of the word. Roxy just thinks they're having a day out. His main destination is the supply house in Owensboro." Del scraped the remaining syrup from his plate with the last piece of bacon. "How are the wedding plans coming along?"

Nick held up his hands. "As far as I know, swimmingly. Lisa said she would let me know when she needed my help, which is fine by me. At this point, we both want to have this planning stuff over and be married, already."

"You could always elope, and then I wouldn't have to wear a tux." Del looked at him hopefully.

"You know that's not going to happen." Nick shook his head. "Lisa is worried about leaving anyone out. I told her nobody cares as much as she does, and that just made her mad."

Del laughed out loud, causing Darcy, Mandy, Jimmy in the kitchen, and several customers to turn their way right about the time the door bells jangled again.

"Keep it down, man." Nick looked around, embarrassed.

Del tried to stop laughing, but couldn't. "I could have told you that the one thing Lisa Reno can't stand is when you tell her a truth she doesn't want to hear."

"Now you tell me."

———✍︎———

Lisa Reno jumped from the driver's seat of her Ford Explorer and made her way to the door of the café, glad the sun had come up, at least. Poor Nick. He'd had to leave before sunrise. The sunny almost-summer day was a blessing after all the rain they'd had in the last few weeks.

The aroma of baking biscuits and breakfast food reached her before she heard the bell on the door emit a loud "clang," and instead of everyone looking at the door, their attention was on her boys, Nick and Del. She sidled up to her fiancé and kissed him on the cheek, surprising him.

Lisa laughed at the guilty expression on his face. "What?"

"You surprised me, that's all. Good morning." Nick turned and claimed her lips with his, driving all thoughts of questions out of her mind.

Mmmm...Maple syrup...

"What are you guys having for breakfast?" She claimed the stool next to Nick, unrolled her silverware, and placed the napkin in her lap before checking out their nearly-empty plates. "Looks—and tastes—like something that requires syrup, surprise, surprise." She grinned, looking at what little food was left. "Ooh, pecan waffles. Nice choice."

"Hey Lisa, need some coffee?" Mandy was manning the coffee pot this time while Darcy took orders from customers who had come in right before Lisa.

"Hi, Mandy." She thought a minute.

Do I have time for a full breakfast? Do I WANT a full breakfast? She sighed. "Yes to the coffee, and I'll just have a sausage and biscuit sandwich."

"Good deal," Darcy said, nodding. "Jimmy made up a bunch for a to-go order and had a few left. Still fresh."

"Perfect. Thanks." Lisa watched Darcy walk away, wondering.

"How do you run on such a small breakfast?" Del snorted at her order.

"For one thing, my breakfast won't be loaded with sugar, so I won't have a sugar crash around eleven o'clock, and for another, I have a dress fitting tomorrow." She shrugged. "Besides, you're nearly done, and I'd hate to make you wait for me." She winked at Nick and gave her brother, Del, the stink eye, which only made him laugh.

"Who said we were going to wait?"

"I think the 'Reno' in 'RenoVations and Associates' includes me, right?" Lisa smiled when Mandy filled her coffee cup with the steaming elixir. "I may be a coffee snob, but you can say one thing about the coffee here. It's amazing." She took a whiff and then brought the mug to her lips to check the temperature. "Mmmm, perfect."

Darcy presented her sausage-biscuit with a flourish. "Here you go, Lisa. Jimmy's outdone himself in the biscuit department today."

She admired the flaky height of the steaming buttermilk quick bread expertly split to contain the over-sized sausage patty, which had been fried to perfection. "I'll say. I hate to bite into it." She held up a finger, and then pulled out her phone to take a picture of the masterpiece. "I'll tag you on Instagram."

Darcy laughed. Lisa could sense that something was bothering her, but she didn't want to ask her here in the café.

"Darcy, I have a dress fitting tomorrow. Want to come with me? If you do, it will give me an excuse to eat out and do a little wedding shopping." She cut her eyes at Nick. "And it's for sure that Nick can't go with me, because I don't want him to have any idea what my dress looks like."

Darcy tilted her head, seeming to consider. "What time? I planned to take off a little early tomorrow to do grocery shopping."

"My appointment isn't until four o'clock. We could fit in a supermarket stop." Maybe they'd have a chance to talk.

"I'll see what I can do with the kids. I'd hate to think about my two Tasmanian devils in a bridal shop." Darcy shook her head.

"Hey, that's my niece and nephew you're talking about." Lisa grinned. "I'm sure they'd be fine, but you need some time out, too." She looked at Nick and Del for backup. "Right?"

Del had a thoughtful expression on his face then eyed Darcy. "I don't mind watching them."

Darcy paused, a tiny frown between her brows. "Are you sure?"

He waved off her concern. "I'll be here working anyway. How hard could it be? I can pick them up at preschool and feed them supper, and then I can take them to my place or come to yours. Whatever works for you?" He seemed worried that she wouldn't accept the offer.

Lisa did a double-take. *He's never babysat kids in his life.*

Darcy was thoughtful. "It would be easier to keep them here at the apartment - all their stuff is here, and they can go to bed earlier. And you have a key." She bit her lip and looked across the counter at Del. "You're sure?"

"Wouldn't have offered if I wasn't."

Lisa stared at her brother. *He wants a shot at this.*

While she was pondering this new development, she watched him shoot Darcy a smile as he got up from the counter and retrieved his check.

"That settles it, then. I will be your babysitter for the evening. I know we'll have a great time."

2

"Are you okay?" Nick frowned a little.

Lisa huffed out a laugh as she shook her head. "Yeah, I'm fine. Just wondering who that guy is and what he's done with my brother."

Nick nudged her shoulder with his. "Our boy is growing up."

Lisa shook her head. "Please. You know better."

"He's been keeping a close eye on Darcy for a while now." Nick went poker-faced as he looked past her to Del laughing at something Darcy had said.

"Look." Lisa whispered. "Oh! She's coming. Don't look."

"Look, don't look," Nick whispered in her ear, which tickled deliciously. "You're going to have to help me out here."

She gave him a swat. "Darcy, I'll send you a text when I know what time we'll be leaving. I can be flexible if you get stuck here." Lisa huffed, glowering at Nick, and then wiped her hands on her napkin. "Nick, I'll go upstairs with you. I need to make a list of fixtures to order."

"I'll be up there in a little bit." Darcy glanced up when the door opened. "Out-of-towners?"

Lisa waved her away. "Go ahead. Do what you have to do."

"I will." Darcy narrowed her eyes. "He looks familiar."

Lisa craned her neck, seeing a man and woman, both wearing suits. "Tourists?"

"I'd say not." Nick got up, a frown on his face. "I remember the man. Agent Stafford."

"FBI?" Lisa's eyes opened wide. "What in the world are they doing here?"

Nick shook his head. "I don't know, but I'm going to find out." He kissed Lisa on the cheek. "I'll meet you upstairs."

"You will not. I'm going over there with you." She put a hand to her hip. "We're in this together, remember. For better or worse?"

Nick picked up their tickets and handed them to Darcy with a large bill. "Keep the change."

"I'll split it with Mandy." Darcy took the money and whispered to Lisa. "Let me know what happens."

"Will do."

Nick put his hand on the small of her back as he led her to the table where the two strangers were sitting. "Agent Stafford?"

The gentleman looked up, recognition on his face. "Nick Woodward. Just the man I came down to see."

"Your lucky day. This is my fiancée, Lisa Reno."

Lisa cut her eyes toward Nick, noting the proprietary air accompanying what could almost be considered a scowl on his face.

The agent smiled pleasantly. "I remember you from last summer."

"Were you part of the FBI team investigating the

tunnels?" They had come in and finished so quickly, Lisa had barely seen them. Apparently, he had seen her.

"I was, and you're the lady who was more concerned about a litter of kittens than the dead body rotting in the basement." He chuckled and stood to shake her hand. "Special Agent Frank Stafford, Chicago Field Office. Special Agent Julia Rossi, Louisville Field Office." Both agents flashed their badges.

Lisa shook his hand, and then Agent Rossi's. "Guilty as charged. By the way, those cats are very good mousers." She grinned and looked from one to the other. "What brings you to our small burg?"

Agent Rossi gave her peer a look of irritation, then focused on Lisa and Nick. "It seems that evidence from the investigation last year had been improperly processed, and that led us to believe there may be additional tunnels, perhaps hidden."

Nick blanched a little, and Lisa felt it in the pit of her stomach. Her beautiful house. Was it going to be a crime scene again? *Please, God, no.*

Agent Stafford returned to his seat and gestured for Lisa and Nick to join them. "Would you like us to fill you in? Unless you'd rather go somewhere private?" The special agent looked around, seeming to mentally document every person in the café, including the uniformed customer coming in the door, making a beeline for waitress Mandy Reno.

Nick met the eyes of the new customer, Sheriff Clay Lacey, then turned and gave the agent a nod and half-grin. "May as well. I've got nothing to hide." Nick and Lisa sat across from one another.

"I appreciate it." He took a deep breath and looked across at his partner. "Agent Rossi wasn't involved with the original investigation, so the regional office thought it prudent to send new eyes down here, and since she was in the state—"

"I drew the short stick." The young woman smirked at Nick and Lisa.

Agent Rossi wasn't just pretty. She was gorgeous. Even other women would recognize that. Tall and willowy, she had nearly black hair pulled back in a heavy bun and almost perfectly symmetrical features. Italian? Maybe. She could be one of Michelangelo's sculpture models.

Fortunately, Nick doesn't seem to notice.

"Do we need to include Sheriff Lacey in this conversation?" Nick spoke abruptly.

Lisa glanced at Nick. The question surprised her.

"Not at this point." Agent Stafford pulled a document out of his inside jacket pocket. "We do have a warrant to search the house and tunnels."

Del walked around the upstairs apartment waiting for his sister and future brother-in-law. What was keeping Nick and Lisa? He went to the larger bedroom with the bath attached. Darcy had moved all her stuff to the kids' room, and they were doing their best to close the room off and keep from tracking dirt as much as possible. One of the things he'd learned a long time ago, from his dad, was to keep the woman of the house happy. Keeping Mama happy meant the project was happy.

Del shook his head. Dad had a point.

There was still a small amount of plaster on the walls in the bath they were transforming, but he had no illusions of being able to keep it. Between the plumbing and electrical, it was easier to rip it out and start over with drywall. It hurt his heart a little, ripping out the plaster.

He had an affinity for the craft. The layers of material, getting smoother as they went on: the thin strips of rough wood lath, the pressed-into-place scratch coat with lime, sand, and animal hair; the brown coat, smoother, without the hair of the first coat; and the thin, smooth finish coat.

It was a process where adding to the layer made it smooth, as opposed to wood, where sanding was required to remove the rough edges and splinters.

Plaster was experience. It was adding to what you already knew and making sense of it.

He took out his phone to check the time.

They'd better hurry up and get here before I start waxing poetic about plumbing fixtures.

Del shook his head and snorted. He wanted this project to be perfect. He wanted all their projects to be excellent, but this one was different. He wanted Darcy and the kids to feel safe.

The door opened downstairs and he could hear Lisa and Nick talking as they came up the stairs to the door he'd left open. They came in, Lisa still chattering.

"You don't think they'll seal it off again, do you?" His sister looked at Nick, a little fear and nervousness on her face.

"No, I don't think so."

"What's going on?" Del felt like he'd walked into the middle of a movie.

Lisa and Nick looked at one another. Nick spoke first. "Remember the FBI agent, Stafford, who was here last year when we found the tunnels?"

"Yeah?" Surely this wasn't coming back to haunt them.

"He's here again, and he has an agent out of Louisville

with him this time." Nick shook his head. "I thought this was over."

"Just the two of them?" Del tensed.

Lisa was concerned "They think there may be another tunnel down there, and there was evidence from last year that was overlooked, so they were sent back."

"Do you need to go out there?" Del could see the worry on his best friend's face, and his sister's. "I can get the information about the apartment from Darcy."

"You sure?"

Del waved them off. "Sure. I take it they want to go out there now?"

Nick took a deep breath and looked at Lisa. "They do. Lisa, you don't have to go." He rubbed his hand up and down her arm.

"Oh, I'm going all right." She wrinkled her nose at him. "It's my house too, remember? You can't get rid of me now."

He put his arm around Lisa. "Wouldn't want to." Looking up at Del, he shook his head. "Sorry, bud."

"No worries. You go solve a crime, and I'll solve the countertop choosing and the placement of the bathroom fixtures. Nothing I haven't done without you a dozen times."

Lisa sighed. "Then we'll leave you to it." She narrowed her eyes and poked him in the arm. "Don't talk Darcy into any shortcuts that you know would make me mad."

"Oh, it's so hard to make you mad."

"Watch it. I'll have Darcy to myself tomorrow." Lisa dipped her chin.

Del thought a second and realized he didn't want Lisa to plant any negative thoughts in Darcy's head.

With a point, a smile, and a wink, he responded. "Gotcha."

Nick opened the passenger door of his Ford F-150 for Lisa to hop in. He got in behind the steering wheel, put the key in the ignition, and then looked over at his love before starting the truck. "What's going on in that red head of yours?"

She twisted her lips in an annoyed grimace. "Honestly, I can't believe this is happening. About to follow law enforcement into the basement of our house. Again."

He shook his head. He knew what she meant. Last year's mystery had garnered more information about his own family than he wanted to know, but it had answered so many questions. Why did he get the feeling he'd learn even more this go-round?

"I'm sure this is just standard procedure when they come across additional evidence."

She turned and looked him in the eye. "And why was the evidence not processed?" She frowned, the little line between her brows begging him to smooth it out. "It all seems a little fishy to me."

He reached for her hand and drew it to his lips. "Let's go and see what they want. At this point, I'd like to get it over with and seal off the entry to the tunnel."

"I know. I'm torn. She took in a breath. "Part of me wants to fill in the tunnel and forget it was ever down there, but then the history lover in me wants to know what happened. If we close it off, we'll lose the opportunity to learn more."

Nick started the truck and pulled into the street from his parking space along Broadway. Considering all three businesses in town plus the post office were on one side of the road, calling the main drag in Clementville "Broadway" must have been someone's idea of a joke back in the day.

"It was enough for me to find out my grandfather was

killed and left down there." He shook his head. "And who killed him? His own father?"

"That doesn't even bear thinking about." Lisa shivered.

"Could be, though. Dad said his grandfather was a tough old bird, and if he'd been rum-running for decades, he had protected the business for a long time. Maybe Zebulon belonged to the lawless element that ran things in this part of the country."

"We may never know."

"Or we might learn something if we find another tunnel." Nick turned down the gravel lane toward his house. "Will it be a problem if we can't get in for a few weeks?"

Lisa sat, deep in thought. "No, it won't. I've got enough to do finishing up Darcy's apartment and wedding stuff. I'm almost done here." She turned and looked at him with excitement. "Did I tell you that I—I mean WE—got the KitchenAid mixer?"

Nick laughed. "I'm so happy for us."

She whacked him on the arm. "You'll see. It makes making chocolate chip cookies a snap. Who knows? Maybe I'll get up the nerve to make cheesecake?"

"In that case, I'm thrilled." He cut a glance her way and put the truck in Park in the driveway of the house.

She reached out to touch his arm. "Are you okay?"

"I'll be fine." He winked at her and leaned in for a kiss. "You sure you don't want to elope?"

"I'd love to, but Mel and my daddy would kill me."

"Your matron of honor maybe, but your dad? He might be glad to get you off his hands."

"Like I've been on his hands for the last five years." She opened the door. "You getting out, or do you want to keep putting this off and talk about wedding stuff?"

"I plead the fifth."

3

Darcy stood next to the ancient metal shelving in the basement, frowning at the somewhat large, footprint-sized shape of dried mud on the floor.

Is that a footprint?

She shook her head. *No, I'm being paranoid. But am I?*

It hadn't been there the day before when she'd come down to retrieve cornmeal from the walk-in freezer. She knew she was particular about cleanliness, but that wasn't the point. Not only was there dirt on the floor, but there was also no reason for it to be there.

She'd been the last person in the basement last night, and it wasn't there, then. The stair steps from outside came in a door where three staircases met: the apartment, the kitchen, and the basement. They came out on the sidewalk around the corner from the front door, which was adjacent to the paved street. No mud to be found.

A prickle of fear worked its way from the top of her head to the tips of her toes. Someone had been down here, and it chilled her to the bone.

This could explain a lot.

Over the last few weeks, she'd noticed that things in the café dining room had been moved around. She hadn't told anyone. It was simply stress, lack of sleep, and raising twins. Wasn't it?

But now...

Darcy bit her lip. She didn't want to alarm her employees and she certainly didn't want to call Mom. She'd just worry herself to death. Besides, Darcy was in charge.

Nick and Lisa had gone out to the house to meet the FBI agents.

Del is upstairs.

Thinking about it made her stomach flutter a little. She felt safer knowing he was there. Should she go upstairs and get him? No, he might be in the middle of something.

Be sensible, Darcy.

This part of the basement had the least bit of light, so she got closer. She couldn't see it clearly, but the shape was there. A flashlight would be helpful.

She'd go upstairs, grab a flashlight, and see if Del could come down and check this out. She could be reasonable when she had to be.

When she got to the main level, she locked the basement door behind herself and pocketed the key. She usually left it unlocked, open to the stairwell and the apartment. Fear, and a remnant of anger, swept through her. If Justin hadn't been killed, she wouldn't be here to be afraid. She'd be safe and sound in base housing somewhere in the world, raising her kids and waiting for her husband to come home.

But that was neither here nor there.

Climbing the second set of stairs to the apartment, she talked herself down, almost to the point of turning around and going back to the kitchen. She probably would have if the door hadn't swung open, and if Del hadn't met her on the landing. It seemed like he was always standing where she was going.

"Hey, Darcy. Did you want to look at countertop samples now?"

He was right there in front of her, and her mind seemed to go blank. Why was she here again?

Oh, right. Dirt. Basement.

She swallowed thickly.

"Are you okay?" Del bent, frowning.

She shook her head and closed her eyes for a second to regroup. "I'm fine. I just..."

She looked him in the eye. "Would you come to the basement with me?"

Del cocked his head. "Something wrong?"

She hesitated as she turned to go down the stairs, Del following close behind. "I'm not sure."

They got to the landing between the two sets of stairs and she pulled the key from her apron pocket to open the door.

"You locked it?" He seemed puzzled. Of course he was. She usually left it unlocked so they could get in and out of the basement where the electrical panel and HVAC systems were located.

She closed her eyes for a second. "I think someone has been in the building, and I think they were in the basement."

Del froze. "What about the apartment?"

"No, I've not noticed anything out of place upstairs." She looked down, then back up to him, eyes widening in fear. "I have noticed some things moved around in the café kitchen and dining room."

"What?" He knew he was staring, but he couldn't believe what he was hearing. "And you haven't said anything?"

She shrugged and looked at him, tears standing on her lashes. "I thought I just forgot. People are in and out of the kitchen and dining room constantly, but not the basement." Her lips clamped shut for a moment. "I did notice the box of receipts had been moved from when I put it inside the desk. When I came down the next day, it was on top." Her face was a picture of humiliation and fear. What he wouldn't give to wipe that look off her face for good.

But for now, the idea of someone in the building without her knowledge made his blood run cold. "So you think somebody that isn't supposed to be in the basement, has pilfered around in the kitchen and dining room, and you didn't tell anybody?"

She narrowed her eyes, her voice dripping with sarcasm. "I wouldn't have come to you for backup if I thought it was Jimmy, would I?" She paused, taking a deep breath. "Wait here. I need to get a flashlight."

"Something wrong with the lights down there?" He was thoroughly confused.

She sighed. "Just wait here."

He held his hands up. "Want me to go on down?"

"No, you might step on the evidence." Her hand was on the doorknob to the kitchen.

He blinked. "Evidence?"

She looked up into his eyes. He could tell she was worried. "There's dirt on the floor."

He frowned. "I know you run a clean ship, but is a little dirt cause for alarm?"

"It is when it wasn't there yesterday, and when there's no place for dirt to come from." She glared at him. "Will you please wait here while I get the flashlight?"

"I'll be here." He put his hands in his pockets and stood there.

It took her about thirty seconds to retrieve the flashlight and lead him down the steps to the basement. "The place where I found the dirt is in the back, where the lights aren't as bright."

When he got down there, he realized that his dealings with this particular basement had been on the other side of the room, not the side to which Darcy was leading him. "You're right. It's darker over here."

She gave him a look that said, "See, I told you."

"Here it is." She shone the light on it.

He crouched, carefully touching the edge of the dirt. "It looks like dried mud." He peered up at her. "And this wasn't here yesterday?"

"No. This is where I keep the to-go containers and glasses, cleaning supplies, and stuff I don't use often. I just happened to need a bag of cornmeal yesterday and a stack of containers today."

He stood and took the flashlight from her, shining it around the area, and then back at the object in question, noting the definite detail of the sole of a boot. "It's a footprint."

She rubbed her arms nervously and glanced up at him, grimacing. "I thought so, but I didn't want to say it and make it so."

Del looked down at the shoe-shaped impression and then back at her, his lips twisted in a grin. "Saying it doesn't make it so. Being here does."

"I know."

He didn't want to irritate her, but it was humorous. Not the situation, of course. Just her.

He turned the flashlight to the floor around the shelving.

"Look at this." He pointed to the second site of dried mud halfway under the shelf. "How is that possible?"

Darcy put her hand on her mouth. "Del, the shelf has been moved. Look at the floor."

He turned the flashlight beam onto scrapes on the vinyl flooring where the unit had been moved away from the wall and put back.

He turned off the flashlight and looked at her grimly. "Is Clay still in the dining room?"

———— ✺ ————

"And you haven't heard anything, or had anything go missing?"

Darcy had been relieved when she'd entered the café to see young Sheriff Clay Lacey at the counter, paying his bill and flirting with his girlfriend, Mandy. She'd wasted no time in asking him to follow her to the basement, and once she mentioned what she'd found, he was all business.

"No." She paused a moment, thinking. "Now that you mention it, Jimmy told me yesterday that we were out of bleach." She looked from Clay to Del. "We should have had plenty."

The two men looked at one another. Clay cleared his throat. "Darcy, I'm going to need to fill out a report on this."

"Good." She laughed nervously. "I mean, somebody has been here, while we've been here, and nobody knew it, and... I'm a little freaked out by this. " If she wasn't careful, she'd work herself into a lather. The more nervous she was, the more her sentences became stream-of-conscious.

"I'm sure you are." Clay took pictures with his phone, making note of the measurement of the footprint. He looked at the shelving unit, glanced at Del, and back at her. "Can we move this out from the wall and see why it was moved to begin with?"

"Of course. Whatever you need to do." She stepped back, hugging her arms around her waist, feeling chilled.

The two men carefully shifted the storage piece, and when it was moved out from the wall, a piece of plywood, painted the same color as the walls, fell forward, toward the shelf. Del shoved it out of the way and looked at Clay, and then at Darcy.

"Houston, we have a problem."

The gaping hole in the wall had been well-hidden.

"Darcy, do you know how long this shelf has been here?" Del inspected the unit, old by any standards. It wasn't used for food storage, so the rusty spots hadn't been a problem.

"No clue." Darcy shivered visibly. "Honestly? It may have been here when we moved in fifteen years ago."

"The hole looks pretty old, but the plywood looks new." Clay pointed out the raw, freshly cut edges, shining his flashlight into the hole, the damp smell indicating that the heavy rains of the last few weeks had percolated down to the tunnel. "I'm thinking this is where your muddy footprint came from."

"It's the north side of the building, Clay." Del stared at Clay until he finally looked at him, confirming he'd thought of the same thing.

Clay nodded, shining his flashlight into the dark interior. "Toward the river." He put the light down.

Del removed his cap and raked his fingers through his hair, then replaced it. It was what he did when he was thinking. Lately, he'd been thinking a lot.

"Well?" Darcy looked from one to the other, impatience at their lack of motion evident on her face.

"Looks like Nick's not the only one in town with a secret tunnel." Del gave Darcy a sideways glance. "What do you think, Clay?"

"I think the FBI agents out at Nick's place will want to see this."

"You're not going to cordon it off as a crime scene, are you?" Darcy was worried, he could tell. "I mean, I have a restaurant to run, and if we can't get to our supplies..."

"I don't think closing down will be necessary." Clay glanced at Del.

"I'm taking you at your word." She pointed a finger at the two men. "I'll go up top and see if I can get Lisa on the phone." Darcy pulled out her phone and, as she walked up the stairs, began scrolling through her "recents."

"When are you going to ask that girl out?" Clay stood, hands in the pockets of his tan uniform, studying Del closely.

Del shook his head, his eyes still following the direction Darcy had been traveling. "Waiting for the right time, I guess."

The sheriff sighed. "Del, did I tell you what Mandy told me at Christmas?"

Del laughed. "No, what words of wisdom did my baby cousin have for you?"

"She said we'd both grow old before I ever asked her out on a date." Clay's face twisted. "She was probably right. If she hadn't said it, I don't know if we'd be dating now."

Del snorted. "Mandy doesn't come with as much baggage as Darcy."

"You mean the kids?" Clay frowned.

The idea of Benji and Ali as a discouragement to anyone

pursuing a relationship with Darcy was beyond wrong. Dead wrong. "Good grief, no."

"Then, what?" Clay shook his head, confused.

Del looked Clay in the eye. It wasn't his place to discuss Darcy's personal and spiritual life with anyone but her. "I've been praying about it."

Clay's gaze was direct. "Best thing you can do. I won't ask, but I'll pray with you, brother." Clay clapped a hand on Del's shoulder. "Or maybe I should say, 'cousin'?"

"Let's not get ahead of ourselves." Del sent his friend a glare and then softened it with a shaking head.

4

Excitement welled up in Darcy as she hit the stairs, jogging up to the kitchen from the basement. When she saw the evidence, her first thought was for her children. Normal. Now she was intrigued. She'd spent so much time taking care of things and people that she'd forgotten how exciting a crime scene could be from a purely academic standpoint—although to be honest, she would rather it be in someone else's basement. This was the most excitement she'd experienced since her mom told her she was marrying Steve Reno. That had been a shock, but a good one. Mom deserved to be happy in her later years.

She chuckled to herself as she opened the door of the kitchen. *Later years.* Mom would love that. At fifty-seven, Roxy Reno was anything but an old grandma. She was the young, perky, cool grandma.

Pushing the door open, she sighed. This place made her happy. She hadn't consciously thought about being happy in a long time, and it surprised her. She glanced into the dining room to see Mandy training Gail, the new waitress. They were sprucing up the dining room for the lunch crowd. Things were peaceful up here.

There was one table filled with a group of old men they'd dubbed "the elders at the gate," because they seemed to solve all the problems of the world in the two hours they sat, sipping coffee and eating an early lunch.

"What's goin' on downstairs?" Jimmy looked concerned, and she turned her attention to him, wondering how much she should say.

Chewing her lip, she decided to err on the side of caution. "Not sure. I'm going to be tied up for a little while. You okay at the helm for an hour?"

Jimmy gave her a jaunty salute. "Aye, captain." He laughed and tilted his head. "You sure everything's okay?"

"I'll let you know." She looked around. Nobody was within earshot, but she didn't feel comfortable talking about what might or might not be down there. No need to worry him.

"I saw the sheriff go down there, and I'm sure he doesn't normally investigate missing cleaning products." He narrowed his eyes. "But you'll tell me when it's time for me to know."

"You're a jewel, Jimmy." For some weird reason, she had the impulse to hug her employee, but she didn't. Instead, she smiled at him as she opened the kitchen door. "I'm keeping the outside door locked for the time being, and if you need anything from the basement, let me know and I'll get it for you."

"Ten-four." He went back to the bread he was kneading, then stopped and turned back to her. "If you need me, holler. You hear?"

"I hear, and thanks." She wondered if he could see the excitement and a little bit of dread in her face.

Del knew his face lit up a little when Darcy came back downstairs. Hopefully, she didn't notice. By the snort coming from Clay, Darcy was probably the only one who hadn't figured it out. Clearing his throat, he frowned and tried to sound serious as he took his cap off, ran his hand through his hair, and replaced it. "'Bout time. Did you get her?"

Darcy drew her chin in and gave him a look boding nobody any good. It was an expression that must come along with becoming a mom. Or a wife. He'd seen the same look on his mom's face, and on Roxy's, his stepmom's, face in recent months. Come to think of it, his sister Lisa had already perfected "the glare," so it must be a woman thing.

"Some of us have a business to attend to, you know. I have a restaurant upstairs." She shook her head.

"I'm sure the girls can keep the old guys' cups filled for a little while." Del was pleased when she twisted her lips into a grin. He sensed a little excitement in the normally private Darcy.

"I'm sure." She looked from Del to Clay. "Lisa must be out of range, so I left a message."

Clay's expression was serious. "First of all, don't touch anything. Darcy, I know your fingerprints will be all over the basement, but from now on, any time you or anyone else is in the basement, wear gloves." He looked at her. "Do you have any on hand?"

"Does a fireman have an ax? This is a food-service establishment. Of course, I do." She reached out and grabbed a couple of boxes of latex gloves, sizes large and small, showing the "large" box to the two men. "The last thing I want to do is destroy evidence."

Del stared, surprised at her turn of phrase, and when he caught Clay's glance, he saw that Clay was curious.

"Yeah." Clay turned off the flashlight and put it on the shelf next to the stairs. Turning to Darcy, he chuckled. "You must watch a lot of police procedural television shows."

Del watched the expression on Darcy's face alter at the question. There was more to this girl than he even realized.

"I majored in criminal justice when I went to college."

"Seriously?" Del looked surprised.

She held her head high. "I was all set to transfer from West Kentucky Community and Technical College to Murray State when I met and married Justin. Then we moved to California, and he was shipped overseas. He came back, I got pregnant, he went back to Afghanistan, and the rest is history." She shrugged. "There went the education."

"What about now?" Del couldn't keep himself from asking. He hadn't been wrong in sensing excitement in what could be a scary situation.

"Now, I'm running a restaurant and raising two kids." She shrugged. "Another lifetime. As for now, how about we get this show on the road."

"Better watch letting stuff like that slip. You may find yourself deputized, young lady." Clay looked from Del to Darcy as he picked up his official sheriff's campaign hat from the top of the chest freezer. "You two going out to Nick's place?"

"I'm in." She grinned. "Oh, and if you need any undercover work or a confidential informant with my contacts through the café, I'm your girl."

Lisa leaned against the side of the truck and sighed. Nick's grandmother used to live in this house. The house that brought them together.

"What's the sigh all about?"

She pondered a minute. "I guess thinking the wedding will never get here and that I'm doing you a disservice not letting you move here before the wedding."

Nick got comfortable leaning next to her and grabbed the hand that sparkled with his engagement ring, then brought it up to his lips. "If you recall, it was my idea, not yours, so you're not doing anything to me—unless you want to go ahead and elope and put us both out of our misery?" He sidled a glance at her and winked.

Lisa turned her hand in his, weaving their fingers together, and squeezed. "We've waited this long. A few more weeks won't kill us."

They stood there, not saying much, waiting for the agents. Nick's arm came around her waist and tugged her closer. "Look at this place."

She did. It was perfect if she did say so herself. When she looked up at him, he shook his head. "Not me, the house."

She took a deep breath and stared at the restored farmhouse. "Okay, what am I looking for?"

He waved a hand toward the house and yard. "Imagine five, ten years down the road."

She closed her eyes for a moment, contentment written all over her face. "I'm imagining."

"What do you see?"

She smiled even wider. Would she freak him out if she told him everything she could see? A laugh bubbled up and out her lips.

"You see something funny?"

She chanced a glance up at him. "Not to me, but you may think so."

He gazed at her, wondering. "Let me have it."

She stood straight, gazing at the house. "I see a swing in the big tree over there." She pointed to one of the ancient maple trees that had survived last year's tornado. Glancing up at him, she continued. "And I see balls, bikes, toy dishes spread all over the yard. Maybe an additional dog for Minnie to train." Minerva, Minnie for short, was Nick's beloved dog, and Lisa loved her, too.

"I like what you're seeing."

She turned and pulled herself to him, standing on her tiptoes. "I see as many kids as we can have in that length of time, and if we can't, we'll find some, somewhere." She felt tears pricking her eyelids even as she smiled. This was something they hadn't talked about, in-depth. While they'd joked about having a bunch of kids, what if they couldn't have their own children? "But that's a discussion for another day."

He held her as close as he possibly could, tucking her head under his chin on his chest, and squeezing the breath from her, it seemed. "I think your vision is perfect."

Relief. "I'm glad. I thought I'd freak you out."

"Hey, I'm not getting any younger, you know." He pulled back and kissed her softly.

"Me, neither." She tilted her head to gaze at him. "That still doesn't tell me why you won't move in."

He grinned, the love in his eyes shining out at her. "Because when we get married and I carry you across the threshold for real, I want it to be our forever home. I want both of us to start fresh." Waggling his eyebrows at her, he added, "And we can start our family that very day if you want."

"Sounds like a plan." She ducked her head, knowing her

face was flaming, and giggled as he goosed her in the ribs, making her laugh even harder.

When they heard an SUV drive up, Nick pulled his arms from around Lisa and kept her hand clasped in his. "Looks like Agents Stafford and Rossi found their way out here."

Lisa grimaced. "I'll be glad when this is over." She looked up at Nick, twisting her lips in a frown. "Don't you think we deserve a break?"

He shook his head. "You know better than that. We don't deserve anything except what God puts in front of us." He laughed when she rolled her eyes at him.

"I know." She gave him a disgruntled look.

Nick heard Lisa take a deep breath. This was certainly not the way he'd planned to spend today. He, Lisa, and Del were going to go up to Darcy's apartment, see what else they needed to do. He'd thought they could finish roughing in the plumbing and get started framing the closet, taking space from the bedroom.

"What are you thinking about?"

"To-do list."

Lisa nodded, smirking. "Work or wedding?"

"Work." He twisted his lips. "Like you didn't know the answer to that. I'll let you take care of the wedding to-do list."

"Sounds like a plan."

Nick looked at the SUV, curious. Agent Stafford appeared to be talking to someone on his cell, and the way he held it, had it on speaker so Agent Rossi could be in on the conversation. "Must be reporting in."

"I wouldn't think there'd be anything to report yet." Lisa frowned.

When they finally walked toward them, and the house, both agents glanced at one another.

"Did you have any trouble finding us this time?" Nick remembered last summer when the team came to investigate and got lost when their cell signal gave up.

"No trouble. Sorry to hold you up. We had to call into the office."

Agent Rossi checked her phone. "I've got a missed call from about five minutes ago." She called off the number. "Sound familiar?"

Nick looked down at his fiancée. Recognition was written all over both their faces, he knew. "Clay."

"Excuse me?" Agent Stafford leaned forward.

"Sheriff Lacey." Nick spoke louder.

"I'll call him back when we get done here. He didn't leave a message, so it must not have been an emergency." Rossi pocketed her phone and looked at them.

Lisa startled and pulled her phone from her pocket. "Phone is vibrating. Darcy tried to call." She tried to call her back. Nothing. "Going to voicemail." She heard a faint "ding" and another vibration. "Wait. She left a message, probably while I was trying to call." She touched the icon and listened, a confused look on her face. She put it on speaker and replayed the message. "This is Darcy. We may have some information, and we're on our way out there."

Agent Stafford's expression closed when Lisa relayed the message, then seemed to come to himself. "Right. We can get a head start here. Are you ready to give us the grand tour?"

Nick led the way up the sidewalk and opened the door, gesturing for Lisa and the two agents to go in ahead of him.

"Nice place. Looks a lot different from last year." Agent Stafford seemed to be trying to be as conciliatory as possible.

"We've done a total remodel since then." Nick glanced

back at Lisa, who was chewing on her bottom lip. "We'll be moving in after our wedding in June."

"Congratulations." Agent Rossi cracked a smile for the first time since they'd met her. "I'm getting married in August."

Nick led them through the living room and into the kitchen where the basement door was found.

Historical significance notwithstanding, Nick noticed that Lisa shivered a little when they went down into the basement of the house. Their house. The house they would set up housekeeping in on a date not too far away.

Nick led the two agents and Lisa to the opening they had found on her first visit to the house, over a year ago.

"I'm not sure what kind of evidence we will find, considering how many people have been in and out of here." He could tell Agent Julia Rossi was a stickler for a clean crime scene.

"We haven't been selling tickets." Nick looked at the two agents squarely, knowing it wouldn't take a whole lot to get his ire up.

Agent Stafford raised his hand. "I'm sure you've not contaminated the crime scene any further."

"We didn't know it was still a crime scene." Lisa crossed her arms and stood beside Nick.

"Officially, it's not." Agent Stafford looked at Agent Rossi, shaking his head in frustration, repeating his orders as he'd told them earlier. "We've been tasked with looking at a particular part of the tunnel, and since I was there for the first investigation connecting it to Chicago, the Special Agent in Charge wanted his Kentucky agent involved." He tilted his head, looking Nick in the eye. "You are not under investigation."

"Good to know." Nick took Lisa's hand. "We've been through enough delays."

When he looked back at Lisa, seeing what he'd come to recognize as tears hovering, he gave her a half-grin and turned back to the agents, gesturing to the opening. "Our tunnel is your tunnel."

The two federal officers pulled out their flashlights, and Nick grabbed the large four-battery flashlight from a shelf near the opening.

Lisa spoke nervously. "We thought about closing this entrance off, but haven't gotten around to it yet."

Nick turned toward her, raising his eyebrows in question, to which she gave him a shrug and turned red. Lisa always felt the need to fill in the conversation. Her way of diffusing tension.

"I'm glad you didn't. We might have had to open it back up." Agent Stafford shone his light around the first room that she and Nick had discovered in their initial investigation.

"I understand another body was found further down in the tunnel?" Agent Rossi was beginning to look interested. Who wouldn't be interested in a secret tunnel in an out-of-the-way place like Clementville?

Nick swallowed. He hoped they didn't hold his forbears' sins against him. "We found one, and then the forensics team found another one. My grandfather."

Agent Stafford jerked around. "How did you find out?"

"DNA test. I'm surprised it wasn't in the report. It was after you guys had closed the investigation."

"We'll add that information to the report." Agent Rossi looked up at Agent Stafford, who was making notes in his notebook. "This could make a big difference in the investigation."

"How?" Now Nick was concerned. Glancing over at Lisa, he could tell she was, too.

The agents looked at one another, then at Nick, and Agent Stafford spoke. "Too early to share, now. Believe me, as soon as I get the go-ahead, you'll be the first to know."

"I'd appreciate it." The longer he was with the agents, the more anxious Nick became. Was someone in his family related to the current investigation?

5

Del pulled up to Nick's house and parked next to his pickup truck, a very quiet Darcy in the seat next to him. She'd hardly said a word since they left the café.

Of course, that was only five minutes ago.

They exited the vehicle and stood in front of the house, waiting for Clay to arrive in his SUV.

His mind was swirling with unanswered questions. Who had been in Darcy's building, and why? He took peeks at Darcy's face, trying to gauge what she was thinking.

"Have you been out here?" Del propped an elbow on the bed of his 1999 Ford truck.

Darcy followed his lead, leaning against the vehicle. "Lisa's brought me out a few times."

Now, what to say? "Nice place."

"Beautiful." Darcy paused, then looked at him sideways. "Somebody's been in my place, Del."

"I know." He stood, staring at the house, trying to formulate his thoughts. *It's hit her that she and the kids could be in danger.* "We'll take care of you, Darcy." He turned his gaze on her and watched as she visibly relaxed her shoulders and closed her eyes for a moment. When her eyes met his, they were bright. Tears?

She nodded, and Del grinned when she stiffened her spine a bit.

The roar of an engine turned their heads as Clay's four-wheel-drive SUV pulled up beside them. Clay jumped out of the vehicle. For a big guy, he moved quickly.

Del crossed his arms in front of himself, eyeing Clay. "I'm surprised your noisy vehicle doesn't alert every crook around."

"The price you pay for extra power." Clay joined them. "Were you guys waiting for me?"

Del uncrossed his arms. "Lisa and Nick didn't come out when we drove up, so we assume they're already in the basement or the tunnels."

"Probably." He gestured to Darcy. "Ladies first."

"Thank you, kind sir." Darcy walked along in front of them, up the brick sidewalk and onto the wooden porch, her light footsteps quiet in contrast to the heavier steps of the two men.

Del had teased Lisa for wanting to keep the wooden porch instead of replacing it with concrete or composite decking material. After she'd fallen through the rotten original floor right in front of Nick, he figured she'd want it as sturdy as possible. But no, she wanted to be able to hear people walk up on her porch, so wooden porch, it was.

He opened the front screen door and heard footsteps clomping up the basement stairs. "Sounds like we got here right on time."

Nick, Lisa, and the two FBI agents emerged into the living room.

"Hey. What's up?" Lisa looked at her brother, Darcy, and

Clay with a slight frown. "Not that I'm not always glad to see you."

Clay acknowledged her with a tight-lipped smile. "It's not a social call, unfortunately." He looked behind Lisa to the agents. "Del, Darcy, this is Special Agents Stafford and Rossi."

Both agents held out their badges as protocol insisted. Del took a close look at the badge numbers, especially Agent Stafford. He wasn't overly fond of the way he was eyeing Darcy.

"I didn't figure. I got Darcy's message as we were about to go down to the tunnels." Lisa looked at her brother. "And I thought you were checking out Darcy's apartment project?"

Del shrugged and then shook his head at his sister. It was nice to have something on her, for once. "I was until said apartment dweller came and got me to investigate a mystery in the basement underneath the café."

"You're joking." Nick stared at them, his gaze finally resting on Del.

"Not even close." Putting his hands deep in his pockets, his mouth went dry. "It seems you're not the only one with special features in your house."

Special features. Darcy shook her head. "It seems that I, well, Mom and I, have a tunnel leading to our basement, and someone has been using it." She glanced over at Del, her backup.

He shook his head. "It was the darnedest thing—an opening similar to what you found down in the basement here, except that it's been used recently, looks like."

Her mind was spinning. It was an odd situation, for

sure. Why was someone coming into her building? Did the FBI agents or Clay suspect her of being involved in whatever was going on in those tunnels? She chided herself. *Of course not. But...* When they'd found evidence of criminal activity last year, she had overheard some of the agents and analysts from the FBI talking in the café, calling into question Nick's innocence. Clay wouldn't, but these agents didn't know her from Adam. *Well, maybe from Eve. Focus, Darcy.*

Agent Stafford was watching her closely. Great. She tried to refrain from giggling nervously, but it was going to be difficult.

"Have you seen evidence of a break-in?" Agent Rossi was on the ball. She narrowed her eyes at the three newcomers.

Clay spoke up. "Darcy...er...Mrs. Sloan had noticed some items in the dining room and kitchen moved around, but didn't think anything of it since there are a few different employees in and out."

Darcy chimed in. "But then I remembered the receipt box."

"Receipt box?" Agent Ross was taking notes.

"I had put it in my desk drawer the other night, and the next morning, it was on top of the desk. At the time, I thought I'd forgotten, but I know I didn't." Darcy glanced up at Del.

"This morning she found muddy prints in the basement, one of which was partially hidden underneath the shelf. When we moved it out from the wall, we found the other part of the print, plus a piece of plywood leaned up against the wall covering a hole."

"Which led to a tunnel." Stafford took in a deep breath and looked squarely at Agent Rossi. "I'd say this merits investigation, wouldn't you?"

The female agent looked like she was annoyed at her

temporary partner, but was prepared to do her job. "Yes, in light of this new finding, I would say so."

Rossi took out a small notebook and jotted down the story Clay told them. "We'll need to look at the entrance in the café basement and see if the tunnels connect."

"I would be surprised if they didn't." Nick had been shaking his head the whole time. "This is crazy. When I think about the system of tunnels out here, and then to think there are more, closer to town? What's been going on around here?"

Rossi closed her notebook and tucked it into her pocket. "When we know more, we can fill you in. Now it's become an active investigation."

Lisa rubbed her hands down the front of her jeans and shivered. "I hope we don't find another body."

"Don't even mention it." Darcy closed her eyes. This was the last thing she needed. Not only was she trying to take over the café for her mom, but she was also enduring a renovation with two preschoolers.

And a home invader. I have all the luck, don't I?

"You can't stay there." Del looked down at her, deadly serious.

"Where can I go? I can't just go out and rent a hotel room for myself and the kids. If you notice, there isn't one within thirty miles of here. Besides, I need to be close to the café."

Stafford's brows went up. "We can secure the entrance."

Del nodded as he faced Darcy. "We'll work something out. We'll be starting electrical work in the apartment soon. It would be better for the kids if nobody's there, anyway. Safer for everyone." Del was staring at her as if she were the only person in the room. The only person he could boss, perhaps?

Her small stature was no match for her temper. She raised herself up as high as her height allowed. "Del…"

Lisa put a hand on her arm. "The idea of something happening to you when we know someone has been in the building has us worried, that's all." When Del opened his mouth to say something, Lisa glanced at her brother and shook her head. "We'll talk to Roxy and Dad. They'll know what to do."

Her breathing calmed, and she closed her eyes. "Fine. I'll call Mom on the way back to town." She looked at her watch, avoiding Del's eyes, wondering if she had to ride back with him. At this point, she wished she'd driven herself. She could use the alone time. "I need to get to the café as soon as possible. I told Mandy and Jimmy I'd return before the lunch rush."

"I'm ready when you are." Del pulled out his keys and opened the screen door for her to precede him out to the porch.

Apparently, she was riding with Del.

Oh, joy.

The basement underneath the café seemed smaller to Del when he, Darcy, Clay, and the two FBI agents were all down there. Lots of tall people in a room with a low ceiling.

All but Darcy. Darcy was the petite one of the bunch. Was there a height requirement for FBI agents? Agent Julia Rossi was five ten if she was a foot.

Del kept an eye on Agent Stafford. Entirely too friendly, if you asked Del.

"When did you first notice evidence of someone's having been here?" Agent Stafford had his notepad out, writing down Darcy's answers. He seemed to hang on to her every word.

Her eyes flitted over to Del. He could see the tremor in her hands, and watched as she pulled them together to still their movement. He smiled, sending encouragement her way. She visibly relaxed.

"The first time I noticed something missing or moved from the kitchen was about three weeks ago." Darcy lifted her shoulders in a shrug. "I didn't really think about it. We have three part-time waitresses, a cook, and then Mom and me, so it's hard to pinpoint exactly when it started."

Frank Stafford nodded. "I understand. You noticed it in the basement, this time?"

Darcy's eyes were wide. "I wouldn't have if not for the footprints."

Agent Rossi took pictures of the dried mud and the hole in the wall, and measured the footprint on the floor. With the increased lighting, it was clearly a large men's-size boot print. Crouching, she looked up at Stafford. "Do you want me to process, or should I call in a unit?"

Stafford was all business. "Go ahead and stabilize it, then call in the unit from Louisville."

"Got it." Rossi continued spraying the footprint with a hardener to lift the shape, size, and particulars of the sole of the invader's footwear. While it dried, she stood and made her way up the stairs to get a better signal, and, Del figured, to have some privacy.

Stafford looked from Darcy to Del, then back to Darcy. "Agent Rossi and I will take prints of your employees so we'll have elimination prints on file." He focused on Del. "I don't suppose your fingerprints are in the system?"

Darcy's eyes, if possible, grew rounder. "Possibly. When we lived on the army base, we were printed and issued an ID. She turned to Del. "You?"

Del shook his head, dropping his gaze from her for a few

seconds. There was only one time he might have been printed, but he hadn't been, and it was a long time ago. "Not that I'm aware of."

Darcy was nervous, as expected. "I'll go tell Mom and Jimmy, and they can tell the waitresses."

Roxy and Steve Reno had cut their day off short when Darcy had called with the news of the findings in the basement. Darcy was tied up with this, and somebody needed to be at the helm in the café.

"Good. If we could get those by the end of the day, it would be helpful. We'll try to get the CSI team in from Louisville in the morning, and then it will be marked off as a crime scene."

"What about the tunnel?" Del was surprised they hadn't asked to enter it yet.

"I'm getting to that." Stafford looked at the three locals sternly. "Did all three of you go in the tunnel?"

Clay shook his head. "No, I just saw as much as possible from the entrance, with the flashlight."

"Good. Otherwise, you would have ruined additional footprint evidence." He noted their response.

Clay took out his investigative notebook. "I couldn't see more than about fifty yards and then it branched off. From what we could tell, one tunnel goes north, and one goes northwest."

"Toward the river?"

Clay nodded affirmation. "Yes, toward Nick Woodward's house."

"Interesting development."

Clay's face was grim. "I thought so, too. We thought it best to get out of there and find you guys."

"Good call." Stafford was stern as he considered Clay.

Agent Rossi came down the stairs. "I've got Agent

Brannock and his team coming down from Louisville in the morning. Should get here around nine o'clock. They'll gain an hour traveling, which is in our favor." Her city accent gave her away. She wasn't from south of the Mason-Dixon.

"Good." Agent Stafford faced Darcy. "Is it going to be a problem for you to close tomorrow?"

Darcy's hand went to her chest. "Is it necessary?"

The agent frowned. He looked at Darcy and softened. "Maybe you can stay open while we check the tunnels. Three days?"

"It will give me time to let the regulars know we'll be closed." Darcy cut a glance at Del.

Del had to speak up. "Should she and her kids be here?" Maybe advice from the FBI would get her to a safer place. She wasn't thinking. Was Darcy was more worried about the loss of business than her safety?

"I think the upstairs apartment is fine unless you think the perpetrator has been up there?"

"I haven't seen any signs of anyone upstairs. I have two preschoolers, and they need to be in their own house." Darcy glanced up at Del defiantly.

"I understand. Until we find evidence to the contrary, I think you'll be okay up there. It's the café kitchen and dining room, as well as the basement that we're interested in examining." Stafford glanced between the two. "Sound good?"

"Yes."

"No."

Darcy's "yes" and Del's "no" came at the same time, causing them to look at one another sternly. Didn't she know she could be putting herself and her twins in danger?

"I'm the one who lives here, and I think we'll be fine. I

have Clay on speed dial if anything out of the way happens."
She arched her brow at Del triumphantly.

*And it'll take Clay fifteen minutes to get here from
Marion. A lot can happen in fifteen minutes.*

"We can arrange for FBI surveillance if it would make
you feel better." Stafford ignored Del and concentrated on
Darcy. Fair enough.

"We'll be fine. I'm going to be out of town tomorrow
afternoon and Del has graciously offered to keep the kids."
She looked up with an expression that spoke volumes.
Volumes of "Take THAT."

"Good. Just remember, the offer stands."

"We'll take care of her safety." Del stared at Clay and
Stafford until Stafford gave in and acknowledged him.

"Very well." Stafford turned to include Rossi in the
conversation. "We'll get those elimination prints done this
afternoon if you can call in your part-time employees. Can
you limit your trips down here to get supplies?"

"We can." Darcy hesitated, and then turned her eyes
toward Del. Was she at least a little bit concerned? Her
expression told him she was torn between listening to him—
the voice of reason, in his opinion—and proving her mettle in
protecting her family.

Whatever her reasoning, he'd help her any way he could.
Maybe without her knowing it.

6

"You should have brought Mom. She eats this stuff up." Darcy sighed.

Lisa could tell Darcy's emotions were close to the surface and she was doing her best to tamp them down.

Lisa turned this way and that in the three-way mirror. The bridal shop was busy with teenage girls looking for last-minute prom dresses. Fortunately, the bridal portion of the store was separate. She had this side to herself. Just her, Darcy, and the seamstress.

"I brought Roxy with me when I bought it." Lisa chewed her bottom lip as she looked at herself in the flowing gown. She'd chosen ivory because, with her red-haired complexion, a stark white made her look more like a ghost-bride than a blushing bride.

Darcy smiled at her in the mirror. "It's perfect, Lisa."

"Is it?"

The seamstress laughed and put her face in her palm. "Honey, I've seen this dress on lots of girls, and believe me, you're the one it was made for."

She could feel herself blush. "Aw, I bet you say that to all the brides."

"I'll let you in on a little secret." The good lady was talking surprisingly well, considering she was holding straight pins between her lips as she bent over, pinning up the hem.

To Lisa, it looked scary.

"What's that?" Lisa met her eyes in the mirror, as she had Darcy's.

"Some brides think enough of themselves that I don't have to say anything."

Lisa was in awe, her eyes again on her reflection. "I can only imagine. I've been in on enough bridal shopping trips to know that." She caught Darcy's eye in the glass. "You'll tell me if I start turning into 'bridezilla,' won't you?"

The sheen of tears belied the broad smile on Darcy's face. "That's what sisters are for."

A bubble of laughter worked its way up." Okay, I can be your sister, but my brother is NOT your brother, kapisch?"

"Got it." Darcy stepped up beside Lisa, looking at her. "She's right, you know. It was made for you. I can't imagine this dress looking as good on anyone else."

Chicken nuggets eaten, Del looked around the living room at the toys strewn all over the place. He would pick them up, except for two little heads resting on his lap, asleep, in front of the television.

He'd carefully arranged his crossed feet so as not to interfere with the Candy Land game they'd been playing when Benji had climbed up in his lap and promptly fallen asleep. He promised Ali he wouldn't put it away so they could finish it later. She soon said she needed a break, and before he knew it, she was down for the count as well. Had he slept a little, too? Probably, because when he heard quiet footfalls coming up the stairs to the apartment, he cleared his throat softly and hoped it was Darcy.

Darcy opened the door slowly, then looked confused as she came in. Until she saw them on the sofa. Then, she smiled, and he couldn't help but return it.

"You three look awfully comfortable." She spoke softly and stood there for a moment, shaking her head. "It also looks like the kids had a good time."

"I didn't dare put away the game after Benji went to sleep. Ali wouldn't have it. Thought we might come back to it after her 'break.'" He laughed silently, his smile growing when Darcy covered her mouth to control her mirth.

"That's my girl. Never give up." She looked at her children with an adoring gaze. "Who was winning?"

"Benji."

"Ooo, I'll bet that was going over well."

He chuckled. "Yeah. When he drew the 'Princess Frostine' card, I thought we were going to have a meltdown."

She flinched. "Ouch. I should have warned you."

"I'm confused. When we were little, Princess Frostine was Queen Frostine. When did she get demoted?"

Darcy grunted. "About the time the next marketing generation showed up, I imagine."

Del chuckled quietly, doing his best to keep it light between them. "Don't tell her I told you, but when Lisa was just old enough to play, she had a redheaded tantrum if she didn't get 'Queen Frostine' first. We finally learned to stack the deck in her favor."

Darcy's laugh exploded, and she turned away to compose herself when Ali stirred. She whispered. "Sorry."

"Hey, nothing to be sorry about. I get to leave, remember?" He waggled his brows.

"Very funny." She put her hands on her hips and tilted her head, looking lovingly at her two babies. "I should get them to bed." She bent to pick up Benji, stopping at his words.

"Need help?"

Her head jerked up in surprise as their eyes met. He could see them softening. "No, but I won't turn it down."

"Good." He began by gently pulling his feet from the large ottoman-coffee table to the floor, trying his best not to wake either of the twins. "Take Benji. I think he's on top."

Her lips pursed in a cross between a smile and a contained laugh. She picked him up, all forty-plus pounds of him, putting his limp arm around her neck and adjusting his weight on her slight form.

"You're good."

"Not really, just experienced."

Del eased Ali into his arms and stood a moment as she wriggled around, finally winding her little arms around his neck before sighing and going limp. She didn't wake, burrowing into his arms as if she belonged there.

He could get used to this.

Children in bed, light out and the door closed to their room, Del tiptoed into the living room to dismantle the game pieces.

"You don't have to do that." Darcy suddenly sounded nervous.

"Hey, I made the mess, I'll clean it up. I just hope Ali doesn't think I've reneged on my promise to continue the game." He looked at Darcy and his eyes widened. "She won't, will she?"

"Del, she's four."

"Yeah. Sometimes she seems much older than four."

"Tell me about it. I always say she's four-going-on-fourteen."

"Sounds about right." He had continued picking up the pieces, putting them in their respective places, as they talked. "She's very discerning, isn't she?"

"To a fault. I can't get anything by her." Darcy shrugged. "I remember being in tune with Mom, but I was twelve when Dad died. Ali doesn't know anything about her dad except for what I've told her, and pictures."

Del raked his hand through his hair, put his cap on, and stood, pushing his hands deep into his pockets. "They're good kids."

"Thank you." Her expression was filled with pride and thanksgiving. "I like them."

"You should be proud of yourself."

"I haven't done anything except try to roll with the punches."

"And you've had lots of those." He stared down at her. He wanted to draw her out, but she was tired and needed sleep before the morning shift at the café tomorrow. Another time. He took a deep breath and mentally shook himself. "I'd better get going."

"Del, I can't thank you enough for keeping the kids." She put her hand on his arm, which he felt to his very core.

"I'd be glad to do it anytime. Just holler." He smiled and winked at her, his hand covering hers briefly. He enjoyed the slight blush he thought he noticed, even in the shadowy room.

"Thanks." She opened the door. "I'll follow you down and lock the door."

Reality crashed in. "I wish you were more secure."

"We'll be fine."

He noticed she stiffened slightly. "I know. Did you lock the door from the basement to the stairwell?"

"Of course I did. I'm not a moron." Was she getting angry? It was the last thing he wanted.

He held his hands up in defense. "Sorry. I was just double-checking."

She sighed and closed her eyes briefly. "I know, and I'm sorry, too. It's been a long day."

"It has. We'll both double-check the locks." He started down the stairs, and when they got to the landing, he turned to her before opening the exterior door. "I could check the basement before I leave."

She opened the door and pushed him. "Go. Rest. You may be needed to save another damsel in distress tomorrow."

A corner of his mouth lifted. "Not many damsels around here, but I'll try my best to be in top form in the morning." He tugged at the bill of his cap in salute and made his way down the stairs.

An idea had planted itself in his mind, and he wondered if he could get away with it.

7

Del woke to the sun beaming into the truck window and a gentle knock next to where his head rested against it. His brilliant idea of sitting in the truck and watching for Darcy's intruder had yielded no information except that it still gets cold at night in May in Kentucky. He knew better than to ask Darcy to let him stay inside, which would have made more sense, but he at least wanted to be handy, just in case.

Clearing his throat, he rolled down the window to face his punishment from the beautiful woman standing outside his truck with her hands firmly planted on her hips. Uh-oh.

"What on earth are you doing out here?" She was fuming. "And in the same clothes you left in last night?"

"I was just..."

"You were just keeping an eye on the place. I get it, but good grief; do you not have confidence in me that I can ask for help when I need it?"

Del tilted his head and looked her in the eye, at a more even angle than usual, considering his height and her lack thereof. "Of course I do."

She looked up and down the empty street. "If people see your truck out here, they'll think something is going on." Now her face was red, and he felt a little guilty. But not much. Another part of him made him want to push the idea she'd sparked further down the road.

"Do you know how much traffic we get through here between the time I left the apartment and now? Zilch." He opened the door of the truck to step out and stretch, forcing her to move back. He didn't want to tower over her and intimidate her, but he was getting a major cramp in the leg he broke last year. If he didn't change position, he would scream.

She crossed her arms in front of herself. Classic defensive gesture. "I know there's not much, but I've made it this long, and Mom for years before me."

He held his hands up to ward off her ire. "I get it. I do. There has been an intruder in your place." As usual, he stuffed his hands in his pockets to give them something to do. He dipped his head before looking up and speaking again. "The idea of you guys up there all alone made me feel sick."

"It was probably the fast food you ate." She was softening. Her forehead relaxed and she took a deep breath. "Where'd you hide the evidence?"

Del grinned, unable to meet her eyes because if he did, he would laugh. Fast food? Not hardly. "Oh, I got rid of the evidence before I was sidetracked by adorable four-year-old urchins." He raked his hand through his hair, wondering about his level of disarray. He couldn't exactly look in the side-view mirror and check, with her standing there and all. She would find out he was just as vain as anybody.

She tilted her head and looked up into his eyes, all anger aside. "Listen, I know you're worried, and I appreciate it. I just need to prove I can take care of my own business."

"Who are you trying to prove it to?" He frowned a little,

narrowing his eyes at her serious expression. He could see a tiny vein bulging on the side of her forehead, indicating stress.

Darcy paused, thinking. He had noticed she did that when backed into a corner. When would she realize that there were people around her willing—and wanting—to help?

"Myself, I suppose." She couldn't meet his eyes after she said it.

That was the problem.

Pride.

She wanted to prove to herself that she didn't need anything or anyone —namely God—to rely on. He'd seen her push even her mother away from time to time, and he knew it hurt Roxy. Maybe he needed to back off. She was letting him know in no uncertain terms that she didn't welcome his help, so he would take her at her word.

But he would keep an eye out, anyway.

———— ∽ ————

By the time she made it around the side of the building, Darcy was so mad she could have spit nails. When the phrase came to mind, she felt a surge of humor, considering she was angry with a contractor. She closed her eyes and stood on the sidewalk for a few moments.

Get it together, girl.

Jimmy and Mom would be there any time.

She swung the door open as her cook drove up. Jimmy Whitaker was a treasure. Retired from a chemical plant in Calvert City, just up the highway from Marion, he had come to her mom first thing, asking for a job. He didn't need the money, but he'd always wanted to be a cook and needed something to do to keep out of his wife's way, so he insisted on minimum wage. Mad money, he'd said, to buy hunting and fishing equipment. He'd proved to be a good addition to their little operation. Both women-bosses had agreed on the superiority of his biscuits, and that was saying a lot.

Jimmy hailed her as she tried to slip through the door. "Mornin', Darcy."

"Mornin', Jimmy. You doin' all right this morning?"

"Nothin' movin' around won't cure." He laughed as he limped from his camo-painted truck to the door.

"Knee again?"

"Yeah, according to my left knee, we're in for a thunderstorm at about..." He held a finger up to the air and grinned. "...eleven o'clock."

Darcy laughed. It was good to have Jimmy in her kitchen. He knew as much about her as anybody around here, and he loved her anyway. "We'll try to work in an ice-break for you."

He held the door open, gesturing for her to go in ahead of him, as usual. "Aw, it'll be okay. Once I'm on it a while, I hardly notice it." He eyed her closely. "What are you doin' out here this early? You're not usually this far from the kids this early in the morning."

Was her color rising? "I had to take out some trash." She avoided his eyes as she pulled out filters and beans to start the morning coffee. "Didn't sleep a lot last night."

"Not surprised." He looked around the kitchen. "I don't see anything out of place, do you?"

She stuck her head through the doorway to the dining room, taking in the long counter. "No, I don't think so. We locked it up pretty tight last night."

"The extra lock on the basement door may have helped." He shrugged and hung his coat on the hook next to the door. "I don't imagine it made you feel any better."

"No, the idea of a stranger in here with access to the building is worrisome enough."

"No question." Jimmy narrowed his eyes at her. "How did the babysitting go last night with Uncle Del?"

She started the coffee grinder, which sounded like an airplane taking off, strategically timed so she didn't have to answer his question immediately. It needed consideration. Thinking about it, she remembered coming in the door to see both of her children sacked out on the couch, literally on top of Del. That made her feel things she had thought she would never feel again. It was a picture she didn't want to forget, but probably should. Del had looked exhausted, but happy.

Unlike this morning. This morning, he was just exhausted, and it served him right. What right did he have to park outside her residence and place of business all night? Didn't he know people around here would talk? That was all she needed. The more she thought about it, the madder she got.

The coffee grinder finally stopped, and the minutes she took to come up with an answer to Jimmy's question came up empty.

"They made it fine. I'm sure he filled them up with fast food and junk. I guess it's a small price to pay for free babysitting." She shrugged, avoiding Jimmy's eyes.

She was surprised when the first thing out of his mouth was a loud guffaw. "What's so funny?"

"You. I know for a fact he fed them grilled chicken nuggets and baked potato wedges, and for dessert, grapes cut in half."

She stared at him. "And how would you know?"

"Because I helped him fix it while you were getting ready to leave." He winked at her and turned back to his biscuit making.

63

Darcy calmed down before it was time to greet Mom. She knew Del meant well, but she needed him to realize she intended to do this on her own.

"Mornin', honey. How was the wedding-dress trip?" Mom gave her a quick hug. "Isn't it gorgeous?"

"It is." Darcy smiled at her mom. "Y'all did good."

Mom waved her off. "Nothing about me. Once she had it on, it was set in stone. No other dress would do."

Darcy nodded. "I remember the feeling."

A sheen of tears came across Mom's features. "I do, too." She sniffed. "You were a beautiful bride, sweetheart."

"You were, too, Mom." She walked into her mom's arms, for a moment relaxing in the care she felt. She wouldn't let the feeling linger, but she would enjoy it for a few seconds.

"Well, I've had experience in it, that's for sure." Mom winked at her as she let her go to pull on her apron.

Darcy wouldn't say anything to Mom about her disagreement with Del.

Mom gave her a bare-bones account of the happenings while she was out the evening before. "Have you decided on the specials for today?"

"I'm thinking meatloaf. It goes over well during the week." Darcy wrote it down on the legal pad and looked up to see her mom nodding her approval. "Plus, if we're closed for a few days, it'll keep."

"Sounds good. How about mashed potatoes, mac and cheese, green beans, lima beans, and salad for sides, and cornbread?"

"And biscuits." Darcy grinned as her mother chuckled.

"No worries. Biscuits are always on the menu." She looked at Darcy with a worried frown. "Is it okay to go down to the basement?"

"I asked the agents yesterday, and they told me if we limit

our trips, it'll be okay. Do you need something?" Darcy tried to save Mom from going up and down the steps when she could.

Mom handed her a list. "'Bout out of lard in the kitchen pantry." Mom had opened the large double-door pantry to check her ingredients. "And all-purpose flour. We're getting low." She pulled out a large plastic container, which was more than half-empty.

Darcy added flour and lard to the list. "I'll bring them up. I say until they tell us otherwise, it's business as usual." She turned back to her mother before heading down the basement steps. "Is there room in the cooler up here for a couple of big roasts, for tomorrow?"

Mom opened the refrigerator unit, standing to the left of the full-sized freezer. "Should be. I think three would be safer. That way if we get shoved out, we can at least make beef stew."

"Good idea." She started down the stairs and called back to the cooks in the kitchen. "Be right back. This will take more than two trips."

"Where's the elevator when you need it?"

8

Showered and shaved, Del arrived at the door of the café. He was glad to have a key to the alleyway door so he could avoid Darcy. When he saw her a couple of hours ago, she was livid. If looks could kill, he'd be six feet under right now.

He entered from the outside door about the time Darcy was heading to the basement. She looked at him in surprise when they came face to face in the small landing where the stairs split. No avoiding her now.

Her face flared as she took a deep breath and clenched her lips shut. "Del."

"Darcy." Would she act as if they'd not had words earlier? Could he be so lucky? And was that even the right tactic? He didn't want her mad at him, for many reasons.

In the meantime, he stood there, their eyes meeting, time slowing down. He watched her face soften. Her shoulders relaxed, and she tilted her head to one side as she shook it, a massive sigh coming from her.

"Del Reno, you're going to be the death of me."

His ire went up a few notches. "That's what I'm trying to prevent." *Good job. Way to go, Romeo.*

The shoulders went back up and she looked to the ceiling. The moment was over. "I've made it just fine before you came along, and I'll make it just fine when this project is over and you're just another customer."

He couldn't help it. His lips twitched. "And stepbrother."

"That doesn't even count."

Hmmm. "Lisa can be your sister, but I'm not your brother?"

"No." She stared at him for what felt like a full minute.

He stared back, relaxing a bit. "Okay."

The last thing he wanted was for Darcy to look at him as her brother. Did it even count when your parents were in their fifties and you weren't raised together? In his opinion, no. They were two people who were in high school at the same time and lived in the same town. That was all.

She put her hands on her hips and huffed. "If you'll excuse me, I need to go down to the basement and get some lard and flour."

She'd been staring at him, hoping he'd take the hint that he was in the way. Maybe in more ways than one. He stepped to one side. After all, she was impeding his progress upstairs as well. "Sorry. Anything I can carry up for you?"

"I think I can manage."

A voice from behind her interrupted. "Darcy Emerson Sloan, you just said you'd need to take two trips, and here's Del, offering to help." Roxy's eyes sparkled from the doorway behind her daughter. When had she appeared?

"Fine." She gave him a dirty look and started down the stairs to the basement and potential crime scene.

"Her bark is worse than her bite." Roxy patted Del on the back.

"I'm not so sure. Her bark is pretty definite." Del met Roxy's eyes and then turned to follow Darcy's form as she descended into the basement.

Roxy sighed. "She's going through a difficult time. It was four years ago, you know."

"When Justin died?"

She wiped her nose with a tissue. "Four years since the soldier showed up on her doorstep to tell her he'd been killed."

Darcy hadn't meant to take out her frustrations on him. He wished he could get it across to her that he would gladly shoulder some of the burdens for her. He glanced up at Roxy. "I'd better go help her before she tries to carry it all upstairs just to spite me." He started to head down the steps and stopped. "Thanks for telling me."

Roxy nodded. "Oh, and we need another can of baking powder."

"Gotcha." He grinned at his stepmother. "I've been praying for her, you know."

"I had a feeling." Tears gathered in her eyes. "Thank you. She needs to start praying herself. If she won't, we'll have to do the praying for her."

"I think we can do that."

———⁂———

"I thought you'd gotten lost on the way from the kitchen to the basement." Darcy knew she sounded petty and disgruntled, but she didn't care. Why wouldn't people leave her alone and let her do things for herself? Let her make her own mistakes instead of wrapping her in cotton wool for protection.

"Your mom told me she needed baking powder, as well as the other stuff." He appeared at her side.

She could feel her face redden, and it only served to irk her more. "Fine."

"What's the heaviest thing you need carried up?" Del's voice was calm.

She looked down at her list. "We need three large prime rib roasts from the freezer, ten pounds of ground round from the cooler, ten pounds of flour, and the baking powder."

"That's all?" He pulled open the freezer door and saw the size of the beef cuts. "Okay, now I know why you thought it would take at least two trips." He looked at her, humor simmering in his eyes. "It would have taken you four."

"Not hardly."

"Well, four without hurting yourself." He teased her, and her defenses began to drop.

"Maybe I exaggerated my abilities just a tad." She couldn't help it. She grinned back. How nice would it be to have someone on hand to do little things for her, carry stuff up from the basement, cheer her up...?

He pulled the packages of meat out, stacking all three in the crook of his arm. "I can carry the flour."

"Are you kidding? You're already carrying about thirty pounds of meat."

"And?" His eyes were mischievous. "I feel the need to prove myself."

She jutted her jaw and considered him as he stood there holding thirty pounds of meat. "Let's see what you've got."

She stacked the ten-pound bag of all-purpose flour on top of the meat and smiled with satisfaction when his arms went down with the extra weight. "Ten extra pounds is more than it sounds like, isn't it?"

His face was reddening, and the veins on his muscular arms were beginning to bulge with the weight. "I'll be fine." He shifted it so the flour wouldn't fall off the top. "Can you get the rest?"

"I can." She pulled out a plastic container and put the thawed ground round in it. For a cook, it was funny that the one thing she hated was touching raw meat. Good thing there were plastic gloves.

"Don't forget the baking powder." His voice strained a bit.

"I won't." She gave him an imperious glance. "You may go on up."

"You don't have to tell me twice." He headed for the door and up the stairs, with Darcy following him.

He had made it to the kitchen, Darcy close behind him, when she saw clumps of dried mud on the floor. The makeup of the soil looked exactly like what she'd seen in the basement. How had she missed it? She'd missed it because she was concentrating on being mad at Del. This time it was next to the door.

The door leading up to her apartment.

Del heard the clatter as he put the last roast in the cooler. He wondered what was taking Darcy so long. She was right behind him. Wasn't she?

"Del!"

He could hear the distress in her voice. "Was it too heavy, after all?"

"Del, come here." Her voice brooked no argument this time. She was serious.

He turned and looked at Roxy, whose eyes were wide.

She'd taken the double-wrapped bag of flour off the top of the frozen meat and set it on the counter.

"Go see what's wrong."

Del didn't wait. He figured a mom knew when her kid was serious and when she was just peeved.

He met her on the small landing, where she gazed at the floor. She'd dropped the container, but didn't spill the meat. He followed her eyes and what he saw made his blood freeze, and not just from carrying a large amount of frozen meat. He saw the soil she was pointing to.

She looked up at him, her face drained of blood. "It's..."

"...at the door to the apartment." Del finished the sentence and rubbed his hand down over his face. He'd staked out the building from the outside to stay in her good graces when he should have been inside. He should have known this would happen. Should have been there to protect them.

Darcy was staring at him, now. Could she see the clashing emotions on his face? He schooled his features and put on what he hoped was a stern, focused expression.

"Del, it's not your fault." Her eyes widened as she spoke.

She knew what he was feeling. He wasn't sure how he felt about that.

He swallowed thickly and nodded. He pulled out his phone and scrolled his contacts until he found Clay's number. The sheriff had told them to call him if they saw anything else. Fortunately, he answered on the second ring.

"Sheriff Lacey."

"Clay, Del."

"What's going on?" The young sheriff was all business. He knew Del wouldn't call at this time of the day to shoot the breeze.

"We've found more dried mud like in the basement."

"Where?"

Del glanced up at Darcy. She still looked scared. "On the landing."

"I'll be right over." Clay paused a second. "I'll give Agent Stafford a call, too. They'll want to be in on this."

Great. The last thing he wanted was for the smooth, well-educated, good-looking Frank Stafford to hang around here. He'd seen him looking at Darcy. "Fine. I'll be here." He saw Darcy put her hand on her hip and revised his statement. "Darcy and I will be here."

Clay's voice sounded like he was trying to cover up a laugh. "Fine. As long as somebody is."

9

It had been a long day. The soil found just that morning in the stairwell leading to the apartment had been analyzed and found to be the same makeup as in the basement. The same as what was in the tunnel system beyond the opening.

Tonight, the federal agents, Clay, and Deputy Ben Carson were conducting a sting operation, and Darcy and the kids had to be out of the way while letting the intruders think she was there. The idea was to limit how many people were in and out, to make whoever was involved think they weren't being surveilled.

Darcy noted the darkness outside her windows and looked down at the large gift bag she had filled with clothes, shoes, and other necessities they'd need for a few days. Mom was going to take it home with her after the supper rush. She'd gotten the suitcases out, at first, then realized that seeing them leave with suitcases would tip off anyone watching the building. Gift bags? Maybe it will look like they're going to a birthday party somewhere.

Trying to anticipate their needs was hard enough under

good circumstances, but this? This was nerve-wracking. Her stepdad, Steve, had picked up Benji and Ali at their preschool and taken them home with him.

She knew it was important not to let anyone know she wasn't going to be there. It bothered her, a little, that she couldn't tell Del. After he surveilled her apartment from the outside last night, she knew his protective streak had come in full force. It had made her mad when she caught him, but now? Now she felt a stab of regret that she'd been so hard on him. She appreciated his watch-care over them, but it was the reason she couldn't tell him. If the intruder had seen him outside the night before, he wouldn't think anything about Del's truck being outside on the street.

But if Del got hurt in the midst of a sting operation? She couldn't think about that.

She and the kids would be fine at Mom and Steve's house. Del would be out of the way, and law enforcement would be able to do their job.

Looking around the empty apartment, she tucked her toiletries into a tote bag that could double as a purse. She was waiting for Agent Rossi to take her place, so she turned on the television to the channel she would normally have on at this time of night. Clay was waiting downstairs to meet Agents Stafford and Rossi, and then he would deliver her to her mom's house.

So much to organize. She'd studied law enforcement, but this was several notches above the level of investigative techniques she'd learned. Would she have gotten to this point? As a college student, she'd dreamed of being an FBI agent, but that was before she had Ali and Benji. Exciting? Yes. Dangerous? Too much for her taste, these days.

A soft knock on the door drew her attention, and she grabbed the bag, then headed to the door. Looking through the peephole, she saw Clay, and behind him, Agent Stafford and a blond woman. A blond? When she opened the door, she startled a bit, recognizing Agent Rossi, usually a beautiful brunette, with a blond wig and porcelain-tinted makeup. From a distance, no one would know it wasn't Darcy upstairs, but a decoy.

"Come in." Darcy stared at her double, except for the eight inches difference in their heights. It was incredible. "How did you come up with such a great wig on short notice?"

Julia Rossi smiled. "I've got lots of tricks up my sleeve. One of the best disguises for me is a blond wig. I can transform fairly quickly."

"Wow." Darcy shook her head, then became the hostess. "There are snacks in the refrigerator, chips on the counter. Make yourself at home."

"I'm not here to eat your food, just to draw out a criminal, hopefully."

"I hope you do. I'd like to get my life back to normal." A tinge of regret touched her. What was normal? She looked up at Clay, waiting by the door. "I'm ready when you are."

He picked up the bag and opened the door. "Got everything?"

"I think so. Hopefully, this is just for one night."

"Sorry you have to close earlier than we thought." Julia grimaced a little. "We don't prefer to disrupt lives unnecessarily, but we've got to get to the bottom of this."

Darcy took a deep breath. "I'm ready."

Clay gestured for her to precede him and turned back to Agent Stafford, who would be stationed in the kitchen, out of sight of the door. "I'll be back in fifteen minutes."

Stafford nodded, relaxed, but vigilant. "We'll be fine. I've got coms in, and Deputy Carson is on the street in a panel van. He can get here in three minutes."

"Good." Clay gave him a small salute and pulled the door shut behind him.

When they arrived at the bottom of the steps where they'd found the second set of footprints, Darcy paused.

Clay nodded encouragement. "My SUV is in the alley behind the post office."

They made their way there, hopefully unnoticed.

Del was tired after a long, stressful day. He could be at home, relaxing, but no way was he going to leave Darcy to fend for herself tonight. He couldn't believe Clay and the agents in charge were being so lax in their regard for Darcy and the kids. He should be inside.

Slumped down in his truck, the seat leaned back as far as he could without impeding his visual of the café and apartment above, he settled in with popcorn, a couple of granola bars, and a bottle of water. When he'd been in the café earlier, eating supper, Darcy had walked all around him, avoiding contact, which aggravated him. Didn't she know he was only looking out for her?

Women.

He kept an eye on the building as he munched on popcorn. His phone, set on silent, vibrated in the cupholder. Nick. "Hey, bud. What's up?"

"What's up with you?"

"Nothing much." He didn't take his eyes off the upstairs windows.

"Are you stalking that poor girl?" He could hear Nick's chuckle coming.

"It's not stalking if it's for her own good."

"You just keep telling yourself that."

"I shall."

"Hey, I talked to Stafford earlier."

Great. He wasn't real pleased with the way the guy seemed to be hanging around the café at supper time. Eating at the counter, monopolizing Darcy, who looked very nervous, by the way. And why wouldn't she be nervous? There'd been somebody outside the door of her apartment, for goodness sake.

"What did he want?" Stafford was probably fishing for some way to impress Darcy. Harsh? Maybe, but he wasn't the guy's biggest fan.

"He asked if we could supervise their crew shoring up the tunnels in the weaker places."

Del noted when the light came on in what was Darcy's bedroom. It was ten thirty. The kids had been in bed for a couple of hours already.

"Del?"

"Yeah. I'm here." And he wished he was in there.

"Can we meet them at eight in the morning to get started?"

"Sure. Do they have the supplies coming, or will we need to get them?"

He could see Darcy's shadowy figure moving around in the upstairs room. Did she double-check the doors? For a little bit, he thought he would go and check, but after getting caught out last time, he didn't dare. So, he sat.

"Did you hear me?" Nick was beginning to sound impatient.

"Yeah. They're having supplies delivered. Got it."

"Good. See you in the morning."

"See ya."

Del hit the red "hang up" icon and checked the charge on his phone. Forty percent. Better plug it in. Fortunately, his truck would charge his phone even if it wasn't running. The beauty of an old pickup. He leaned his head back and closed his eyes for a few seconds.

When he opened them, he realized he'd been asleep for an hour. An hour that could have meant life or death to Darcy, Benji, and Ali. He jerked, then stared at the windows on the second floor, seeing nothing but darkness. When his eyes dropped to the front of the café, his heart came up to his throat.

Smoke.

10

No thinking. Just doing.

Del called 9-1-1, then ran from the truck to the side door, for which he had a key. The priority was to get Darcy and the kids out of there before the smoke got upstairs. If he wasn't too late. *Don't even think it, Del.*

The door led to the landing where the doors to the kitchen, the basement, and the apartment met. Before he could get the door opened, he was grabbed and pulled away.

"Stay back." Clay's voice hissed in his ear.

"What are you talking about?" Del stared at him in unbelief. "We've got to get them out of the apartment. Smoke rises, you know."

"They're fine." Clay had his eyes trained on the door from their vantage point behind the dumpster.

Del shook his head. "What's going on?"

Clay glowered at Del, then looked back at the door. "We've set a trap for whoever has been coming through the tunnel."

"With Darcy and her kids in there?" He knew his voice

was rising and he could feel his hands balling up into fists. As his hand drew back to strike, Clay clapped his hand over Del's mouth and pushed him against the aging brick wall.

"Shut. Up."

Clay was bigger than Del by about twenty pounds, though they were of a similar height. He had always been tougher. Football defensive lineman to Del's quarterback. Funny, the things that ran through your head when you wanted to punch someone.

Clay got in his face and whispered loudly enough for Del to hear him, but quietly enough that the sounds of the smoke detectors and the loud scream of the firehouse alarm summoning the local volunteer firefighters would drown him out. "Darcy and the kids are at your dad's house."

"I just saw..."

"You saw Agent Rossi."

Del's eyes narrowed.

Clay spoke. "Are you going to be quiet and listen?"

He looked Clay in the eye. "What can I do to help?"

"You called 9-1-1, didn't you?"

"Of course I did."

Clay took a deep breath and shook his head. "Now that you're here, stay here and watch the door." Clay touched his ear, listening. "Coms. Stafford is in the kitchen pantry. The guy went up the stairs toward the apartment, and likely set the fire in the dining room. I'm going in to block him from leaving. You stay here, and if he gets by me, you can stop him."

"With what?" Del tried to think of something he could use as a weapon.

Clay held up the object in his hand. "Maglite?"

Del grabbed it, feeling the weight of it.

"I'd give you a gun, but I don't have my spare with me."

"I've got one in the truck."

Clay shook his head. "No time. If somebody comes out this door, clock him with the flashlight."

Del gave him a grim look. "Let's get this guy and see if we can connect it to Nick's house."

"That's the general idea."

Clay quietly opened the door and entered.

Del knew he'd been hard on Clay, mainly because he had set his sights on Del's sister until last year. Clay finally figured out that Lisa wasn't the girl for him, and now he had a girl of his own. Del looked up at the bricks in the darkened alleyway.

He's doing better than me.

There was a security light in the street, but the shadows were deep where he was hiding. The relief of knowing Darcy was safe allowed him to concentrate on the job at hand. He didn't like the idea of Agent Rossi up there, but she was a trained FBI agent and was probably tougher than he was.

Hopefully tougher than the guy who was up to no good.

There was a loud crash from the front of the building and Clay yelled. "Del, get in here."

He jerked the door open and rushed through a second door leading to the kitchen. Agent Stafford was on the floor, unconscious. Clay knelt over him, checking his pulse.

"Is he okay?"

"Call 9-1-1 again. Ask for an ambulance along with the fire truck, then get up to the apartment and check on Rossi. She should have been down here by now. I'm going after the guy. He went out through the front window." Clay stopped. "Tell Darcy there was no fire. Just smoke."

Clay went into the dining room and traced the intruder's steps to the jagged glass frame. He stopped short, then carefully climbed through and ran to his SUV.

Del made the call as he made his way to the apartment, giving the dispatcher Clay's info and Stafford's badge number. Good thing he'd memorized it back at Nick's place. He'd had a feeling it would come in handy. Where was Agent Rossi?

He went to the apartment door and looked up the stairs, still smoke-filled. Had the female agent been overcome with smoke? He quickly made his way up to the door and found Agent Rossi huddled on the floor, unconscious. Del was more than thankful Darcy and the twins were as far from here as possible.

Rossi was alive, but not well.

--- ⟨∽⟩ ---

Darcy shook as she drove to the café. When she arrived, it was chaos. Ambulances, state troopers, and some unmarked black SUVs had stopped, haphazardly, in front of her place of business. In front of her home.

She saw Del next to the ambulance and made her way to him, ducking under the crime scene tape. Until she got to him, she didn't realize tears were streaming down her face. He looked at her strangely, then over at Agent Rossi, who was in a gurney with a bandage on her head and oxygen attached to her nose. She was conscious, at least.

"What happened? How much damage?"

"There wasn't a fire. Somebody set some rags on fire in the trash can to fool us."

Darcy closed her eyes and drew in a deep breath. "Thank goodness."

Del nodded. "Clay isn't back yet. He followed the intruder after he got past Stafford and Rossi."

"He wasn't alone." Agent Rossi's raspy voice stopped them.

Darcy looked up at Del, and then they both looked down at the injured woman, who had pulled the oxygen mask away to speak, and was now coughing with every breath.

Darcy went to her. "Did you get a good look at them?"

She shook her head. "Came up behind me. The one I saw had on a ski mask. Thought I had the guy in my sights, then the smoke got too thick. Stafford and I—we didn't expect a second intruder. Didn't think I would need a gas mask for this job." She smiled weakly.

The EMT strapped Julia Rossi in and prepared to put her in the ambulance.

"Is Frank okay?"

Darcy looked over at Agent Stafford. He met her glance and gave her a small smile as he held an ice pack to his head, continuing his conversation with the officials.

"I think so." She glanced back to see him walking toward her, his tall, lanky frame weirdly reminding her of Del, if he worked in a suit and tie.

Agent Stafford came their way and stopped at the gurney before they loaded Julia up. "They'll take good care of you."

"I'm sure."

"These are nice folks here."

Stafford looked down at Darcy with what she thought was the first real smile he'd sent her way since he'd been here on the case. He'd been nice, but a little stand-offish. Maybe that was just her perception.

"Did you get a look at either of the guys?" He watched his partner closely.

"Medium height and build, the other a little taller. Couldn't see him as well. Ski masks, maybe a filter underneath," she choked out. "If Sheriff Lacey hadn't been on the ball, we would have had a different outcome."

Del spoke up. "If you guys hadn't been here, it might have been Darcy and her kids."

Darcy's eyes went to his and she saw the anxiety on his face. She didn't want him worrying about her. It created complications.

She heard the roar of a four-wheel-drive SUV and saw Clay getting out. He walked to them quickly, but confidently. Darcy had a thought that it was like watching everything in slow-motion.

"You guys all right?" He stood, hands on his hips, looking from the patient on the gurney to the agent with an icepack, and then to Del.

"Did you find anything?" Agent Stafford seemed angry. Probably at himself for underestimating their criminals.

"I'll be able to see more when daylight gets here. They think they got away clean, but we've got blood evidence at the window."

"The window?" Darcy looked at the beautiful plate-glass window on the front of the café and wilted. "The window."

Clay's face was grim. "Looks like when they couldn't get to the basement and couldn't break out the safety glass in the door, they went for the next-best-thing."

"I'm sorry, Darce." Del put an arm around her shoulders. "That's what insurance and family contractors are for."

Del stayed until the last emergency vehicle except Clay's and Stafford's left the scene of the crime. He shook his head as he looked at the damage done to the front window. It would have to be completely replaced, and the lettering re-done.

When was Clementville ever the scene of a crime? Thinking about it, he huffed. Maybe it had been the scene of more crimes than they knew. If the series of tunnels underneath their community was any indication, clandestine activity had been going on for a long time.

"Hey."

Del had been so deep in thought, he hadn't noticed that Clay had walked up to stand next to him until he spoke.

"What do you think, Clay? Isolated incident or part of something bigger?" Del looked the sheriff in the eye.

"If this were the only thing going on..."

"Yeah." Del snorted in disgust. "That's what I thought."

Clay shook his head. "The FBI wouldn't be interested if it was a simple case of breaking and entering. Agent Stafford thought they had a shot at catching at least a foot soldier in whatever operation was going on here. To tell you the truth, I'm a little surprised they didn't catch them."

Del faced east, watching the sun rise over their little town. "Do you ever think we're just a few steps away from God thinking we're too much trouble to fool with?" He shook his head again, glancing at Clay, who, to his surprise, was smiling.

"If we got what we deserved, mankind wouldn't have lasted this long." Clay glanced at him and motioned with his head toward Darcy. She'd come out and stood there, apart from the fray, staring at the building containing not only her livelihood but her home. "Somebody needs some support."

Del shifted his gaze to Darcy, sad to see the slight slump in her usually strong, if petite, shoulders. He closed his eyes for a second. *Is this my opening, God? Do you want me to comfort her?*

When he opened his eyes, Frank Stafford, the FBI agent, was standing next to Darcy, talking. Now her back was erect, her bearing confident. Maybe it wasn't Del's place to be a strong arm to lean on. Maybe God had someone else in mind.

"Seems that the job is taken for the moment." Del's jaw ached. He made himself unclench his teeth.

Clay shrugged, twisting his lips in thought. "Maybe. Maybe not. God's timing."

Del stared at Darcy and Stafford. "As long as she's okay. That's the main thing."

Steve and Roxy drove up, and Roxy exited the truck as quickly as possible, then made her way to her daughter. She clasped her to herself and held on. "Oh, honey."

"I know, Mom." Darcy wiped tears from her cheeks. "It looks worse than it is."

Dad walked over to Del. "What were you doing here, son?" He looked angry, but Del knew better. It was his immediate response to worry, and when he was worried, he came across as, at the very least, quite annoyed.

"I thought I was watching out for Darcy and the kids, but apparently I came close to interrupting a sting operation." Del glanced at Clay, who was chuckling.

"Seriously, if Del hadn't been here, I wouldn't have been able to go after the guy that went through the front window." Clay shook his head. "I didn't catch them, but I surprised them to the point of their leaving some pretty good evidence on the premises."

Dad nodded. "Good deal."

"Who's with the kids?" Del knew before he said it that they wouldn't leave them home alone. Hypervigilance.

"I called Lisa, and she's over there. They're still asleep."

Relief washed over him. "Good."

Dad squeezed Del's shoulder. "Lots of people taking care of Darcy, Benji, and Ali."

Del looked past his dad at the FBI agent talking on his

phone a little apart from anyone else. "Seems like it." He was glad God put people in place to watch over these three. He just wanted to be the one doing it.

———— ❦ ————

Darcy's attention wandered as her mother fussed over her and their building. She felt like she was floating above it all, looking at it from outside herself. It was silly, she knew, but she'd known those feelings before in times of great stress in her life. Her gaze wandered across the scene, which got brighter by the moment as the sun rose over their sleepy little community. There was talking going on all around her, and her focus stopped on Del. He stood there, talking to Steve and Clay, his look grim.

She began to relax, knowing so many people were watching out for her.

Thank You, God.

Honestly, she wasn't sure where that came from. She still watched Del, and suddenly his eyes met hers and a jolt of something went through her.

This didn't need to happen. Couldn't happen. He deserved so much more than she was prepared to give. Or did she need more than she was prepared to ask for? It was confusing, and she didn't need that in her life just now.

She pulled her eyes away from his, stiffened her spine, and put on a brave face as Frank Stafford walked up to her.

"I've called my forensics team, and they're leaving early." He studied her. "Are you okay?"

She held her head high. "Of course I am. Just grateful you were all here and I wasn't."

He straightened his loose tie. "Just doin' my job, ma'am."

She arched a brow at him, and he laughed. "Well, I

appreciate it." She had so many questions. Why were people breaking into her home? Her place of business? What was the FBI looking for? She shoved the questions back. They'd tell her when they knew something.

The way he looked at her made her feel a little uncomfortable, but she couldn't put her finger on it. He'd become very attentive. At first, she thought it was just a federal agent being polite. Now? She wasn't sure.

"This may be bad timing," Stafford spoke, looking around to see who was close by. "But I wondered if, when we get this case solved, you'd be interested in joining me for dinner one evening?"

She felt the red swamp her face. It wasn't as if she hadn't been asked out since she became a widow. She had, a few times. Having twin preschoolers was usually a buzzkill for any romantic notions, and she was notorious for using Ali and Benji as an excuse for not going out. But Agent Stafford? He knew she had kids. He probably knew more about her than she'd be comfortable with.

Clearing her throat, she glanced up at him, then over to Del, who seemed to be in deep conversation with Clay, and then back to Frank. "I'm not sure."

"I understand. We've got a case to solve, so you've got time to think about it." He stepped closer and took her hand. "I won't hold it against you if you say no, but it won't stop me from trying to persuade you to say yes."

11

Lisa had pulled a kitchen chair over to the counter so Benji could help her make biscuits. More likely, he was playing with the dough and any "biscuit" he made would be hard as a rock.

Nick came in the back door and moved up behind her. He tousled Benji's hair, and kissed Lisa's exposed neck, making her shiver to her toes.

"Good morning," he said.

"Good morning to you." She turned and kissed him, keeping an eye on the busy little boy and an ear ready to hear when Ali's feet hit the floor. "Benji is helping."

"These'll be good biscuits, won't they?" The boy's wide brown eyes met hers, and her heart melted.

"They will be excellent."

"Ex-slent." Benji grinned and turned to Nick. "Uncle Nick, will you eat one of my biscuits?"

Nick moved over to lean on the counter next to the Benji. His eyes met Lisa's over his head and he winked before turning back to the serious young man. "I would be honored."

Benji kept working the dough, and about the time they were ready to put the biscuits in the oven, Lisa heard the pitter-patter of a certain little girl's feet. Ali was awake, and as soon as she saw Nick, the flurry of pink ran and wrapped her arms around his legs. Nick was a favorite.

"Uncle Nick, did you have a sleepover, too?" She tilted her head as far back as she could to see his face before he picked her up so that her eyes were even with his, her little hands on his cheeks.

Lisa could feel her cheeks becoming impossibly hot, and when her eyes met Nick's, he winked at her audaciously. "No, sweet pea, but come June, your Aunt Lisa and I will have sleepovers all the time."

"June is when I'm going to be a flower girl." Their wedding was nothing to Ali; it was all about being a flower girl. She cupped her hands to whisper loudly into Nick's ear. "I've been one before."

He gave her a solemn look. "I saw you. You were the best flower girl I've ever seen." The compliment garnered him a squeeze around the neck.

Benji would not be outdone. "I'm gonna be a ring bear." He nodded emphatically. "I've been one before, too." He tilted his head and looked up at Lisa. "Why is it called a 'ring bear'?"

"It's actually ring bearer."

"What's a bearer?" The little face kept looking more confused as the conversation went on.

"It's someone who carries something. 'Bear' is another word for carry."

"A bear is a big animal. Cody at school said he saw a black bear once." His face was deadly serious.

Lisa wanted to laugh. Instead, after putting the pan of biscuits in the oven and setting the timer, she sat in the chair

—which was probably covered in flour, but she didn't care—and pulled Benji into her lap. "Sometimes the same word can mean more than one thing."

"That's weird." He frowned. "Did you know that, Uncle Nick?"

"Yeah, buddy, I did. It can be confusing."

"Where's Mom?" Ali had just noticed that Lisa and Nick were the only grownups around.

Lisa looked at the angel in Nick's arms and stood, setting Benji down on his feet. "Your mom had to go to the café to see about something."

"Oh. Do we get to stay all night at Granny's house again tonight?"

"We'll see. Your mom will let us know when they get back." She looked at her assistant baker. "Benji, do you want to help me check the biscuits?"

The thought of checking on something he'd had a hand in was too exciting for words. He nodded his head as hard as he could.

"We have to be careful. The oven door is hot, so you need to step back, okay?"

"I know. Mommy always tells us to take three steps back from the stove when she opens the door."

Darcy was such a good mom. Lisa hoped she would be when it came her turn to be one. "Your mom is right."

She took a potholder and opened the oven door. All four of them peered in. The biscuits were as light and fluffy as could be.

"Those look like Mr. Jimmy's biscuits." Benji looked at her with awe.

Lisa could have cried. "Benjamin Sloan, you just made my day."

———⟡———

Darcy walked through the dining room, shaking her head at the cleaning necessary before they could reopen. She'd left it perfectly clean last night, and now there was a film of ash and grime on everything. Absolutely everything.

Sometimes it was all too hard. Too much to deal with. The idea of carrying on in her mom's footsteps running a business felt ludicrous at times.

She stood at the doorway between the dining room and kitchen, seeing the metal trash can filled with the remains of charred rags they had set on fire to create as much smoke as possible. Smoke was as dangerous as fire, sometimes. Shivering at the thought that she and her two babies might have been here, asleep, and never awakened, she closed her eyes, trying to keep the tears from falling.

Suck it up, Buttercup.

She couldn't do anything until the forensics team got there, but she could open windows and let some of the smoke out. The apartment was probably soaking in smoke even as she stood there.

"Ms. Sloan?"

She looked back to see Agent Stafford coming toward her, so she pasted a serene expression on her face. "Call me Darcy. Everybody does."

"On one condition."

She noticed one of his brows rise minutely. He was a handsome man. She hadn't thought him her type, but nice enough. "What's that?"

"That you call me Frank." He stood, hands on his hips, tie loosened, and a bandage on the side of his head where he'd been hit earlier.

Her nerves must have been getting the best of her

because the small friendly gesture of asking her to use his given name was almost more than she could bear. It would be easier if he were curt and to the point. All business. But he wasn't.

His earlier suggestion that they see each other socially came to mind. Maybe it was time to get back on the horse, and maybe someone like Frank would be a good trial run.

"Doable." She smiled at him. "Frank."

"Good." He looked around and then back at her. "It's a lot. I know. And I hate to be the one to tell you that you can't touch anything until we've gone over every inch of the building."

"I thought as much." She took a deep breath before she thought, and then coughed. "Can I at least open some windows upstairs? Everything we own will be soaking in the smoke."

He shook his head. "Not yet. I'll tell the team sweeping the apartment to open the windows when they finish."

"Thank you. Maybe it will help." She didn't know what to do. In her recent experience, there was always something needing to be done, cleaned, cooked, or wiped, be it the café or for her children. "I'm a little at loose ends."

"I know. It would probably be best if you go back home with the Renos and we'll call you as soon as we know anything."

Nodding her head, those pesky tears threatened again. "I appreciate it, Frank." Her eyes wandered across the scene. She raised her hands and resigned herself to letting them fall in frustration.

"Go. Take care of your kids." He looked down, and then back at her. "I'm glad the three of you weren't up there."

"Me, too." Taking care of her babies was the most important and most meaningful job she had now. Before tears could fall, she waved her fingers and turned away, unable to say more.

She walked out as quickly as possible. And wouldn't you know, Del would be right in her way?

———⟨∽⟩———

Del caught Darcy by the arms before she plowed into him. Not that he would have minded.

"Del Reno, why are you constantly standing where I need to go?" Her face was tear-stained and frowning. She was one of those people who did everything in her power to make sure no one knew anything was the least bit wrong, even when her place had been broken into and vandalized, and if she'd been there, she might have been killed.

He cocked his head to one side. "Just coming to see if you needed anything." He looked behind her to see Frank Stafford talking to one of the analysts.

Great.

He was in no mood.

"I'm okay. There's nothing I can do, so I may as well go back to Mom and Steve's and take care of the kids."

She was decidedly grumpy. Fine. He'd about decided he'd kill 'er with kindness.

Stuffing his hands in his pockets, he looked at her. "Roxy's talking to Clay, and the team from Louisville just got here."

Darcy looked to see the group of analysts heading into her home. "What are they looking for?"

"Who?" Del tilted his head.

"Everybody. The FBI? The people breaking into my house? What's it all about?"

He turned in the direction she was looking. "I don't

know. Something's going on that they're not telling us, that's for sure."

Sighing, she closed her eyes. "I feel so useless."

"You're not, but I know what you mean. It all happened so fast."

"Were you watching the place again last night?" She gave him a stern glare, but it was softened by the glint of tears.

"Guilty as charged." He glared at her right back. "It might have been nice to know there was a sting operation going on. I almost walked into the middle of it."

She closed her eyes. "Del, you could have been hurt. After what those people did to Frank and Agent Rossi..."

"It's a good thing I was here. Clay was the only law enforcement standing."

"I know, but..."

Del looked over Darcy's shoulder. Frank stepped away. "So you're calling him 'Frank,' now." Del's blood pressure was rising, but he was not going to show it.

Her mouth hung open for a few seconds, and then she pressed her lips into a thin line. She put her hands on her slender hips and stared him down, all trace of tears gone. "And what business is it of yours what I call the man?"

"None at all." He clenched his jaw. If Stafford was the kind of man she was looking for, then she should go for it. As she intimated, it was none of his business.

She swept past him and out the door to join Roxy and Dad, still in a huddle with Clay. Looking at his phone, Del saw that it was nearly ten a.m. The truck with the lumber should be at Nick's grandparents' place by now.

He glanced back to see Darcy standing next to her mom, arms crossed, anger written all over her back, and probably her face, too.

If there'd been a wall nearby that didn't need to be dusted

for prints, he'd be punching a hole in it. Two could play at this game.

———— ∽ ————

"Where is he?"

A long way from Chicago, for sure.

Rebecca Durbin paced up and down the dim, damp tunnel, her bodyguard and the closest thing she had to a friend, Clyde Burke, watching her as he leaned against the cool rock wall. The goon her grandfather had hired on the advice of his right-hand man, Gabe Torrio, was supposed to be here half an hour ago.

She raked her hands through her straight, raven-black hair, wishing she had a hair band to pull it back. Her tall, erect body was stiff with anticipation.

"Relax. He'll be here." Clyde was the total opposite of her, and for that she was grateful. Most of the time.

She pulled out her cell. Lots of battery, no signal. How did these people live down here in the sticks? She held it up. Nothing. She walked down the tunnel toward the entrance. Still nothing.

Pacing wouldn't help the situation. She'd had a feeling, in the back of her mind, that when she came back to Kentucky it wouldn't run smoothly. She grew up here. She knew the lay of the land, but she'd worked hard to forget what it was like, and the reminder annoyed her. The only vestige of her Kentucky roots was the occasional slip of the accent, and the surprise she saw on people's faces when she came up with a factoid only a citizen of rural America would know.

That, and the anger she felt every time she thought of her father, who had forced her and her mother to stay by any means necessary, threatening to hurt her and Becca if she considered leaving him. By the time Becca was in high school, Lydia, her mother, had given up trying. Halfway through her college degree, he'd murdered her mom and Becca had been whisked to Chicago by her grandparents. Her formative years were not happy ones, but she thought she hid it well.

When she heard footsteps, she instinctively looked at Clyde, who was on high alert. He pulled her closer to him, which was fine with her.

"Stay up against the wall until we know who we're dealing with."

If it wasn't part of her crew, they certainly didn't want to get caught down here. There was still at least one federal agent in town, possibly more by now.

How could this guy have been so stupid as to try to smoke out the people who lived above the café? An honest-to-goodness fire would have been more efficient. It would have gotten them out long enough for them to finish up. The irritating thing was that now they'd be looking even closer at the crime scene, possibly unearthing the safe before she and her crew could get to it.

The footsteps grew nearer, and the voices she heard an indistinct tune being whistled. It was her partner, although she shook her head at the thought. He wasn't even trying to be quiet.

She stepped out of the shadow as he came around the corner. "Gerry?" The man grabbed at his chest, his face blanching.

"You tryin' to give me a heart attack?"

She stood her ground. "Would it make you work any faster? Gabe wants access to the café, and he wants it yesterday."

Gerry raked his fingers through his hair, grimacing as he

pulled out a shard of glass. The large bandage on his arm had not been put on by an expert. "Tell the boss we've got it under control."

She seethed. "Under control would have us with full access to the tunnels, and the feds out of our hair, and—here's the biggie—not leaving evidence behind." She glared at the bandage and narrowed her eyes at Gerry. "I understand one of them is in the hospital?"

"Yeah, we double-teamed her in the upstairs apartment. Smoke inhalation and concussion, probably. She'll be out of circulation for a few days."

Becca nodded. "Good. I can keep an eye on her."

"You goin' to infiltrate a little county hospital? Don't you think you might be noticed?" Gerry looked at her like she was crazy.

Clyde spoke up. He was usually quiet when he knew she was on a tear, but he had narrowed his eyes when Gerry asked her the question. "Are you sure about this?"

"I've been in there before. It can't have changed that much." She threw a glare his way. "I'll be in and out, and nobody will notice."

"It's been a while since you were a nurse." Clyde knew better than to question her. Sometimes he did it anyway. "You don't exactly have the appearance of the run-of-the-mill overworked floor nurse." He curled his lips, looking her up and down.

She felt the heat on her face, but she raised her chin defiantly. She defaulted to her usual M.O. She let anger take over so she spoke coldly. "It didn't seem to affect the last job." She tilted her chin at Clyde. He was concerned. She could tell. But she had to get this operation buttoned up and get herself out of here before something happened or someone recognized her. Before the good memories became a liability. "I want to get this done."

"Tell me what you need."

"I need you to blend in and see what you can find out about the café. It's changed hands since I was here. I know the woman who runs it is a widow with two young kids, and I know they're onto us, thanks to Gerry over here." She looked at her flunky in disgust.

"I'll be prepared next time."

"You'll be lucky if there is a next time. Vic wasn't too pleased to hear you nearly got caught."

The man looked down at the mention of her grandfather. "What do you want from me now?"

"Start moving the equipment out of the tunnel and be on the lookout for cops. Now that they've found the entrance from the café, we need to get this wrapped up as quickly as possible." She gave him a withering look. "Great job leaving muddy footprints, by the way."

12

When Darcy woke up to the sun shining in her face, she knew she wasn't at home. She was at Mom's house. And it was nearly nine a.m. How long had it been since she slept this long? Usually, one or the other of the kids bounced into her bed around five a.m., promptly going back to sleep and leaving her unable to do so.

Today her children were in the hands of others, and she couldn't go to work if she wanted to.

She grabbed her lightweight robe and slipped her feet into her slippers, then padded to the kitchen where her mom was sitting at the table. The cozy kitchen had been made even more so by the homey touches she'd added to the bachelor home.

"There you are." Mom looked up at her from the magazine she was perusing. "I thought about taking your pulse, but when I went to the door, I heard you snore."

Darcy huffed. "I do not snore."

Mom's eyes widened, a comical look on her face.

"Okay, maybe a little." Darcy's lips went sideways in a smirk.

Mom got up and hugged her. "You were sleeping so well I didn't want to disturb you. It's been a rough few days."

She endured the hug and pulled away from her mom before she was ready. She couldn't break down now. "You should have woken me up to get the kids to preschool."

Mom waved a hand in dismissal and sat back down, leafing through the foodie magazine. "Steve enjoys taking them." She laughed. "He's thrilled to have bonus grandchildren since he doesn't have any of his own yet."

"I have a feeling he won't have to wait long for Lisa and Nick to produce. What do you think?" Darcy sat next to her mom and winked, and they laughed together. How long had it been since they'd been able to simply sit at the table and talk to one another?

Too long.

"I made muffins. Want one?" Mom slipped out of the chair again and poured her a cup of coffee.

Darcy took a long whiff of the magic liquid and closed her eyes. "I usually drink coffee for medicinal purposes."

"Like to wake you up?" Mom laughed.

"Exactly. Today, I drink it because it tastes good." She could feel herself relax even as she drank the caffeinated beverage. "And it may have been the smell of muffins that got me out of bed. No telling how long I'd have been there if not for the aroma of blueberry-lemon muffins."

"They taste like spring, don't they?" Mom put a plate with two muffins and the butter dish in front of Darcy. "Eat up. I think you've lost weight."

"Probably." The muffin dripped with melted butter and disintegrated in her mouth. "These are perfect, Mom."

"Thank you kindly." Mom smiled. "New recipe."

"We need to put it on the menu."

"No shoptalk today, unless necessary. You hear?" Mom was going to be protective Mama Bear today, it seemed.

"Gotcha." She tilted her head and inspected the muffin in front of her. "Although it might be hard to do when I'm getting calls from the insurance agency and the FBI all day."

"I know." Mom paused and looked Darcy in the eye. "There are lots of people praying for you, sweetheart."

Feeling herself stiffen, she had a difficult time meeting her mother's knowing gaze. "We'll be okay."

"I know you will." Mom scrutinized her daughter carefully. "God's got this."

"I'd like to know His reasoning behind all 'this.'" She drained her cup and got up from the table. The last thing she wanted to do on a day off, such as it was, was to get into a discussion about whether or not she believed God was in control.

If He is, He's certainly not doing me any favors.

———— ∽ ————

Del walked out behind his dad's house, and into the springtime woods. His old stomping grounds. Normally the peaceful spot would calm him, the smell of new growth and the mellow aroma of last year's leaves pulling his attention.

Not today.

He knew Darcy was at Dad and Roxy's house. He'd warned Roxy that she might hear some noise. Hopefully, Darcy wasn't still asleep.

Darcy's minivan was parked in the driveway. Maybe he could walk off the irritation that had simmered all night and was once again raging through him. Early, before Dad drove the kids to their preschool, he'd gone to the construction office, steps away from the house. He was at a loose end, and he wasn't in the mood to talk. He wanted to shoot something, so he'd grabbed his dad's '70s edition Winchester 9422 rifle, always kept in the corner of the closet next to the back door of the office. He had poured ammunition into his pocket and stuffed paper targets under his arm. May as well make good use of the anger.

He'd done his fair share of hunting, living in Crittenden County, where people flocked from all over the world for the excellent deer hunting, but honestly, target shooting was enough of a challenge for him. He could kill an animal if it were putting a loved one in danger or if he needed sustenance, but the sport of hunting didn't appeal to him as it did many of the men in his circle.

It was one of the reasons he and Nick had clicked when they renewed their acquaintance in college. They were both more interested in watching sports and playing sports than in spending the wee hours of the morning and early evening strapped to a deer stand in a tall tree or crouching in a duck blind on the ground in cold, rainy weather. Dad wasn't much of a hunter, either. He said when he was a kid there weren't that many deer, and it was a rich man's sport unless you needed to hunt for food. He would rather build something than kill something.

Del agreed.

Yesterday, if looks could have killed, Del would be on a slab in the morgue. Darcy was over-the-top angry with him, and this time, he shared her anger. She was the most stubborn, bullheaded, irrational, obstinate, headstrong woman he'd ever met. He'd dated a girl in college with anger issues, but Becca was nothing compared to Darcy Emerson Sloan in a fury.

Two could play at that game. She had told him to get out

of her business, and he did. When the crime scene was cleared, Nick and Lisa would have to put the finishing touches on the project without him. He was done.

He stopped in the middle of the woods, taking in the sights and sounds of life around him. He took a deep breath to calm down and began the process of loading the gun. It held fifteen rounds, so when he could see the tip of the bullet in the magazine, he dropped the remainder into his pocket.

The first two shots he got off didn't touch the target, but the more he breathed deeply and concentrated, the closer to the bull's-eye his bullet came.

What am I doing here, God? I don't know when I've ever been so angry in my life.

You're not angry. You're hurt.

Del pulled the scope away from his eye. Hurt? Yeah, it kinda hurt when Darcy told him he had no business in her business, but he was more angry than hurt. Wasn't he?

You care about her.

Uh, I think we know how Darcy feels about me, so what's the point?

Del shook his head. Sometimes these "conversations" with God went in directions he wasn't prepared for. Sure he cared about Darcy. She was a friend. He wanted the best for her. She was practically family.

He looked down to see how many rounds he still had in the gun. At least one in the chamber. Probably five or six. He pulled the scope back to his eye and trained it on the second target he'd put on the fencepost. It was lower than the first, and he had to concentrate a little harder on this one.

You care about her.

Was this God talking, or the other guy, on the other shoulder? Why would God want Del to pursue a woman who didn't want him, much less a relationship with God?

He got off a few more shots. The gun was getting lighter, so he would have to stop and reload pretty soon.

Sorry, Father. I think that ship has sailed.

Give it time.

Give it time. Was He serious? Of course He was. God's always serious. He paused and looked heavenward. *I'm not getting any younger, you know.*

When the time is right, you'll know. I'll tell you. For now, be patient.

Del couldn't help but think of the book of James, chapter one, the first few verses:

Consider it pure joy, my brothers and sisters, whenever you face trials of many kinds, because you know that the testing of your faith produces perseverance. Let perseverance finish its work so that you may be mature and complete, not lacking anything.

Joy. Was that what they were striving for, here? Del shook his head as he took his last shot. Consider it pure joy. The only time he saw joy from Darcy was with her kids. Any other time, she seemed to be hiding from everyone, maintaining the wall she'd built around herself to protect her from further disaster.

He looked down the barrel to see if he'd expended every round, and he had. Walking over to the tree and the fencepost where he'd hung the paper targets, he studied them. The first one, on the tree? Pretty pitiful. But the second, while he was talking to God, was consistent. The middle of the target was completely gone because all his shots had met their mark.

Joy. He'd been a stranger to that emotion for a while, as well. Maybe when he found it, he could help Darcy.

Until then, he'd let her stay mad at him and he'd avoid her like the plague.

13

Del, Nick, and the construction crew were almost done shoring up the tunnel where it had been blasted shut last summer. It was irritating that what had been a perfectly viable tunnel a year ago had been damaged to the point that it put Nick and Lisa in danger when the tornado struck their community last summer. Del, covered in dirt and mud, sat on the back stoop with a bottle of water, staring off toward the river.

"You're deep in thought." Nick, as dirty as his future brother-in-law, walked up to Del, straightening his ragged Murray State Alumnus cap.

"Hey Nick"

Nick turned when he heard his name from one of the crew.

"Where do you want the extra timbers?"

He paused for a minute, then called out instructions. "Stack 'em over by the barn for now. I might find some other use for them."

The workman sent him a thumbs-up and directed his

crew.

"I guess we could use them to build a pergola." Del took a long drag from the water bottle. He was back in the present, trying to get his mind off the situation. Nick seemed to be taking all this in stride, but then, what was all this when a guy was about to get married? Del guessed that trumped pretty much everything.

Nick considered for a moment. "That would be nice. Maybe put a swing in it?"

Del could see the wheels turning. "I feel an extra job coming on, and one for no pay." He grinned at his friend. "Good idea, though."

"It was your idea." Nick's brow arched and he laughed.

"That's why it was such a good one." It was good to be with Nick. He could always pull him out of a funk. He hadn't felt like this in a long time

"Heard you went shooting yesterday. You should have called. I've wanted to do some target shooting."

"I'll call you next time. Maybe shoot at clay pigeons." Del stared out at the river again, shaking his head. "I needed to blow off steam."

"I hear you." Nick took a seat on the step next to Del, staring along with him. "Any problem in particular?"

Del snorted. "What do you think?"

"Woman trouble?"

"Not all women, just one specific one."

"I figure it's not Lisa, because she's been making herself scarce lately with all the wedding prep." He cut his eyes over at Del. "Darcy?"

Del dropped his head to look at his hands, clasped between his knees. "I've been praying a lot, and it seems like the more I pray, the madder she gets."

Nick chuckled. "Sounds about right." He turned to look

his friend in the eye. "You do know that the closer you get to somebody, the more they're able to hurt you and frustrate you half to death." It was a statement, not a question.

"Trouble is, I think Darcy's pulling further away from me instead of closer." He shook his head. "Maybe it's for the best. I think God wants me to be with someone who cares as much about Him as I do."

"Maybe. And maybe your timing is off. Give it time, Del. The more you hurry things along, the more things can go wrong, because you're the one pulling the strings instead of God."

———————— ⟨∽⟩ ————————

Lisa, Darcy, Mandy, and matron of honor, Melanie, arrived at the bridal salon just in time for their appointment. The bridesmaid dresses were done, and they were there for a final fitting.

Lisa laughed at her best friend, Mel. "I'm glad you didn't get pregnant with child number three before my wedding."

"It wasn't in the plan." She rolled her eyes at Lisa.

Darcy spoke up. "Neither was the last one if I remember correctly." All three girls laughed as they approached the salon, causing the clerks and customers to turn their way when the door opened. "Oops. Better get out my town manners."

Lisa doubled over in laughter. "Darcy, I'm so glad you were able to come with us today."

Darcy harrumphed and gave her stepsister the stink eye. "Well, I can't do anything at the café." Then she grinned. "I'm glad, too. It's kinda nice to have a day off with other people for a change."

Mel sighed as she looked at the bridal gown in the window. "It seems like a lifetime ago since I got married."

"Don't rub it in." Lisa gave her a mock glare. "My engagement feels like it was a lifetime ago."

"Believe me, it will be worth it when you walk down the perfectly appointed aisle into the arms of your betrothed." Mel had her hand on her chest as she spoke dramatically.

Lisa giggled when she saw Darcy gagging next to her. "It had better be. I could have eloped and been an old married woman by now if it weren't for you."

While Darcy and Mel wandered around aimlessly, having experienced this all before, Mandy, in the beginnings of her love affair, was enthralled at the sight of so many bridal gowns. "Lisa, this may be what Heaven looks like." Her eyes were round when she beheld the featured gown on the mannequin.

Lisa put her arm around Mandy's shoulders, taking it in with her. "Maybe. Somehow I think it'll be even better than this."

They meandered through the racks, basking in the beauty in the store as they waited for their appointment to begin. Lisa tapped her chin in thought. She hadn't been able to go to Darcy's wedding to Justin. It was while she was in Texas.

"Darcy, what was your wedding dress like? I don't think I ever saw any pictures."

Darcy paused at the rack of petite dresses. "It was perfect." She pulled a few out, and when she got to the end of the rack, she stopped. "It was similar to this."

Lisa saw the tears poised on Darcy's lashes. "It's beautiful."

"Sometime I'll show you my album. Since we've been in the same family, there's been one thing after another, and that's the last thing I've been thinking about." Darcy sighed wistfully.

"I'd like that." Lisa put an arm around Darcy's shoulders and squeezed.

Mel walked up to them, in charge, as usual. "They're ready for us. Who wants to go first?"

Lisa looked from one to the other. "All three of you. I want to see how you all look together."

The consultant focused on the bridesmaids and agreed. "Good idea. We saw them when you picked each one out, and they coordinate beautifully, but you haven't seen them standing side-by-side." She ushered Mel, Mandy, and Darcy into dressing cubicles next to the larger bridal dressing room, then came back to Lisa, whispering. "And how about yours?"

"Is it done?" Lisa's insides jumped up and down in excitement as she was shown into the larger dressing room.

Donna, the seamstress, came in, carrying the long bridal gown high above her head, her face wreathed in smiles. "I finished it this morning, and if I do say so myself, I think it turned out amazing. Are you ready to try it on? If it works, we can cancel your later appointment."

"Of course I'm ready!" She tossed her purse into the chair in the familiar dressing room, toeing her shoes off in preparation. "We can see them all together."

"Exactly. I had a feeling you'd be in." The seamstress hung the dress on the tall hook. "I'll be right outside to check it when Barb gets it on you."

Lisa had looked forward to spending time with her bridesmaids and getting the final touches on their dresses, but this was a bonus. She could surprise them by appearing in her own dress. They'd each seen it, but not at the same time, together.

As Donna helped her with the dress, she stared at herself

in the mirror. Four weeks. Four weeks until she became Mrs. Nicholas Woodward. "It's perfect."

The consultant peeked in. "You decent?"

"More than decent." Lisa chuckled, unable to take her eyes off of herself in the mirror. "Are the girls ready?"

Barb chuckled. "Dressed and waiting by the mirror."

Donna pulled the curtains back, allowing the three young women to see Lisa in all her glory.

"Oh my." Darcy seemed mesmerized. "I'd forgotten how beautiful you look in your dress."

"The ivory color is perfect." Mel's jaw had dropped and recovered, but she still looked a little starstruck. "Girl, you're going to outshine us all in the bridal department."

Mandy was speechless for a moment. "I don't see how anyone could look as pretty in a wedding gown as you, Lisa."

Lisa felt the heat creep up her neck, and tears smart in her eyes.

"Quit it." Mel fussed. "Your chest is getting all mottled."

Lisa rolled her eyes. "Sorry. I'm not great with compliments."

"Well," Darcy stated, "You don't have to break out into hives over it."

They all laughed and then sighed in tandem, which made them laugh again.

Lisa looked at them together in the mirror. "You girls look amazing."

"I wasn't sure about yellow, but you know, it works." Darcy twirled a bit in her A-line strapless gown.

"I've always thought blonds and redheads looked good in yellow." Mel studied Darcy carefully. "And on you, it's perfect."

"I may have found my new favorite color to wear." Darcy

laughed. "And on you and Mandy, with your dark hair?" She shook her head. "You look amazing."

"Well, now that we've established a mutual admiration society, I say we get started with our fitting. What do you say?" The seamstress held her pin cushion up.

"I say yes." Lisa turned and swayed, observing herself from all angles. "Do you think, seeing as how the dresses are done early, we could move up the wedding?" She gave Mel a cheesy grin, then laughed when her best friend gave her a glare that would sink a ship.

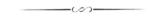

Nick walked through the dim tunnel from the entrance in the basement of his house, slowly taking video of each nook and cranny. Their end had been removed from the "active crime scene" category, and he wanted to do some exploring on his own. He had to chuckle. Lisa had been interested in exploring too, but two dead bodies in one tunnel system were enough for her. If it weren't for possible historic significance, he'd have the tunnel sealed off at the basement. He wanted to get the opinion of a historian he knew, first.

Clive Harper, a former classmate of Del and Nick at Murray State, was now a history professor at their alma mater. Nick had promised Clive a video before he made the trip out to see for himself.

It smelled damp, but it could be worse. He remembered the sickening odor of that first expedition. Worse than bad. Putrid wouldn't even cut it.

Nick kicked something on the floor. His foot hit a large rock, which made him think of the rolled-up rug that had covered evidence found on their first trip. This time it wasn't a body, thank goodness. And not a cat and kittens, either.

He'd never forget the scream Lisa let out when she thought she'd been attacked by a rat, only to find a mama cat guarding her babies. Of course, it wasn't long until they stumbled on corpse number one—and a rather fresh one, at that—the body discovered to have links to the mob in Chicago.

Further in the tunnel, he came to the larger room where they'd found the remains of a moonshine still. The FBI unit had taken it to perform tests on it, and he doubted he'd ever see it again. A shame. It was a part of his family's history. Not a great part, but it was history.

You can't change it, no matter how much you try to cover it up.

The right fork in the tunnel led to the opening at the site of his great-grandparents' house, whereas the left led to the river bluff where evidence had been found of a smuggling operation active as little as a year ago.

Was it active again, in a different part of the network?

He hadn't gone far when he came across a small crevasse, barely big enough for a person, and not a very big person. It would be easy to miss upon first inspection. He remembered the portion in Mammoth Cave National Park called "Fat Man's Misery." This one could be called "Tall Man's Misery." He crouched down, stopping the video and turning on his flashlight. The phone wouldn't cut it here.

What looked, at first glance, like mere shelving of the sandstone was an opening. Natural or not, it was big enough for a person to get through. Nick was glad he'd put on coveralls.

Leopard-crawling through, he couldn't help but wonder what made people go to such lengths to hide their illegal activities. He understood Depression economy, but there had to be a better way of providing for a family. Had his great-grandfather killed his own son over a disagreement, in this very tunnel system?

When he found an even smaller spot, he thought he would have to crawl back out, backward. A hundred years ago, people were smaller.

He made it through and breathed a sigh of relief when he came out into the center of a full-sized cavern. Another naturally occurring cave linked by man-made tunnels. All his life he'd heard there were caves around here but had never found any in the limited amount of time he'd been here with his grandparents.

Nick stood up and stretched, looking around. The air was stale here, which told him it didn't go toward the river. Opening the compass on his phone, he shook his head. He was heading southwest. Toward the café. He looked in the other direction and saw what appeared to be another tunnel, heading the opposite way. Did it meet up with one of the tunnels the FBI had found when they discovered his grandfather's skeletal remains?

Heading toward the café was probably a bad idea. It was cordoned off, the forensics team from Louisville doing their job looking for evidence of the intruder into the café. There was nothing, however, keeping him from exploring the other route. He had a feeling his property was directly above him. He'd gotten turned around enough that he couldn't be sure how far he was from the opening at the old home place.

He'd started in the direction of what he expected to be a passageway to another opening in the tunnel heading northeast, toward the river, when he heard voices. They weren't close, and he was having trouble pinpointing where the voices were coming from. Since he didn't know what was ahead, he couldn't be sure.

All he knew was if he ran into the guys who tried to smoke Darcy and her kids out of her place, he'd be in trouble.

———————————

Clinking water goblets together at the tiny little Italian restaurant in downtown Paducah, Darcy, Lisa, Mandy, and Melanie were finishing their outing in style. Bread-sticks and Alfredo dip had arrived, and from the aroma coming from the region of the kitchen, their entrees would be nothing short of amazing.

Darcy took a deep breath and felt herself relax for the first time in several weeks. Mom kept asking her if she was putting too much on her, and she kept saying, "Of course not." Maybe she had downplayed it. Just a bit.

"Could we do this once a month?" Melanie looked longingly at the ladies around the table. "One night away from my kids. Just one. It might get me through to the next month."

"I hear ya." Darcy held up her glass again. She grinned at Lisa, who looked conflicted, and whispered. "Hey, Mel, look at Lisa."

"Yeah, she's about to become a newlywed. No once-a-month girls' night for her—not in the foreseeable future, anyway." Mel shook her head. "Bless her heart."

"Exactly." Darcy laughed. "I've needed this for a while, ladies."

She'd no more gotten the words out than she heard her silenced phone vibrate in her purse. Wincing when she saw "Del" on the notification banner, she muttered under her breath. "Now what?"

Lisa, Mandy, and Melanie were talking over details about

the wedding, so she leaned over. "Excuse me, ladies. I'll be right back."

When they all looked up in acknowledgment, she pulled her phone out and walked toward the restroom, next to the exit.

"Del?"

"Yeah."

"Hang on a minute." Unable to hear anything for the kitchen noises, she went out the exit to the sidewalk. "I'm headed outside the restaurant."

"Good. Are you with Lisa?" He sounded tense.

"What's wrong?" Her first thought was that the criminals had succeeded in burning down the café. Maybe that was reaching.

"I can't find Nick." He paused. "I wondered if she'd heard from him this afternoon."

"And you didn't want to worry her." She might be mad at Del for all kinds of reasons, but she would admit when a guy was being sweet. And Del was. Most of the time.

She heard him expel a breath. "Busted."

"If she has, she hasn't said anything." Darcy paused, thinking. "You got the tunnel braced, didn't you?"

"Yeah, we finished yesterday. Nick was going to do a little exploring."

She knew her mouth was hanging open, and her eyes were drying out, so she'd forgotten to blink for a few seconds. "Does Lisa know that?" She had an image in her mind of Del running his hand through his hair and adjusting his cap. His nervous tic. She'd always wondered what his hair felt like.

Focus, Darcy. On the problem, not the man.

She shook her head, wondering what was wrong with her.

Del was speaking, and she needed to pay attention. "Not the full scope of his activities."

"Oh, Del." She closed her eyes, and when she opened them, she glanced in the window. Lisa and Mel were still deep in discussion, only looking up when the waitress refilled their water.

"I know. He's got a professor from Murray State coming out to look things over, and he wanted to send him a video ahead of time."

"You've got to go find him, you hear?" The glare she knew was on her face was ineffective on the phone, but her voice carried some of her frustration.

"Hey, he's a big boy, you know."

"I know, and I also know there have been criminals down there. Did you hear me? Cri-mi-nals." She spat out the last word, trying to be forceful without screaming, but it was hard.

"I'll go. But don't tell Lisa."

"I won't, and don't YOU go down there by yourself, either." The very thought of something happening to him made her stomach turn. Why? She had no idea.

Nothing. Darcy narrowed her eyes and looked at the phone. Did she hear—no, it couldn't be—laughter??

"Promise me, Del. Get Clay, your dad, anybody, but don't go alone."

"I promise." He paused. "I'm a big boy, too, you know."

She sighed, and felt like every bit of oxygen in her body came out in the process. "I know." She rubbed the sidewalk with the toe of her shoe, studying it carefully. "Just be careful."

"Yes, ma'am." And he hung up.

That man.

———————⌀———————

Smoking out the café hadn't been such a bad idea, after all. The FBI and local cops were busy processing the crime scene, which diverted their attention away from the undiscovered tunnel. Becca couldn't relax, though, until they were done and she was a hundred miles from Clementville.

Becca was on the riverbank, close to the tunnel entrance on the river. It was the easiest way to get the chemicals and equipment out. There was a naturally occurring landing there, hidden by willow trees and underbrush, so they didn't have to have a boat moored there all the time. It could come and go, taking the various objects away a load at a time.

Part of her wished she could explore the area where she'd had a somewhat happy childhood, maybe retrieve those happier memories that were just out of reach. If it hadn't been for her dad...she wouldn't go there. They'd lived in a house on the outskirts of town—if you could call Clementville an actual town. More of a stop in the road.

She wished she felt free to walk into the café and order a burger and fries, the way she and Darcy did from time to time when she was a kid. She'd learned that Roxy, who ran the café when they were kids, had gotten married and that her daughter, Darcy, was running it now.

It would have been nice to know that before they tried to smoke out the place. She remembered Darcy from elementary school on, envying her cottony blond hair and the cool loft apartment over the café, comparing it to her natural mousy brown hair and unhappy home. Thank goodness for hairdressers, at least. Her long black tresses would be nothing without them. Most people in her current circle never knew her with lighter hair.

"You gonna give us a hand, or what?" Gerry came up

behind her, lugging a box of drug paraphernalia, bringing the smell of chemicals with him. She didn't want to think about that.

"That's your job, not mine."

He snorted and continued out of the opening.

Becca was feeling pretty good about herself. At least she did as long as she didn't think about Darcy. That was a lifetime ago.

When she went to the hospital it was more different than she realized. There had been several additions, and the hallways didn't look familiar from her time doing clinicals for her nursing classes.

She'd garnered a few strange looks as she went down the hallway. Her expression was bright and hurried as if she were extremely busy or on an important mission, so no one questioned her presence. If it was like when she lived there, the small hospital had the occasional nurse from other area hospitals, so it wasn't completely out of reason for a stranger to be there.

When she entered Special Agent Rossi's room, she found her asleep. Picking up the chart on the wall next to the door, she scanned down the medical jargon, glad she knew what most of it meant. Agent Julia Rossi was set to leave the hospital the next morning, and that wasn't going to happen.

"Hey, Becca, could you come here a minute?" Clyde's voice brought her back to the present. He was at the opening, beckoning, vigilant, as usual, making sure he was aware of every single thing around him. Why couldn't he be ugly and repulsive like three-fourths of the guys she had to work with?

She walked out into the sunshine and took a deep breath. "What's up?"

"Gabe called." He looked at her closely. "He's coming down."

Becca took another breath and exhaled slowly. Grandfather—Vic when it was business—was checking up on her. It was the only possible reason his right-hand man was on his way. "I should have expected it."

Clyde gazed out toward the river. "We need to step up the pace getting the tunnels cleared out." He turned toward her. "You okay?"

"I'm fine." She frowned. "I wish Vic would trust me to get this done." Trust her, period. If she was going to carry on the business after he was gone, he'd have to start sometime.

"He trusts you, but he can't seem to keep his finger out of every pie." He shrugged. "How did it go at the hospital?"

"I put a generous dose of sodium pentothal in her IV. That should keep her asleep awhile and lower her blood pressure enough that they won't let her leave the hospital tomorrow."

"Lasting effects?"

"She'll be sleepy for a while. Sodium pentothal isn't just used for truth serum, you know." She glanced up at him. "It's also used to induce comas."

He looked at her, his face carved in stone. "And to sedate inmates sentenced to lethal injection. How much did you give her?"

"Don't worry. I checked her weight and age before I gave it to her." She gritted her teeth. "I know what I'm doing."

"No question about that. Just wanted to make sure we weren't looking at a long-term situation." He narrowed his eyes. "Like her death."

He thought she would do that? The idea he even imagined her capable of murder bothered her more than she wanted to admit. "I'm not a murderer." She felt tears prick at her eyes, but she wouldn't let them come.

"Never said you were." He stuffed his hands into his pockets and stared out at the rolling river.

Did he think because her dad murdered her mom, that she had it in her to do the same? And, considering the business she was in, why was she surprised? Had Clyde ever killed anyone? After what she'd learned about her grandparents, she had no illusions about the fact that they were part of the reason their daughter was dead.

14

"Everything okay?" Lisa looked up at Darcy as she came back to the table.

She'd promised Del she wouldn't tell Lisa until there was something to worry about. Was telling a small lie out of the question, if it was to protect someone?

Melanie looked up at her and pointed to something on her tablet. "Darcy, wouldn't an archway like this be amazing?"

Saved by the Mel. Darcy sat quickly, taking the tablet from her. "Beautiful." She smiled up at Mel, ignoring Lisa's question. "Justin and I had a similar arch at our wedding. It made for beautiful pictures."

Lisa leaned over, thoughtful. "Where can we get something like that?"

Darcy stared at her stepsister in disbelief. "Are you kidding me? Del and your dad could whip up an arch like that in no time." She laughed. More with relief that she hadn't questioned her further than at her playful comment.

"That's true." Lisa checked her phone and saw the time.

"I can't believe it's nearly two o'clock." She paused. "I think I'll call Del now, and see what he thinks. Mel, could you text the picture to me so I can send it to him?"

Darcy's eyes widened, and she knew, she just knew, her face had blanched.

"Are you all right?" Lisa looked at her with concern. "You're pale, all of a sudden."

Darcy chuckled. "Somebody walking over my grave, I guess."

"I've never understood that one." Mel shook her head.

Thanks, Melanie, for the distraction.

"It's how the old-timers described the unexplained shiver you get sometimes. I'm sure there's a reason for it, but who knows what it is?" Darcy shrugged her shoulders and smiled.

Mel sent Lisa the image via text, and she heard the tablet give a gentle "swoosh" tone and Lisa's phone a soft "ding."

Lisa picked it up. "I'll text it to Nick. That way he'll have it."

"Good idea. Who knows what those boys are up to today." Darcy wanted to wipe her brow in relief, but she restrained herself.

"Nick was supposed to go to the house to measure for blinds. I'm not sure if Del was going over with him or not." Lisa frowned slightly. "Well, it sent, but he didn't reply."

"Men, right?" Darcy tried to laugh it off.

"You're not kidding. When I text Jake during the day, I'm happy if I hear from him by bedtime." Mel shook her head in disgust. "He justifies it as 'That's the beauty of texts—you don't have to answer if you don't have time,' and I tell him if it wasn't important, I wouldn't have sent him a text in the first place."

Mandy laughed. "Maybe he'll see it later. Who knows?"

She lifted a brow. "He may be at your house with no service. You know how unreliable it is out there."

Lisa nodded, "Probably."

"I'm sure that's it." Darcy didn't exactly lie; she just let Lisa believe what she wanted.

The waitress brought the tickets to the table, and Lisa grabbed them. "My party, my treat."

"I would have come anyway, but thank you." Darcy took a deep breath. "It was glorious being out of town. Especially now."

"I know." Lisa gave her a sympathetic look. "It must be hard being closed, not knowing what's going on."

"It is, but everyone's been nice."

"Especially Agent 'Frank,' right?" Lisa batted her lashes and tried, unsuccessfully, to hide a grin.

"Maybe." Darcy looked at her friend from beneath her lashes. "He may or may not have asked me out for dinner once this craziness is over."

The surprise on Lisa's and Mel's faces was priceless.

"Y'all, your chins are going to touch the ground if you don't pull 'em up." Darcy laughed at her two friends. How long had it been since she'd had a pack of girls to run around with?

Mel recovered first. "Agent 'Frank?' And you? I thought..." Melanie shot a look at Lisa.

Mandy went ahead and said what they were all thinking, she was sure. "We thought, maybe, you and Del...?"

She could feel her face redden. The heat was a dead giveaway, and boy, there was heat. Almost as much as when she'd watched Del tenderly carrying her daughter to her bed the night he stayed in his truck all night, watching over them all.

"Del and I are friends." She busied herself with checking

her phone unnecessarily. "Really." She avoided their eyes. "And we're family."

Lisa and Mel looked at one another, then at Mandy, and back at her, brows raised on all their faces.

Lisa smirked. "If you say so."

"You're kidding, right?" Mel and Lisa spoke the two sentences in tandem.

She gaped at them both, exasperated. "And I used to wish I had sisters."

Del drove up to the house where Nick and Lisa would "take up housekeeping," as the old-timers would say. Nick's grandparents' house stood, pristine with its white body and blue trim after a complete remodel last year, not revealing the system of hidden passageways that had aided no telling how many illegal schemes over the years.

Nick was still here. His truck was parked in its usual spot. Del checked the truck bed and saw the toolbox open—it looked like he'd taken his flashlight with him. Good call. Del grabbed his from behind his seat and looked at the pistol he kept there. Would he need it?

Darcy had made him promise he wouldn't go in alone. Of course, if he found Nick, he wouldn't be alone, would he? Since it didn't make sense to anger her further, he pulled out his phone and looked at the lousy reception out here. He walked up to the porch and got an extra signal bar. He knew it was even better upstairs, but this would have to do.

"Clay? Del."

"Yeah, what's up?"

Clay sounded a little tense. But then, why wouldn't he?

Recently, every time he'd talked to Del, it had been to report a dangerous crime.

"Hopefully, nothing." He paused and surveyed the open fields around the house. It was beautiful out here. His house in "downtown Clementville" was nice, but close to people. Five backyards backed up to his. Without a fence, it would be impossible to keep kids or dogs safe.

Kids?

He cleared his throat.

"You still there?" Clay's voice brought him back to the present.

"Yeah. Sorry. Signal blanked out for a minute." *Forgive me, Lord. I know I told a bald-faced lie.* "Nick came to his house to check out his end of the tunnels, and I haven't heard from him in a few hours."

"Was he supposed to check in?"

Del twisted his lips. "No, but he came this morning, and he hasn't picked up when I've called. Straight to voice mail."

"That happens when you don't have a signal, too."

"I know." He frowned, knowing Clay couldn't see him. "That's why I didn't haul you out here with me."

Clay took a deep breath. "Do you want backup?"

"No, I wanted someone to know where I was." Del chewed on the inside of his cheek, a nervous habit. "I promised Darcy I wouldn't go in the tunnels alone."

The burst of laughter coming from the sheriff made Del close his eyes and long for a floorboard to open up and swallow him.

Clay recovered himself. "Sorry, Del." He cleared his throat. "I understand."

"I'm sure you do." Del shook his head. "And it's nothing like that."

"Um-hmmm. How about this? Call or text me every

hour. It's one thirty now, so if I don't hear from you by at least three o'clock, I'll head out there. Will that keep her at bay?"

"Maybe. I'm hoping he lost track of time or is out of signal range."

"Me, too. Thanks for giving me a heads-up." Clay sounded more serious. "Honestly, right now I don't think we can be too careful." He paused a moment. "Do you have a gun?"

"I do." He hadn't planned on taking it with him.

"I'd take it." Since Clay wasn't one to advocate gunfire unless necessary, Del took him seriously.

"Are you sure I need to?"

"I figure an ounce of prevention..."

Del took a deep breath. "Okay. I'll carry it unloaded and put ammo in my pocket."

"Sounds good. And Del?"

"Yeah?"

"Be careful down there. I would drive out there right now if I weren't babysitting the FBI team."

"I understand, and thanks. I'll keep you posted."

Del ended the call and took another look around at the exterior of Nick's house. They'd done a good job if he did say so himself. Dad had been pleased, and it was the first project they'd completed without his help.

He stuffed his phone into his pocket, then pulled it back out to make sure the ringer was on, and that it was loud enough to hear it. Check. He walked back to the truck and took his nine-millimeter handgun from behind the driver's seat, and slipped an ammo magazine into his other pocket, sticking the gun in his belt. Fortunately, it would load quickly if he needed it.

He didn't want to need it.

When he got to the front door, he tried the knob and

found that the door was unlocked. No surprise there. Nick hadn't planned to be there long, he figured, and they were far enough off the road that people didn't stop and break in for no good reason.

Considering all they'd been through, locking the door while at home might not be a bad idea.

He walked through the house, calling Nick's name, and got no answer. In the kitchen, the basement door stood open, and when he got down the steps, he saw that the door leading to the system of tunnels was also open.

That narrowed his search.

———— ⟨∞⟩ ————

Nick crept along the passage as quietly as possible. He could still hear the voices, and the location of the source was getting clearer.

He was exploring new territory. Had the FBI or Clay and his deputies found this section of the cave in their investigations? Probably not. There were many hiding places in this section. More small cavities both natural and excavated. Shining the light on the floor, he saw multiple footprints, different shapes and sizes.

When he had gained on the sounds, he pulled back to the wall. According to the voices he heard, there were two men and a woman in the natural cavern ahead of him. The woman seemed to be in charge. The short man's accent gave him away as being from a more northern region of the country. Chicago? New York? Parts in-between? Shifting around, he found an opening behind some rocks that gave him a view of the back of one man's head, the top of another, and a woman. He couldn't see her face, and they couldn't see him.

The taller man spoke. No discernible accent there. "You

clocked a federal officer. You know how much time that can get you?"

The shorter man waved him off. "I think we can safely say the fed is fine, and won't exactly press charges. I could have bled to death going through the plate-glass window." He turned, and Nick could see a large white bandage with evidence of continued bleeding.

The tall, dark-haired woman held up her hands. "Guys, shut up." Hers was the only trace of a southern accent in the group. She shifted to the side and he got a glimpse of her face before it went out of view. She looked familiar, but he couldn't place her. Had she been in the café, or around town? Possibly. Was she someone he was supposed to know? He wished Del were here. Del knew everybody in a four-county range.

"Who you telling to shut up?" The injured man returned.

"Both of you." She put her hands on her hips and looked from one to the other. We're fine, the woman is fine."

"How do you know?" The taller of the men spoke belligerently.

"I went to the hospital, remember? Rossi is the only fed admitted."

"Yeah, and you could have gotten caught." The tall guy shook his head. "If you think he would do time for assaulting a Fed, you can only imagine what it would be for killing one."

"I didn't kill her." She shrugged. "Just slowed her down a little."

Nick couldn't move from his spot behind the rock formation. Not until they left, anyway. Why hadn't he grabbed the gun he kept in the glove compartment?

The conversation continued, all arguing whether they were right in smoking the place or if they should have burned it down completely. As it stood, any charges would be harassment or maybe attempted murder. If they'd burned the place down, the authorities would have found the safe before them. Smoke was the better option.

Then something the woman said grabbed his attention.

"If anybody finds out I used to live here, and that I'm in the family, we're all done for."

What did she mean, "in the family"? Was she talking about a family here in Clementville—his family, perhaps—or in the broader scope of possibilities, "the family," as in, organized crime?

"Vic won't let anything happen to his favorite hillbilly." The short guy leered at her, earning him a dirty look, which made him laugh.

"Look. You are only here because Gabe recommended you. Understand? I can give him a call at any time and have you taken out of the picture."

"Hey there, I meant you no offense. Who knew under all that southern sweetness was a bucket of nails?"

Nick strained to hear. They left his sight-line, and their voices seemed to be moving away. He slowly moved over to get a visual of where they'd been standing. They were gone. Probably down the tunnel he'd intended to explore.

About the time he got up the nerve to follow them, he began to hear sounds from the direction he'd come.

Great. Here he was, caught in the middle of two different sets of people, not knowing if they were friend or foe.

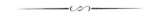

Del made his way through an unfamiliar part of the tunnel and almost had a heart attack when Nick emerged from behind the rocks along the worn passageway. The expletive he let fly was not in character for him, but in this instance, he felt it was justified.

"Nick, what's going on?" He tried to modulate his breathing, his heart beating a mile a minute.

Nick held his finger to his lips. "Quiet."

He didn't know what was going on, but he trusted Nick with his life.

"There are three people back there—two men and a woman—and they were talking about the invasion at the café."

"Whoa."

"Yeah. That's what I thought. They went further down the tunnel. I don't think the FBI or Clay's crew found this one." Nick looked at Del and shook his head. "Speaking of finding it, how did you?"

Del focused on Nick. "I tracked you until I quit seeing your footprints and found the crevasse. Kinda tight, isn't it?"

"You got that right. Not excited about returning the way I came." Nick considered the tunnel in both directions. "And, I can't decide whether to follow them and see what they're up to, or get back to the surface and call for backup."

"You know what Lisa would say."

Nick grimaced. "She'd say get backup." He looked into Del's eyes. "What if they get away?"

Del paused, thinking. First, he was no longer breaking his promise to Darcy, because he was with Nick. Second, one of them should go up top and one of them should follow the criminals. The second thought eliminated the good intentions of the first. "We need to split up."

"I know." He looked down the darkened tunnel where the three had gone ahead, probably to another exit. To the home place door, or the river? Or maybe even somewhere else?

"Lisa's not going to be happy, period, when she finds out you came down here by yourself." Del didn't mention Darcy. That would open another whole can of worms he wasn't ready to deal with at present.

"I know." He stared off, and then back at Del. "You head to where you can get a signal, and I'll follow these people."

"Do you want my gun?"

Nick's eyes brightened. "You read my mind. I'll take it."

Del handed over his handgun and magazine of ammunition.

Nick held it in his hand, holding it as if testing the weight of the pistol. "It's the same model as mine."

"Good, then I don't have to tell you how to use it." Del twisted his lips a little.

"You might get a signal before you get out. Some of the tunnels seem to go uphill and some downhill. Probably where they dug out around rocks."

Del paused. "Be careful, brother." He compelled Nick to look at him. "I mean it. I don't want to be the one telling my sister you got hurt, or worse."

"Don't worry. I don't intend to delay this wedding in any way, shape, or form."

"You know what they say about good intentions." Del glanced in the direction of possible danger.

Nick nodded solemnly. "I'll be careful. You, too."

Nick quietly crept down the tunnel in the direction he'd seen the intruders go in and caught up with them. He tucked himself into an opening in the rocks, hoping to hear what was being said. They were still bickering over something, but he couldn't quite hear well enough to figure out what it was all about. When his cell phone buzzed in his pocket, he almost jumped out of his skin.

A text, from Lisa, sent to both him and Del, with a picture of an archway for the wedding. "Not now, sweetheart." He whispered the words as he flipped to Settings to turn off even vibration as a signal. He didn't want to give away his position.

His fiancée wouldn't be happy with him right now, he knew, but with everything happening at the café, he wanted to find out if his family had anything to do with it. Putting people in danger was bad. When there were small children involved, it was unconscionable.

Memories of spending time with his grandparents had been tainted with the brush of crime stemming from his great-grandfather, Zebulon Woodward's, time. When he'd found out that Granddad—Mac to everyone else—wasn't his grandfather, it had taken a while to put it together.

Mac was a Woodward, as was his biological grandfather, Daniel Senior. He'd been a cousin, and when his grandfather had been killed, his great-grandfather had brought him in to help out on the farm. The rest, as they say, was history. And such a convoluted history it was. He'd never considered that his dad was a "junior," and that Granddad's name wasn't Daniel. He had thought maybe he went by his middle name and hadn't thought about it. He'd just been Mac Woodward.

Had he been involved with the illegal activities? Nick couldn't reconcile the idea with what he'd known about Granddad. He was the one he went to when he had questions about life, girls, God. Dad wasn't approachable, but Granddad was.

Nick heard the three moving, and he pushed himself back against the wall of rock. He was hidden about as well as he could be.

"The feds have part of the tunnel closed off where we need to be. Boss isn't going to like it." The shorter of the two men was pacing, back and forth, as if he'd had practice doing so in a small space. A prison cell, maybe?

The tall woman tossed back her dark hair and snorted with disgust. "You should have taken care of it before the FBI got involved. It's not doing us much good to have someone on the inside. If either of you gets caught, I'm out of here. I can't be placed with you."

"I wouldn't be so sure, lady. Somebody may have seen you at the hospital."

Nick was pretty sure that was from the shorter of the two men. The hospital?

"They wouldn't notice me, Gerry. I know how to blend in. I'm a nurse, remember? Or used to be. Anyway, we need to get in there when we can. They won't work all night." She turned toward where Nick was hiding, her gaze settling near his hiding place. He was thankful he'd thought to silence his phone completely.

"What if they have somebody standing guard?" The taller man spoke. "They've brought in another team. The manpower is available, now."

The shorter man, the one she'd called "Gerry" shook his head. "I don't think they will. They won't take a chance on the woman and kids being there after the break-in." He looked up at the woman and sneered. "I don't suppose you want to be the one to chance it?"

"I think not." She raised an eyebrow and gave him a look that bespoke no love lost between them. "I'll keep an eye on Rossi. She'll be out of commission for the next day or so."

The man standing next to the woman hadn't said anything until now. "That works. If you've been around, they won't think anything of your being there. If one of us showed up, we'd stick out like a sore thumb."

Gerry's laugh burst out. "Speak for yourself. Me, I can be a charmer when I want to be."

"You keep thinking that, if it helps." The woman shook her head and looked to the taller man. "We've got to get the rest of the merchandise and equipment out of there before someone finds it. You hear me?"

"Your hick accent is showing, dear." The taller man put his hand on the woman's shoulder.

"You've got your job, I've got mine. Don't you forget it."

Nick hadn't moved a muscle, but for no apparent reason —gravity, he supposed—a rock shifted and fell to the floor of the cavern. Three sets of eyes turned, and three people, two of them armed, made his position.

15

Two thirty.

Had it only been an hour since Del had talked to Clay? He'd said he would come out here if he hadn't heard from them by three. Trouble was, the last thing they needed was for a posse to roar through the tunnels and scare off the criminals. He'd need to tell him to come in quietly.

He felt his phone vibrate in his pocket. Lisa.

"Where's Nick? I can't get him to answer."

Del could have bet money Lisa would text him when she didn't hear from Nick. He sent her an answer quickly, pausing when he saw the reception waning as he walked through the living room.

"Checking on him. Probably out of range."

Maybe that would keep her at bay. He had Nick's keys, and he was heading to the truck to retrieve Nick's handgun. No way was he going to tell Lisa.

The reception was dismal here. It was one of the downsides to country living, but it might be worth it. On one end of the porch, there was nothing. On the other end? Four bars of service.

He punched in Clay's number only to have it go to voice mail. Frustrated, he looked up at the color on the porch ceiling. "Haint Blue," Lisa had called it.

He'd have to leave a message and get back to Nick. "Clay, Del here. We've got a situation at Nick's house. He's okay. There are three people in the tunnel that shouldn't be there, and Nick heard them talking about the break-in at the café. Call me or text me, but I may be out of range. You probably want to get out here, and you may want to include Agent Stafford." He started to hang up, and a thought came to him. "We entered through Nick's basement, and I'll leave the back door open. Come in quiet. Repeat. Come in quiet."

Call made, he shoved the phone into his pocket and walked over to Nick's truck. With a click of the key fob, he was in the shiny, late-model truck, and sure enough, there was Nick's handgun, the twin of his own.

He hoped neither gun would need to be used.

As he walked back onto the porch to enter the house, his phone rang.

"Clay."

"Del, what's going on out there?" Clay sounded rushed. "I'm headed your way now, and Stafford is with me."

"Nick's down there keeping an eye on things, I came up to call you and get his gun out of the truck." Del perched on a rocker so he'd keep the signal. "He's got mine right now."

"Good. No SWAT team, huh?"

"No, we don't know where they're getting in from the other side, and you'll lose them if you come in gangbusters."

"Got it."

Del could hear Clay filling Stafford in, and then his voice came through loud and clear. "Don't try to engage them."

Del snorted. "Don't worry about us. We have no intention of getting involved. If anything happened to Nick, Lisa would kill me, and if anything happened to me, Lisa would kill me—if I'm not already dead. I lose either way."

"Point taken."

"I'm heading back in and locking the front door. The back door to the kitchen will be unlocked."

"We'll be there, no sirens, in about ten minutes."

"See you then."

Del pushed the red End Call icon on his phone and turned off the ringer. You could never tell when you'd have a glimmer of a signal down there, so the last thing he wanted was to broadcast his whereabouts to shady characters.

He locked the door behind himself as he entered, then made his way through the kitchen and the basement door. Good thing he'd worn his sneakers instead of his work boots. Much easier to keep a low profile. How the television detectives—especially the female ones—did their job in dress shoes both amazed and amused him.

Del was where he estimated to be about halfway through the tunnel when he heard a scuffle. Not good. When a shot rang out, he froze. Nick was in there. His best friend. His brother in so many ways. He gave up stealth and broke into a run, only to have Nick crash into him in the tunnel.

"They found me. Get out." Nick didn't even slow down. "They're coming up behind us."

He didn't stop to think, he just put it in high gear about the time he heard footsteps running behind him. Were they leading them right to Nick and Lisa's house? Unacceptable. In his hurry, his mind slowed down enough to look around as he traveled. Since he'd been through here several times by now, he was familiar with some of the off-shoots, both natural and man-made.

He remembered the tunnel hidden by a natural outcropping. The one leading to the Woodward homestead. Unlike the one heading directly to the river, it was still viable. He'd go that way, try to misdirect them. Couldn't call out to let Nick know, and he hoped when he noticed he wasn't behind him, he wouldn't turn back. If nothing else, splitting up would divide the opposition, evening the odds a little.

They were getting closer. Del tried to take in his surroundings. There was a dark spot up ahead. If need be, he could dive into it. If he had time.

A shot rang out in the same instant he realized he'd been spotted. He plunged himself into the dark unknown, not knowing if it was yet another tunnel, a crevasse, or simply a hollowed-out spot. When he hit the bottom of whatever it was, all he felt was searing pain.

But not from falling. The thought came to him as even the light of the opening began to turn dark.

I've been shot.

Nick raked his hand over his face, the cool air of the cavern doing nothing to stop the sweat from running into his eyes. Nerves and physical activity had caught up with him.

He'd heard a shot ring out, and he was sick. Not only had they potentially led gangsters to his house, but when Del didn't catch up to him...

Taking deep breaths, he stood in the dark, listening. He no longer heard footsteps behind him, and he wanted to retrace his steps and check on Del. Maybe he was hiding along the way? *Keep him safe, God.* He closed his eyes for a minute and said it over and over as he pulled the ammunition magazine out of his pocket and loaded the pistol. He shone his flashlight toward the chamber to make sure it had loaded properly

Finally, he heard sounds coming from the other direction. From the house. Reinforcements?

Nick quietly made his way toward the basement opening, trying to listen both ahead and behind himself. When he got to the tunnel that led from the first room to the larger opening, he stopped short when he met Clay and Agent Stafford, with Clay's deputy—Ben—right behind, all carrying guns.

"Nick." Clay stopped and took in a deep breath. "Where's Del?"

Nick paused a beat and closed his eyes. "He was right behind me. I met him when they spotted me." He gulped in air. "We split up at some point, and I heard a shot."

Clay's face was grim. He turned to Ben and Agent Frank Stafford. "I'll go first, Ben, you bring up the rear." He put his hand on Nick's shoulder. "Del's probably fine." He looked at the other two men. "Let's go. I'm ready to get this settled, once and for all."

Agent Stafford snorted but followed Clay. He whispered, "If that happens, we'll be lucky. Chances are, if we catch them, they'll send more."

Clay held up his closed fist, silently telling them to stop.

Nick peered down. They were at some kind of opening. To what, he wasn't sure.

Agent Stafford shone his light around, and on the ground, squatting as he pointed at something at their feet.

"Blood." The agent looked up at Nick, then at Clay. "Clay and I will follow the tracks, Nick, you and Ben check and see if Del is in there."

Nick rushed in.

"Hang on." When they turned back to him, Stafford

spoke. "Watch your step. I didn't get a good look, but it may be a drop-off."

Clay and Frank went down the tunnel, the way Nick had traveled both ways just minutes ago, it seemed. Shining the flashlights around, there was, indeed, a drop-off. As they neared it, they realized it wasn't a pit as much as a crater. Not too deep, but enough to throw you off your feet if you weren't looking for it.

At the bottom, not moving, was Del, blood pooling on the ground from a gunshot wound.

16

Was that Del Reno? Becca was shocked when she got a glimpse of the guy they were chasing. Well, one of them anyway. Clyde pushed her behind a rock formation and pulled out his gun. "Stay here." He didn't leave her side. That was his job.

She was still stunned when she heard a couple of shots ring out. Stunned and more than a little sick. She'd known Del all her life. They rode the same bus through elementary and middle school, and in high school, he was one of the guys that didn't act like he was too "cool" to talk to the younger teens. In college, he had asked her out, and their romance had begun. They'd been inseparable. Until she left.

Closing her eyes, she waited behind Clyde's strong form. She was tall, but he was taller, which made her feel safe. A fleeting thought came to her. What would he think if she leaned her head on his muscular shoulder and relaxed for a second?

Her mind wandered between Del in college and her operation falling apart at the seams. She and Del had dated steadily before her grandfather had her basically kidnapped after her mother's murder. She'd thought maybe they had a chance. Maybe if she'd stayed? She'd never know. The last time they'd been together was an occasion she'd rather forget, and she was sure Del would, too.

Footsteps coming down the tunnel pulled her attention back to the present. Gerry and Keith ran to them and stopped when they saw Clyde.

Gerry was out of breath. For a guy who was liable to get caught at any time, he was out of shape. Becca's mind worked that way. "What happened?"

"There were two of them." Gerry leaned over, gulping air. "By the time we realized they'd split up, I'd lost one guy and was chasing the other one."

"What did he look like?" She narrowed her eyes, hoping she was wrong.

"Blond, shaggy hair." Gerry looked at her strangely. "Needed a haircut."

She closed her eyes and groaned inside. It was Del. Had to be. "Where is he?"

He chuckled grimly. "I got in a good shot. He's at the bottom of a shallow pit." Gerry, breathing restored, almost preened. "He won't be bothering us."

Becca shook her head, her eyes closing again. Tears would come. She had to stop them now, but they would come, later, when she was alone.

"I should never have come here."

Clyde took her arm. "Becca?"

She looked up at him, her face pale in the dim light. "I knew him."

"Him, who?"

"The guy he shot." She swallowed thickly. "It had to be Del Reno."

———————— ⌒ ————————

Darcy rushed through the automatic doors of the emergency room about the time her mom and Steve arrived. Mom had called as soon as she heard there was trouble, and the ladies had left Paducah and hightailed it back to Marion and the hospital.

Del had been shot. All they knew was that an ambulance had brought him to the hospital and that he was unconscious when they left Nick's house.

This was her fault. If Del hadn't thought she and the kids were in danger, he wouldn't have been down there. He would have let the police and the FBI do their jobs, and he and Nick would have been safe. As it was, it could have been either of them. Seeing Lisa in the waiting area, mopping her eyes, she knew her friend and stepsister was as relieved that Nick was okay and by her side as she was devastated that her brother may have been mortally wounded.

Darcy tried to stay on the sidelines, knowing she was an extra person. Steve and Lisa needed one another. Seeing them embrace, Steve patting a sobbing Lisa on the back, Nick's hand never leaving her shoulder.

How would it feel to have such a support system? She closed her eyes and shook her head, willing the tears to stop. When she looked up, her mom was staring right at her, and she walked over to her.

"Sweetie, are you all right?" Mom hugged her, and the tears seemed to engulf her.

"Mom, what if he dies? It will be my fault."

Mom pulled back and stared at her, shaking her head in confusion. "What are you talking about?"

Darcy stared off into space, blinking furiously to stop those stupid tears. It wasn't like they would change anything, anyway, so why give in to them? And, if she told her mother what she was thinking, could she help? Probably not. But maybe? She took in a deep breath. "If Del hadn't been worried about the kids and me, he wouldn't have gone down there."

Mom shook her head. "Sweetheart, you are putting a lot on yourself for no good reason."

Darcy gasped in horror. "No good reason? Del may die, and if he does, it will be on me."

"No, sweetie, it won't." She pulled her daughter to herself again, holding her stiff form until she began to relax, and then held her away to look at her. "Del would have gone in there with Nick whether you were in trouble or not. The idea that these people could get to both Nick and Lisa's house and the café was what drove him. It wasn't only about you and the kids." Her eyes twinkled as she shook her head at her offspring. "Although I'm sure that may have been extra encouragement."

"Mom." Mom winked at her and Darcy gave her a dirty look. "There's nothing..."

Darcy glanced over to see the doctor coming out the doors from the treatment rooms. Steve, Lisa, and Nick stepped over, and Mom and Darcy moved toward them, trying to stay out of the way, but still hear the doctor's update.

For sixty-five, Dr. Maddux's hair was barely sprinkled with gray. "Steve, Lisa." He looked up and smiled cordially. "Everybody." He could speak up because their group was the only one in the waiting room at the moment. "Del's okay."

A collective whoosh sounded as relief spread through them.

The doctor held up his hand. "He's okay, but he's not great." His face became serious. "He has a shoulder wound, almost a chest wound, but it missed all major organs.

Unfortunately, it nicked an artery, which accounts for the blood loss. We've stopped the bleeding and are getting him ready for surgery to repair the damage. He also suffered a concussion, but he's conscious."

Darcy felt the wind go out of her sails and reached back to see if there was a chair behind her. Thank goodness there was. If not, she'd have passed out then and there. The black spots she kept seeing were getting thicker. Once she sat and began breathing again, she felt more like herself. What in the world? She didn't faint.

He was awake. Hurt, but awake. She wanted to see for herself, but she had no right, no right at all, to see him. She'd have to rely on secondhand information.

The doctor was still talking. He'd glanced over at her when she sat down suddenly and was eying her curiously. "Put your head between your knees. Are you all right, Darcy?"

Darcy did as she was told and got her equilibrium back. She stood, still a little shaky, and smiled wanly. "I'm fine. Don't do well with blood."

Her mother clamped her lips together and shook her head, looking for all the world as if she could laugh. Darcy frowned at her, and Mom simply grabbed her hand and squeezed it.

"Doctor Moore, the surgeon, is on her way here from Madisonville, and as soon as she gets here, we'll take care of our boy." The doctor clapped a hand on Steve Reno's shoulder and squeezed. "He's in good hands." He winked at his old friend. "And, he wants to see you."

Steve's eyes were shining with unshed tears.

Why can't I be as honest about my emotions as a man approaching sixty?

His wife kissed him on the cheek and motioned for him

to go. Darcy watched as Del's father followed the doctor through the doors she'd gone through two Christmases ago when Benji fell and banged his head on the side of the tub. Mom and Steve had reconnected that night.

Look at them now.

Her smile withered as she thought of another time, fifteen or so years ago, when she sat here, in this waiting room, hearing that her daddy had died.

What was the phrase? "The Lord gives, and the Lord takes away?" Maybe it was a verse in the Bible. Wherever it came from, it only reinforced for her the idea that God didn't like her very much, no matter what everyone said.

Lisa sank down in the vinyl-covered armchair next to Darcy and closed her eyes. "How does Del get himself into these situations?' She shook her head, then turned to look at Darcy, who was pale. "Are you okay?" She narrowed her eyes. Darcy was pale, and her answer to Dr. Maddux that she didn't "do well with blood" was a crock.

Darcy couldn't meet her eyes, picking an imaginary piece of lint from her jeans. "I'm fine."

Right.

Nick came over to sit next to Lisa and pulled her hand into his lap. "Hey." He bent over their linked hands, then turned to look at her with an anxious smile.

"Hey, yourself." He was worried. She could tell. And he felt responsible. Lisa's attention went from her fiancé to her friend. Both of them looked worse than she or Dad, and shouldn't they be the ones worried about their family member? "What's going on?"

If they'd practiced, Nick and Darcy couldn't have been more in sync when they both blurted out, "It's my fault."

Lisa gazed up at the ceiling and shook her head. "You two goofballs are not at fault, here."

Nick spoke. "It was my idea to go down there. Del was going along so I wouldn't get in trouble for being down there alone."

Darcy shook her head. "I told him not to go down there alone." She snorted. "Of course, I also told him not to watch my house all night, and he didn't listen then, either." Looking at Nick, she shook her head again. "So you two were one another's alibi?"

Nick grinned sheepishly. "I guess so."

"See? Del is his own man. He's not going to do something because somebody tells him to do something, or in Del's case, tells him NOT to do something." Lisa sighed. "It's not the fault of anyone but the criminals who shot him. If they hadn't been around, none of this would have happened."

Darcy still didn't look sure, and Lisa couldn't do the believing for her. Darcy had more going on than guilt over Del's getting hurt. *Help her, Lord.* She was glad God didn't mind on-the-spot prayers because lately, she'd been sending up a lot of those.

Dad came out to the waiting room from seeing Del. Lisa looked up expectantly as Dad came out to the waiting room from seeing Del, and Roxy went to him.

"How is he?"

"Not great, but he talked to me." Dad rubbed his hand down his face, then turned to Lisa. "Said he guessed if he was on crutches for my wedding, he could be in a sling for yours."

Lisa laughed, tears hovering near the surface.

Dad cleared his throat. "They took him to pre-op, and the nurse told me to tell you we can move down to the operating room waiting area." He looked at the group that had gathered. "You don't all need to stay."

Nobody moved. Lisa lifted her lips in a subdued smile. "I don't think you'll get rid of us very easily."

Darcy bit her lip and checked the time. "I want to stay, but I need to pick up the kids from preschool."

Roxy was torn. "I would offer, but..."

Darcy shook her head emphatically. "You need to be here with Steve, Mom."

"I know." Roxy hugged Darcy as she stood up. "I'll keep you posted."

"Please do." Darcy turned back to the group, twisting the strap of her purse, then focused on Lisa. "Can I do anything for you?"

"Take care of my niece and nephew." Lisa could tell Darcy was putting off leaving. It was hard being on the outside, looking in. Something about the expression on Darcy's face made her sad. She didn't want her stepsister to feel left out. She also didn't want her to miss an opportunity, and Del was an opportunity. She couldn't help it. Her arms went around Darcy and she squeezed, glad when she hugged her back.

If only she would get her head on straight and accept it. More importantly, accept the fact that God loved her, and Jesus died for her.

That was what she needed to accept more than anything. Once more, Lisa closed her eyes briefly as Darcy went through the exit.

Help her, Lord.

17

Only one sound at a time pushed through the fog of anesthesia.

First, a quiet beep. Next, voices from far away, getting closer. Then, all at once, every sound around Del came alive in a cacophony of unwanted stress on top of the bitter cold he felt all over.

"Mr. Reno, can you hear me?" The nurse was intent on waking him, and it was the last thing he wanted to do, so he nodded. Maybe that would satisfy her.

"Mr. Reno, are you in any pain?"

There was another nurse, a different one, as he drifted back off. Why couldn't they leave him alone?

"I'm sorry, Del."

He forced his eyelids open a crack to see a tall, dark-haired woman standing over him. As his vision cleared, he recognized her...but from where? When? "Okay." That was all he could get out before the darkness closed in again, and blissful sleep took over.

And then there were the warm blankets. You had only to

mutter the word "cold," and the nurses in the post-op recovery unit started piling them on. The weight, as well as the warmth, was like being wrapped in a satisfying hug, helping you to drift back to sleep, lest you start feeling the pain that was there, just out of reach.

The fog of surgery began to lift, and he moved his legs a little. Okay, legs work. Fingers? They move. Arms? The left one seemed okay, but the right...

Then it came back to him. He'd been shot, an experience he never expected to have. Shot. With a gun. In the shoulder. When it happened, he thought he'd been hit in the chest, and that it was over for him.

What was that last question again? Oh yeah. Was he in any pain? "Not much." He looked up at her. "Who was the other nurse?"

The nurse patted his good arm and grinned when he finally focused on her. "I'm the only one down here today. Let me know if you start feeling any pain, okay? The more we can manage it up front, the better off you'll be."

He remembered. When he'd had surgery on his leg, he'd tried to be all macho and not take any pain meds. He'd pretty much lied, saying he felt no pain, when he had. At least this wouldn't keep him off his feet.

But that face. Somebody had been here.

"You rest. We'll try not to bother you for a little while. I'll let your group know you're alert and that the surgery went well."

"Any permanent damage?" He had to know. He knew he wasn't mortally wounded, but there were nerves, arteries, and who knew what else in the region where he was shot.

Dr. Jessica Moore, the surgeon, came up to the bed and leaned on the rail. "Hey, Del. How do you get into these scrapes?"

Del smiled. The surgeon would have to be Jessica, the girl he'd had a crush on all junior year of high school. Now she was married, with three kids, and a successful surgery practice. "Talent, I guess."

She shook her head and chuckled. "At this rate, you'll have plenty of stories to tell at our next class reunion." Turning on her professional stance, she pointed toward his wound. "I talked to your dad, and I'll tell you what I told him. You'll be fine in a few weeks if you rest and let your body heal. No lifting until I see you again in two weeks. Local driving only, but not for a few days. Sling on when you're not at home. Protect the wound at all times. Change the dressing twice a day until the drainage stops. Shouldn't be more than a few days before it seals itself up."

"No permanent damage, then?" Del grinned weakly.

"Nope. You're young, you're healthy, and the worst part was that it nicked an artery and you lost a lot of blood before they got to you. You were given three units of blood, which is a lot, but even then, you weren't in danger of dying. A little longer, though..." The doctor shook her head. "There are still bullet particles in there, but they're not hurting anything."

Del stared at the doctor. "Is that normal? I thought you had to get the bullet out or it would move around and do more damage?"

She waved a hand dismissively. "That's television for you. By the time a bullet gets inside you, it's done the damage it's going to do unless it's in a joint or a vital organ or made out of lead." She shrugged. "We checked the location of the fragments and tested one to see what it was made of. You're okay."

"Good to know." He shifted in the bed, wincing as he inadvertently moved his right arm. "Thanks, Jessica."

Dr. Moore patted him on the leg. "Glad to be of

service. We'll keep you a couple of days since we had to give you blood, but you should be good to go after that." She winked and fluttered her fingers at him. "See you tomorrow."

He waved, then relaxed against the pillow under his head. Eyes closed, he felt the wound under his collar bone begin to burn, and just then, a machine connected to him beeped, sending him a dose of much-appreciated pain medicine. He wouldn't argue. Right now, all he wanted was to sleep until he was healed up.

Sleep, and push Clay and the FBI to get this solved, because resting was not an option until he knew Darcy, Benji, and Ali were safe in their own home. Add figuring out who the strange nurse could be. He'd have to ask the others if they had seen her.

—————— ⟶ ——————

"Mommy, can we get a Happy Meal?" The high-pitched voice interrupted Darcy's thoughts, which were centered at the hospital, not on the kids—and they knew it.

Ali was the vocal twin. If the two of them wanted something, it seemed that there was an unspoken agreement that Ali verbalized for both of them.

Darcy checked on them in the small mirror underneath her rearview mirror. "Did you have a snack at school?" They didn't like it when she called it "preschool." They preferred to call it, simply, "school."

No answer. She glanced back and saw them conferring between the car seats, then they looked up, saw her, and sat up straight. Busted, much? She wanted to laugh out loud. But she didn't. Sometimes those two were too smart for their mom. Especially these days.

Benji spoke up. "We had cookies. Don't we need 'real food'?"

Yep, too smart for her. They'd heard her say they couldn't have cookies until after they had 'real food,' and took it to heart. Especially if they wanted chicken nuggets and fries. Oh, and a toy. They needed more cheap junk playthings like a hole in the head.

"We'll eat supper soon. We're going to cook grilled chicken for Grandmommy and Granddad." Maybe that would stave off starvation. "We need to go to Food Giant first. What do you want with your chicken?"

"French fries." Ali was not to be trifled with.

"How about mashed potatoes?" Darcy looked back to see her daughter, deep in thought, when an idea came to her.

"With cheese?" Ali sent her best smile to her mother.

"With cheese."

Darcy had been at loose ends the last few days since the café had closed. She needed to cook. She needed to do something, anything to keep busy.

And now Del was in the hospital. No matter what Lisa said, she still felt somewhat responsible.

She pulled into the parking lot of the local grocery store and almost balked at the limited number of spaces. *That's what you get when you wait until school's out to do your grocery shopping.*

The abandoned cart had been left in the perfect place for her to dash over and get it, then put both kids in. She was glad she didn't need much. The kids were in the big part of the cart, and she'd have to use the small part for the food. There wasn't a single aisle that didn't have someone she knew and had to stop and talk to. Somehow news of Del's being in the hospital had already spread. She didn't share any details, only that he was expected to make a full recovery. The beauty of a small town. She loved living back home, but there was something to be said for big-city living, where you didn't know anybody.

Chicken. That was what she was there for. She bent to peruse the deals to be had, and as she put a tray of chicken breasts in a bag, a hand touched her elbow.

She turned. "Frank." She looked at him in surprise. "What are you doing here?"

He laughed. "Same as you, only I'm here for the cooked food, not the raw stuff." He glanced around and then smiled down at the twins entertaining themselves in the cart. At least they *had* been until Frank came over with no cart, juggling his grocery items.

"Mom, can I get out? Ali's bothering me." Benji's sullen eyes flitted from Darcy to Frank, his mouth downturned.

"No, Benji, you need to stay right where you are." She frowned. "Sorry. They've been at school all day, and we're on our way home to cook supper."

He was sympathetic. "Benji, I have a sister, too. She bothered me all the time."

The small boy glared at him, looking distrustful. There was no trace of cheer on his usually friendly face.

Darcy was embarrassed. "Benjamin Sloan, what's wrong with you? Agent Stafford is speaking to you." She looked up at Frank, who was waving it aside. "No, we're working on speaking when spoken to." She put a hand on her hip and gave her son her sternest expression. "What do you say, young man?"

"Sorry." Benji didn't exactly look at Frank, but he threw the word toward him.

"Not a problem." Frank raised his eyebrows and took a deep breath as he smiled down at Darcy. "I can see I have a hill to climb with your son."

Darcy was stymied at her son's behavior. He was usually pleasant, even around people he didn't know.

"Have you heard anything from Del? He'd lost a lot of blood." Shaking his head, he continued. "Gunshot wounds are nothing to sneeze at." Frank spoke, Darcy still pondering Benji's behavior. As soon as he mentioned Del's name, she saw her son's eyes go wide.

"What's happened to Uncle Del?"

"Sorry. I wasn't thinking." Frank looked chagrined.

"That's okay. You're about the tenth person who's asked me about Del, and they were oblivious. No one else went into quite as much detail." Darcy arched a brow at Frank and leaned over to her children. "Uncle Del was in an accident and had to go to the hospital." She was surprised at the expression of fear on both their faces. If she weren't in the middle of the grocery store, she could almost cry. Again. "He's okay. The doctor had to do an operation to fix what was messed up, and Grandmommy will call when he gets out of surgery."

She had been concentrating on the kids, and now all the anxiety she'd felt before the meal-planning thoughts took over came back in full force. Del was hurt and could have been killed. She closed her eyes for a second.

Frank touched her arm again. "Are you okay?" He seemed worried.

Darcy pasted a fake smile on her face. "I'm fine." She took a deep breath and turned to the kids and Frank. "We'd better get a move on if we're going to cook dinner for Grandmommy and Granddad."

"I need to go. I pulled stakeout duty tonight. With Julia still in the hospital, it's Clay and me."

"How is she?"

Frank frowned. "She was doing great, on track to leave

the hospital today, but then her blood pressure bottomed out and she's been sleeping most of the day." He shook his head. "Her parents and fiancé are coming to take her home, but they won't release her until she's more responsive."

Agent Rossi is engaged? Thank goodness.

Darcy frowned, unsure where that thought came from. "I hope she's okay."

"She will be. Clay's assigned one of his deputies to stay and keep an eye on things." Frank seemed to come to himself. "Anyway, to stakeout I will go."

"Hence the cow patty sandwich in the cart?" She looked pointedly at the large half-round layered sandwich made from half a loaf of round bread and filled with meat and cheese. "If I might suggest, some fruits and vegetables wouldn't be amiss in all that junk food." She chuckled at his reddening face.

He held up the potato chips and fruit roll-ups, a mischievous look on his face. "What do you call this?"

Shaking her head, she laughed. "I call it flirting with diabetes."

Becca sat in her car, tears spent. She'd parked as far away from the hospital entrance as possible, knowing a late-model Audi would attract attention. Attention was the last thing she needed.

She shouldn't have gone in there. What if he remembered seeing her? Maybe her hair being different would be enough to keep him wondering. He was still pretty out of it.

Clyde hadn't been happy when she'd told him she needed time to herself. She didn't ask for it often, but today was different. She'd never been a party to one of her oldest friends getting shot. For all she knew at the time, he could have been mortally wounded. Fortunately, he wasn't, and she, Clyde, and Gerry had made it out of the tunnel before the feds and local law enforcement got there. It was good to have inside information.

Leaving him in there, not knowing if he was alive or dead, was almost more than she could bear, but the job had kicked in. They had removed the rest of the evidence that could put her grandfather's entire organization behind bars. Was it worth it?

She thought about Mom and all she'd gone through with Dad. Before they met, he'd hooked up with Becca's grandfather's organization, smuggling drugs and liquor in and out of these Kentucky tunnels, and eventually rose in ranks to the "big time," getting him to Chicago as a trusted member of her grandfather's crime family. He'd met Mom by accident while on business at Vic's house. They soon fell in love and married quickly, cementing his standing with the family.

But then he got caught.

When trouble came, Granddad—Vic—sent him back to Clementville and forbade her mother to go with him. She refused, breaking ties with Chicago.

Becca had never known what happened because it was something they never talked about. She always hoped, when she got older, that they would trust her with the story of why she didn't have grandparents.

Dad's parents were dead and he was an only child, so the few relatives he had weren't close enough to be considered "ties." He'd taken Mom away from everything she'd ever known, and because she was in love with him, she'd followed blindly.

Becca's earliest memories of home were of the house where Dad grew up, in Crittenden County.

Her phone vibrated, and she picked it up. Granddad. "Hey, Granddad."

"Rebecca. Give me an update." His words were brusque, as if she were any other member of the organization. He refused to use the more endearing short form of her name, "Becca," that her grandmother and everyone else in her life used. Always "Rebecca." Why did it hurt so much that a man whom she'd only known for eight years was impossible to please? She closed her eyes and concentrated, hoping he couldn't hear the strain in her voice from her recent emotional breakdown.

"We cleared out the merchandise and the records."

"You're sure?"

"I'm going back in the tunnels to check it out in the morning."

"Morning might be too late. You need to get it buttoned up."

"One of the guys shot someone. I'm at the hospital making sure he doesn't die on us." She made herself sound harsh because it was all her grandfather understood. The tightness in her throat helped sell it, though it was for a much different reason.

"Are you there alone?"

"Yes, I'm staying under the radar."

"Why do I pay Clyde if you're going to run off and get yourself killed?"

It's not like he cares. He just wants someone he can press into telling on me. "He's close by."

"He'd better be. What about the fed?"

"She's still pretty out of it. I helped it along. No lasting effects."

He paused, making her think the line had gone dead for a moment. When he spoke, that fantasy was shattered. "We need back in the café."

She frowned. "I thought the café break-in was a diversion?"

"Just follow Gabe's instructions."

"Okay. Anything I should know?"

"Not at this point." His voice never tendered, never asked if she was okay, never seemed to appreciate the grandfather-granddaughter relationship.

"I understand." She didn't.

"Good. Don't get caught."

She closed her eyes and wanted to scream. "Have I ever?"

"There's always a first time."

"Gotta go. It's shift-change at the hospital and I want to check on the patients one more time. I'll send Gerry out to check the tunnels tonight, and I'll go over there first thing tomorrow." She swallowed and leaned her pounding head back. "When should we expect Gabe?"

"He should be there any time. If you'd talked to Clyde in the last hour, you'd know that."

Becca cringed. She'd missed her check-in call and now Granddad knew it. Great. "Gotta go, Granddad."

"Report in tonight."

"Will do."

She heard the slow beep of disconnection and held her phone out, seeing that he'd cut off the conversation without as much as a goodbye. How would it be to have a loving, caring grandfather? One that put her ahead of his business?

She looked around the parking lot. She saw a few nurses and aides coming out of the hospital and going to their cars. Now was the time. Checking her hair in the mirror, she smoothed on lip balm and gave herself an artificial smile.

Brown contacts went back in her eyes—she'd taken them out when she cried earlier. Her hair was pulled back in a plain knot at the nape of her neck, minimal makeup except where her scar was, on her forehead, and scrubs loose enough to hide the curves of her figure. The idea was to blend into the woodwork. Considering she used to have light hair and her actual eye color was blue, she thought the disguise was pretty convincing.

18

Del had been moved to a regular room and was brought beef broth and orange gelatin for supper. He frowned. "Not exactly the supper of champions," he muttered.

"What are you grumbling about?" Lisa came in the door, Nick on her heels.

Del shook his head. "I can't eat this."

Lisa, ever positive, smelled it and gave her brother a weak smile. "I'm sure the cooks here are fantastic and need encouragement to use their imaginations."

Nick scanned the contents of the tray and wrinkled his nose. "Doesn't look like you eat it. You drink it." He grinned, then sobered. "You doing okay?"

"I'll be fine. I'm still sleepy from the anesthetic, but with the pain med machine over here?" He pointed to the box on a stand with lights blinking, "I'm virtually pain-free."

Nick's eyes went down and then focused on his friend. His head was still ducked slightly, a frown furrowing his brow. "What possessed you to turn down the other tunnel?"

"I didn't want to lead them to your house." Del shrugged

and then winced in pain when he realized he needed to limit his shrugging to one side.

Lisa looked at her fiancé, then at her brother, and shook her head. Were those tears? "You could have both been killed."

"But we weren't." Del gave her a lopsided smile. "And we may have led the FBI closer to catching whoever did the damage at Darcy's."

Nick looked at his toes, quiet. "Maybe."

A thought occurred to him. "Hey, the weirdest thing happened while I was in recovery."

"Pink elephants dancing on the ceiling?" Lisa laughed.

"No, I'm serious. While I was still pretty out of it, a nurse stood over me."

"There's nothing odd about that."

"She seemed so familiar. And she said, 'I'm sorry, Del.'" He stared at Lisa and Nick, frowning. "Why would a nurse say that?"

"Maybe she thought she'd moved something and caused you some pain?" Nick furrowed his brow. "You said she looked familiar?"

"Yeah, but not recent familiarity." He thought a moment. "You know how you see the face of somebody you haven't seen in a long time, and you can't put your finger on it?"

"You probably dreamed or hallucinated." Lisa picked up the bowl of broth and began feeding her brother. "You'll spill it all over yourself if you try to do it."

"Bring me a burger tomorrow?" Del obediently opened his mouth when the spoon came to him. He knew it would be bad, and it was.

"We'll see."

"And a shake?" He tried to pull the puppy-dog-eye trick on her. Sometimes it worked.

"Don't push it."

"I've been shot." He avoided looking at his sister and glanced at Nick, who was hiding his face, laughing silently.

Lisa stood there, hand on her hip as she paused in feeding him. "I think you're going to be fine. You're starting to provoke me."

———————⟨∽⟩———————

Becca ducked into an empty hospital room in time to avoid coming face to face with Lisa Reno and another guy. Nick Woodward? She remembered him from college. He looked different from the twenty-two-year-old she remembered. She probably did too. At MSU, he seemed to always be around when Del was with her. Sometimes it exasperated her, but he was fun, so she usually got over it. It had probably kept them from taking steps that would have changed their lives completely. She should probably be grateful. She'd thought she loved Del at the time, and probably would have done anything he asked. Fortunately, he hadn't asked.

The one time they strayed out of the straight and narrow, they got caught. Underage drinking and a DUI were a wake-up call. She wondered if Del still drank. She had become so used to it with her dad, she didn't even question "going south," as they called a liquor run to Tennessee from Murray State University. Most of western Kentucky was still "dry" at the time, so if you wanted alcohol, you had to drive for it, hence "going south." Unfortunately, it also meant driving under the influence and lots of state police traps to get through. Del had been over twenty-one, she hadn't been. It was their first try, and wouldn't you know they'd get caught when they took a ditch instead of hitting a deer.

She'd never forget Del's look of abject fear when the

officer kindly gave them a warning and a talking-to instead of a ticket or arrest. Becca was treated by a paramedic at the scene, and released, with the suggestion they go to the emergency room for a scan, which they didn't. The scar on her forehead was her souvenir of the evening.

Del said it was a "God thing." They could have been hurt badly or arrested.

Whatever. She'd not seen much of God in the last twenty-seven years of her life, so she wouldn't know. Her philosophy was "go along to get along," and she thought of God as "the boss," patterned after her grandfather, sitting in a big chair with lackeys all around doing his bidding. Right now, she was one of them, which made her angry. Mom had gotten away. She had broken free of her father. Just not of her husband. Then she'd been murdered for it.

Now she was free of everything.

She heard Lisa laugh as they passed the door of the room where she was straightening a pillow without cause, to keep her back to the door. One hurdle crossed. She had a feeling Del was awake. If that was the case, she couldn't go into the room. He'd recognize her immediately if she spoke.

Checking both ways outside the door, she saw that the coast was clear. She walked toward Del's room and stopped just short of his view into the hallway. She could hear him talking.

"I'm good, Dad." He paused, like he was on a phone call. "You and Roxy don't need to come down here. Lisa and Nick left, and Lisa helped me with supper." He laughed at something his dad must have said. "Yeah, considering. I've requested a burger and shake for tomorrow. Feel free to pass my request along to Darcy and Roxy."

She stood there, in the hallway, knowing his attention

was on the call, and could imagine the smile broadening on his face. Darcy? Darcy Emerson?

She'd been gone a long time. Until the last few days, she hadn't thought of Darcy in years. Her childhood and teenage years were a blur. It was as if she were a different person then. Sometimes she had trouble remembering even the most important moments, and Darcy fit in the category of a life that wasn't hers, but someone else's. She wasn't in college with them, was she? No, she'd gone to community college and was getting ready to transfer. Becca had heard she got married and moved away.

And now she was a widow. How long, and how, she wondered?

Maybe her husband turned out like my dad. If she has Del on the hook, she's in luck.

Becca watched as Del ended the call. He was cute in a rumpled sort of way, his light hair always about three weeks past a good haircut. She felt a touch of a smile cross her mouth, letting her mind wander for a second until she thought about her grandfather. What would he say to her hanging around here checking up on an old boyfriend?

The clatter of the supper cart returning for the empty trays roused her from her thoughts. She had to get over to the ICU and check on the agent. If Agent Rossi wasn't starting to come to, she'd need to get the info about the drug she used to the doctor, somehow, without getting caught.

Darcy frowned. She still wasn't used to waking up at Steve and Mom's house. When would this be over and their lives back to normal? Would it ever? As long as there were tunnels out there that organized crime knew about, were they safe?

Were her babies safe? What about Lisa and Nick, when they moved into their house?

Why couldn't those tunnels have been used for something besides crime?

She grabbed her robe and stepped into her slippers before going to check on Ali and Benji. She bypassed the room they shared when she heard them laughing in the kitchen, along with Mom and Grandpa Steve.

"Were you guys going to let me sleep all day?" She glanced at the clock. "It's nearly ten o'clock!"

Mom came over and hugged her. "If anybody deserves a break, it's you, sweetheart."

Darcy hugged her back, then waved her away and picked up a napkin to catch grape jelly before a drop of it fell from Benji's chin. "You're messy, did you know that?" She looked over at Ali, her face completely clean in contrast.

Benji grinned. "I know." And he went right back to his toast and jelly.

"Can I fix you an egg? There's bacon on the platter and some biscuits if you want brunch." Mom looked at her daughter and laughed. "I can't seem to get away from being a short-order cook."

Darcy split a biscuit and broke pieces of bacon to put on it. "This will do nicely." She took a bite and closed her eyes for a second, reveling in the crunch of the bacon and the flaky biscuit. "Mmmm, Mom. This is wonderful."

"I thought I'd fix hamburgers for lunch." Mom leaned on the counter, watching her little family with a smile.

Darcy snorted mid-bite. "Del's request?"

"Yep. I didn't have a son, so I'm enjoying spoiling him a bit."

That hurt a little. Mom hadn't had a chance to spoil Justin because he'd shipped out a few days after the wedding.

She'd never had the opportunity to know him. It was in the past, and there was no bringing it back, now. She frowned, focusing on her bacon biscuit. "I always said you should have had more kids."

Mom sighed a little and looked off into the distance. "I know. We wanted to."

This was new information. "Really?" In the past, when she'd brought it up, in a joking manner, her mom had poo-pooed the idea and laughed, saying one Darcy was enough to make up for a houseful of kids.

Looking up at her from the table, she was surprised at Mom's response.

"Really. When you were about five, I had a miscarriage, and then we couldn't get pregnant again."

"I'm sorry, Mom."

She waved her away. "It's in the past."

"And there's no bringing it back."

"Exactly."

Steve went over to his wife and leaned on the counter next to her, slipping an arm around her waist. "I'm glad to share my kids, and Roxy—" He kissed her on the cheek and winked at her. "I'm all for having another kid if you want to."

Mom swatted him and endured a quick hug and another kiss on the cheek from her husband as they all laughed.

The laughter in the house was what Darcy needed. She'd tried too hard to do everything perfectly, think things out ahead of time, and be a rock the kids could count on. She looked at her mom and Steve, and tears came to her eyes. They were happy. They'd both lived through the tragedy of losing a spouse, and now they were building a life together with their blended family that had jelled like it was meant to be.

Del was such a good big brother to her. Her heart

lurched. Somehow she knew if she continued to think of Del as her big brother, she would never be happy again.

She excused herself and had a hard time meeting her mom's eyes. "I need to get dressed and start the day."

------- ᴄⱭ) -------

Del lifted his eyes to the ceiling and muttered a quick, "Thank You, Jesus," when Darcy entered his room with a Styrofoam cup and a bag. He instinctively waved, and immediately regretted it. *Ouch.*

"I understand you ordered a Clementville Café special and a shake?" Darcy's eyes twinkled.

"When did you start delivery?" Del decided to milk it a little bit.

"Oh, we've been known to deliver to especially sad cases from time to time."

She laughed, and Del with her. "You want sad? You shoulda seen the bowl of broth they brought me for supper last night. Talk about sad."

"I can only imagine. Not a broth guy, huh?" The smile on her face made him feel exhilarated, somehow.

"Only if it's chock-full of beef, potatoes, and carrots." He snorted. "They did let me have oatmeal for breakfast. That's a gateway to a burger and a shake, isn't it?"

"I'd say so." She pulled the burger and fries out of the bag and set them up on his tray, adjusting it while he moved his bed into a seated position.

"Oh, man. This looks so good."

"Thank you, kind sir. Must be nice to be the solitary customer at the café. You got special treatment from the head chef herself. She fixed it at the café's remote location at the Reno homestead."

"And I appreciate it." He grasped the large burger with his good hand and took a big bite, then closed his eyes in ecstasy. "So, so good." He didn't make a habit of talking with his mouth full, but he couldn't help it. There was no way he was going to waste time with the niceties when he had the best burger and shake in town at his disposal.

"How are you feeling?"

"I'm okay."

She shook her head. "So what on earth are you doin' in the hospital?"

Del chuckled as he slurped his chocolate shake, the mixture easing its way down in perfect fashion. "They tend to keep an eye on guys who get in the way of a bullet."

Darcy blanched a bit, and he was sorry he said it. "Don't worry about me. I'm fine." He put down the shake and took her hand in his good one. "Darce." He forced her to look at him. "I'm fine."

"I know. And I don't know why I'm so emotional these days." She shook her head furiously as if trying to clear the cobwebs from her mind.

A minute or so later, he'd finished the burger in record time. "It's been a rough week." He winked at her as a nurse came in shaking her head and carrying a tray.

"You mean you'd rather have a burger than the vegetable soup I've brought you?" She smirked at Del, and then looked at Darcy. "Unless you'd like it?"

Darcy laughed and perked up. "Sure. I'm game."

The nurse cleared away the trash—except for the shake. Del grabbed it just in time.

"Here. You can sit on the edge of the bed. It'll be easier with the tray." It felt good, having Darcy here.

She looked from him to the bed with a question in her eyes, but gave in and sat down gingerly, making sure she wasn't taking up too much space. As if anyone as tiny as her could do such a thing. She took a bite of the soup, made a face, and then looked around on the tray.

"Where's the salt and pepper?" She whispered to him. "It needs help, big time." She rummaged around on the tray, finally finding salt, pepper, and another "low sodium" packet of mixed seasonings under the edge of the plate.

"I wondered how long it would take you to feel the need to spice it up a bit." Watching as she expertly stirred in the extras, he knew he was going to get sleepy pretty soon. "I had the weirdest dream while I was in the recovery room."

She stirred, tasted, and then broke up a few crackers into the mixture, tasting again. "Almost edible." She looked up at him with a pert grin. "Are you sure it wasn't a drug-induced hallucination?"

"Maybe." He sat there, considering. "It felt so real. And I was coming in and out more all the time when it happened."

"Tell me about it. I need something to get my mind off this amazing lunch." Then she spied the pudding cup and grabbed it. "But this? You can't mess up a pudding cup."

"Very true." He thought a minute. "I remember the nurse coming to me a few times, making me talk to her, getting me a warm blanket and such, and then there was this one nurse who looked so familiar."

Darcy peeled the top off the pudding, dipping her spoon into the chocolate dessert. "Male or female?"

"Female. Definitely."

He wanted to laugh when her eyebrows rose at his last remark.

"Did she have on a mask?"

He nodded. "Yeah, which makes it even harder to figure out."

"What did she look like?"

"Like a recovery-room nurse."

Darcy concentrated hard on that pudding like it was the most important thing in her life right now. "Ha. Ha." She shook her head. "I mean physical characteristics. Short? Tall? Hair color? Pretty?"

Considering, he tilted his head and felt his brows gather in a frown, trying to remember. And his head was beginning to hurt, too, which didn't help. "She seemed tall, but I can't be sure. Hair was dark, eyes brown."

Del watched as Darcy licked the last of the pudding off the plastic spoon and sighed. "You can't beat a pudding cup."

Did she have any idea what she did to him?

"What else did you notice?"

Should he tease her? Would she take it the wrong way? He couldn't help himself. It was only fair, after all. He waggled his eyebrows and said, "Rather shapely." Then he laughed at her rolling eyes.

"You are incorrigible."

"I've heard that before."

"I'm sure you have." She put the empty pudding cup on the tray with the rest of the trash, then rolled it to the foot of the bed to await pickup. "Do you have any idea why she seemed familiar?"

"No, and that's what bugs me. I know I've seen her before." He looked up at Darcy. "High school? College? Could be any number of places or times."

"You've been around. You aren't a young man, after all," Darcy teased.

He snorted. "I've led such a cosmopolitan life." As he said it, a thought came to his mind. He really hadn't explored the world like Darcy had, or even Lisa. He'd graduated from the regional university then immediately gone into business with

Dad. Most people would consider him "provincial," and the idea ticked him off. No wonder he was so predictable.

"I'm sure it'll come to you." She picked up her purse from the chair next to the bed and turned toward him. "I need to get out of here. I have to go by the insurance office while I'm here in town, and pick up a few things at the grocery, but I left my list at Mom's and I guess I'll need to call her and see what else we need before I go back. Can I drop anything off on my way back home?"

He laughed. There she went. When Darcy was nervous, her sentences were distinctly in the run-on category. "I can't think of anything. I hope I get to go home tomorrow."

"You probably will. As the old watch commercial used to say, 'You take a licking and keep on ticking.'"

"You need to watch something besides YouTube." Del laughed and shook his head.

"It's one of the only places I can find viewing that is rated G. The kids pick up on everything these days." She pulled out her phone to check the time. "I'd better get on the move. Let me know if you think of something before I leave town."

"I will. Hey." He reached for her hand again, and her eyes met his, finally. If he hadn't needed his hand earlier for eating, he'd have never let go. "Thanks again, Darcy."

"You're welcome, Del." There was a little mist in her eyes as she squeezed his hand back, then took her leave without saying another word.

He'd give anything to see what was going on in that beautiful head of hers.

19

Darcy's heart was pounding by the time she made her way down the hallway of the patient rooms, and she was glad there weren't people around. Only one nurse in sight, at the end of the hall, and she looked very busy, head down, eyes on the chart in her hand. Darcy thought about Del's "mystery nurse," and sent out her usual friendly smile. This woman fit his description perfectly, from what she could see. Amazing the things you think you see when you're coming out of anesthesia. She would have sworn Justin was there with her when they'd had to do an emergency C-section to deliver the twins.

But he wasn't. Her friend Ellie was there, Mom on the way. Their husbands were in the same unit, and to top it off, Ellie's husband Brent had grown up in Crittenden County, in the Tolu area. Darcy vaguely remembered him from high school, but he was a big-time athlete and she a lowly freshman, so their paths hadn't crossed.

Ellie was a jewel. A true California girl, she showed Darcy the ropes, and they were soon inseparable. Ellie was there for her when even her mother couldn't get there in time.

So a story about a stranger in the room who wasn't? Completely plausible, considering the drugs they'd been pumping through him by then.

Just as she was about to come even with the busy nurse, the woman looked up, startled.

Ducking her head, the nurse mumbled a quick "Excuse me," then rushed down the hall in the opposite direction.

"All righty then." Darcy had offered her a friendly smile, but it had not been returned. Frowning, she kept pace and made her way to the lobby and toward the front door. Odd. She had been gone from this town long enough that she had lost touch with a lot of people she went to high school with, and people had moved here since then and weren't part of her past. But this woman looked familiar. Probably someone she'd seen around town at the grocery store, bank, or any number of places. It was curious, though.

As she left the hospital, her phone vibrated in her hand. Turning it over, it read, "Ellie."

"Okay, El, this is weird, but I was thinking about you. Like, just now." Darcy shook her head as she pushed the button to unlock the aging minivan.

Ellie laughed on the other end of the line. "That's cool. I've been meaning to call you forever, but it's been so busy around here."

"I get it. How's Cole? And Brent? Have you heard where you're being stationed? How's the weather out there?" Her questions tumbled out. She'd missed her best friend. Ellie was one of those people destined to be your friend, and you never expected it. Ellie and her babies were on the top of her list of blessings for which to be thankful.

Ellie laughed. "I can't keep up if you spit out questions as if I were in the Inquisition."

"Sorry!"

Ellie took a deep breath. "I have news."

Uh-oh. Darcy's experiences with surprise news hadn't been so great. "Good news or bad news?"

"Ummmm...a little of both, depending on your perspective."

"Spill." Darcy had gotten in the car and started the air conditioner. There was a definite heatwave going on for May.

"Brent is being stationed outside of Cali."

"Whoa." She knew this would be hard on Ellie, a lifelong Californian. "Are you okay?"

"That's the bad news."

"Okay, I'm starting to relax. If that's the bad news, what is the good news? Let me guess. You're pregnant with twins." Darcy laughed.

"No, ma'am," she said emphatically. "Not pregnant again, yet." Ellie paused. "You'll freak. I know you will."

"Spit it out, girlfriend."

"I can't give you all the details or I'd have to kill you." She snickered.

"Ha. Ha. So he's going with Intelligence?"

"You could say that, but you didn't hear it from me. Anyway, he's being stationed in Paducah, Kentucky."

"You have got to be kidding me."

"Nope. He's been keeping an eye out for assignments within two hundred miles of his mom and dad, and this came up. He's been taking classes and getting certifications for cyber-security."

Darcy sat there, dumbfounded. "I can't believe it."

"I can't either."

Darcy detected a note of sadness. It would mean

uprooting Ellie, but she'd been lucky to stay in her home state of California as long as she had. Most people had to move multiple times. "You're going to miss California."

"I will." Ellie's long sigh could be heard across the phone.

"If I say I'm super excited, it's for me, okay? I know it's going to be hard on you."

"Yeah. But I love my in-laws, and I'll be closer to you, which put Paducah above places like, oh, I don't know, Virginia. Or Alaska." The laugh was back in Ellie's voice. "To be honest, Alaska wasn't really in the running. Nice place to visit, but... Anyway, we're coming down next week to find a house. You free?"

Was she free? "Unfortunately, yes."

"Why the 'unfortunately'?"

"It's a long story, and I'd rather tell you in person. Maybe I'll know more by next week. But yeah! I can't wait to see you."

"Me, neither. It's been too long. Brent is so excited, and a little nervous, too."

"I understand that. It's tough to re-integrate into rural life. At least you'll be moving to an actual town."

"He's not sure. We may move closer to you guys. After living in California where it takes an hour to get fifteen miles down the road, a fifty-mile trip in an hour will feel like he's on a racetrack."

"You got that right." Darcy sighed. "I've missed you."

"I know. I've missed you, too. You'll have to find me a group of girlfriends, or I'll bug you to death."

"Not a problem. You'll love my stepsister, and her best friend is great, too. I've connected with them a lot with Lisa's wedding coming up. They'll adore you." She paused. "Just remember who your very best friend is."

Ellie laughed. "I'll never forget." Darcy heard a crash in

the background. "I gotta go. Cole is teething, and when he's not chewing on everything—including the dog—he's pulling things off of tables and out of drawers. One of these days, he's going to bonk himself on the head."

"I hear you. Benji is going to be the death of me." Darcy smiled, feeling tears come to her eyes at the mere thought of Ellie being close enough to hug, to giggle with, and to just be with. "I love you, friend."

"I love you, too. I'll call or text when we finalize our plans."

"Good deal."

Ellie was coming. After a happy conversation, she barely gave another thought to the mysterious nurse.

That was a close one. Becca knew there was a chance of running into people she had known in her life before Chicago. It seemed like another world instead of another city. Running into Darcy Emerson was as close as she wanted to get to being caught.

She was distracted, and distraction put her in danger.

She peeked into Del's room and saw him nodding off. His arm was in a sling, but he looked fine. Becca didn't dare go in there. She had taken a chance talking to him in the recovery room without getting caught. What if he remembered? He would probably think he'd been hallucinating.

A few more steps down the hall, she came to the Intensive Care Unit. The one-story hospital was so small that the ICU and CCU were combined. Looking into the windows, she could only see three patients in there. The two nurses were busy working with the other patients, so she slid into the cubicle where Julia Rossi lay in the hospital bed, oxygen and monitors hooked up to her.

The nurse in her regretted she'd been a party to causing harm, but for her grandfather's part, he didn't think about it. She had to get tough. The smoke inhalation had been bad, but the dose of sodium pentothal she'd injected had slowed down her recovery time considerably.

Eyes flitting from the patient's chart to the other nurses within sight, she paused to check the monitors. Rossi would live. Not that her grandfather cared. To him, one less fed to worry about was a good thing. But Becca didn't want it on her conscience.

She made her way to the exit. Not many cars in the lot at this time. There was a beat-up minivan in the front lot, but nobody close to her car in the employee lot. She would have to pass the minivan to exit the parking lot. If anyone was in it, they probably wouldn't notice a random car exiting the campus of the hospital.

She got in her car and started up the air conditioner, ready to get out of there. Ready to get away from Crittenden County. Sure, she had some good memories, but most of them were painful. For many, school was a painful part of childhood. For her, school was great. It was home that had traumatized her.

Becca pulled closer to the minivan and had to stop for an ambulance to maneuver its way into the emergency bay. She was directly behind the van and looked into the side-view mirror on the driver's side. It was Darcy, and she was talking to someone on her phone. Becca had to get out of there. As if she'd heard her thinking, Darcy looked into the mirror, right into her eyes.

Darcy had been a good friend to her when they were kids. She remembered going to the apartment over the café.

It was so cool, she'd thought, to live upstairs, up above it all. It was part of the reason she'd wanted a loft apartment in Chicago. The soaring ceilings of an old re-purposed building gave her a sense of space she hadn't realized she needed.

She'd probably hesitated, because all at once, she saw Darcy's eyes go round with recognition.

Becca had been made.

———— ⌀ ————

"Lisa, call me back as soon as you get this. Everyone is fine, but...I need to talk to you."

Lisa had checked her messages when she came down to the kitchen for a drink. She put down the hammer she'd been using to hang pictures, then listened to Darcy's message a couple of times to get all of it. She must have been in a rush when she tried to call, and Lisa had been in the house out of cell-reach, as usual.

She found Darcy's name on the list of contacts and tapped it. Darcy answered on the first ring.

"Darcy, what's up?" Lisa was worried. Too much had happened in the last year for her to relax."

"Lisa. Did Del tell you about the weird dream he had?"

Odd. No hello, no "How are you." Right into the matter at hand. "Uh, yeah. Why? Did you see Del today?" Lisa wanted so badly for those two to get their act together and fall in love already.

"I took him a cheeseburger and shake. But that's beside the point."

Lisa paused, twisting her lips in a frown. "Is he still saying it was too real to be a dream?"

"Yes, and I know how hallucinogenic pain meds and

anesthesia can be, so I tried to talk him out of it, too. Did you get him to describe the mystery nurse?"

"No, we didn't get that far."

"I did. He was eating, then I ate his soup..."

"Oh really?"

"Anyway, he said she was tall, as much as he could see, dark hair, dark eyes, and familiar, but he couldn't figure out from where, or from when, for that matter. Hey, we had to talk about something, so after he told me about it, I had him describe her."

"So it was a woman?"

"Yes, and Lisa, I think I saw her."

"You didn't."

"I can't be sure. I saw a nurse in the hallway as I was leaving, and she avoided looking at me. You know how I smile at people I don't know and people with me ask me if I know them and I tell them no, I just do that?"

Lisa chuckled. Darcy was the queen of hurried, run-on sentences. "And?"

"And then, I was sitting in the van because my friend Ellie from California called—she and Brent are moving back! I can't wait! Anyway, an ambulance came in and the nurse was waiting to pull out, and I saw her in her car, while I was sitting in my van. She looked at my mirror, and our eyes met, and Lisa, you will never believe it."

Surely Del had imagined this person. Surely. "Is it someone we should know?"

"I can't be one hundred percent sure, but it looked like a friend of mine from when we were kids."

"Who?"

"Do you remember Rebecca Durbin?"

Lisa's heart pounded with surprise. "Of course I do. She and Del dated while they were at Murray. Then she just disappeared. We found out her dad killed her mom, and we didn't see or hear from her again."

"I didn't know they'd dated."

Darcy's voice went quiet. Hmmm. Lisa was glad Darcy wasn't standing in front of her, or she'd have to hide the delight on her face. She cleared her throat. "Yeah. It was pretty serious. When she left, it did a number on Del. He hasn't dated much since."

"Wow."

There was a moment of silence on the line.

"Do you really think it was her?" Lisa tried to wrap her head around all this. "And if it was, why didn't she say anything in the hallway?"

"That's the strange thing. Rebecca and I were pretty close in middle and high school. She came over to the apartment quite a bit, but I never went to her house."

"In light of what happened, that's understandable. I can't imagine." Lisa shook her head.

"Are you at the house?"

Lisa looked around at her beautiful kitchen, wedding favor supplies dumped on the enormous island. "I am. Trying to get a few things hung on the walls so it'll look homier when we move in. I had the choice of that or putting together wedding favors. I opted for hanging pictures." She paused, thinking. "Did you go back in and tell Del."

"No way. I had a fleeting thought of following her, but my vehicle isn't exactly unobtrusive."

Lisa laughed, thinking about Darcy's burgundy well-loved van. "No hiding in that thing."

"I lovingly call it the Raspberry Bomb." Darcy paused. "Lisa, be careful out there by yourself."

"I will. The entrance to the tunnel under the house is triple-locked, and I have no desire to go down there anyway. I had my fill of it when we found the body." She closed her eyes and shivered. "If I think about it, I can almost smell the foul odor I was afraid we'd be stuck with."

"Good. Keep your eyes open."

A thought occurred to her. "What was Rebecca driving? I can watch out for it."

"A black, very new, very shiny, very expensive-looking sedan." Darcy chuckled. "Don't ask me what model or make, because I was still trying to pick my jaw up from the floorboard when she was gone and it occurred to me I should be thinking of that."

"Got it. I'll tell Nick to keep an eye out, too."

"Good. And Lisa?"

"Yeah?"

"Let's keep this from Del until he's better. I don't know why, but I'm a little freaked out by this."

They ended the call and Lisa stood there thinking. Satisfaction bloomed on her face. Darcy was a little freaked out. About Del's safety. Stood to reason. He'd been shot, after all. And they didn't know by whom.

But Rebecca Durbin? Where did she fit into all this?

———*∽*———

"This may sound weird, but could I just say getting shot is easier than breaking a leg?"

Nick looked across the cab of the pickup truck and saw Del wince as he struggled with the seat belt. His future brother-in-law and best friend had been released from the hospital, and Nick was in town anyway. Therefore, Nick was tagged for pick-up duty.

Nick laughed. "I think getting shot might have more repercussions, possibilities of actually killing you."

"Yeah, but at least I can walk while I recover. The cast drove me nuts. Not driving, going to PT, hurting most of the time. This I can handle."

"Can we take the year off from injuries?" Nick teased. "You're cutting into RenoVation's profit margin."

"I'll see what I can do." Nick heard Del pull in a deep breath. "Nick, I need to ask you something. I know you think I'm crazy, but I haven't been able to stop thinking about the nurse I saw in the recovery room. She stood over me and said, distinctly, 'I'm sorry, Del.'"

"You were pretty traumatized."

Lisa had told Nick about Darcy's sighting. Why would Becca Durbin be here? And if it was her, why wasn't she making herself known? This was where she came from. It was home her entire childhood.

"I know. But it's been bugging me. I haven't had much to do besides think about it, and the more I think about it, the clearer it gets." Del frowned and shook his head. "This is where it gets crazy."

They were at the stoplight, so Nick looked across at Del. "What?"

"Do you remember Rebecca Durbin?"

Nick snorted. "Of course I do. I remember talking you out of asking her to run off and marry you."

Del shrugged sheepishly. "Yeah. Impetuous youth."

Del sobered, apparently needing to talk, but not wanting to relive the last time he'd seen Becca. "After the accident, she was gone the next day."

"That was rough."

"No kidding. Here's the weird thing. The mystery nurse reminded me of Becca."

"Man, you were dreaming. Had to be." Was he? Nick knew better. Maybe it was someone who resembled her, a cousin, maybe? If the person Darcy saw was Becca, where had she been all this time?

"Probably." Del looked straight ahead. "She had brown eyes, though."

"What color were Becca's?"

"Blue. Some things you don't forget."

———— ⌒ ————

"Are you crazy?"

The peaceful setting of her out-of-the-way childhood home was now anything but peaceful. But had it ever been?

That first day, she'd run her fingers across the dusty spines of the "Baby-Sitters Club" books she'd adored and read over and over, and the academic team trophy she'd been so proud of. She was finally able to mourn the loss of what she considered her "real" life.

Becca closed her eyes as Clyde berated her—quietly, but berated, nonetheless. Maybe she'd gone a little further than she'd told him she would. Maybe she had to see for herself that Del was okay. Maybe she deserved this. After all, it was Clyde's job to keep her safe, and she hadn't exactly been helping him along.

"I know." She looked up at him, wishing away the tears trying to form. "I had to make sure he was okay."

"And what about the agent?"

"Secondary, but I checked on her, too. She was improving. I was worried I'd given her too large a dose. Her numbers looked good. I overheard a nurse say she would be moved to a room tomorrow."

"That's a relief." Clyde raked his hand over his face and leaned on the porch rail, facing her as she sat on the swing her mother had loved. It was rickety, like their lives.

When they'd realized their activities were going to take longer than they thought, they'd made the out-of-the-way house their base of operation. Finding it would take someone familiar with the area. It was out of sight and the well-hidden drive was off a winding secondary road in the middle of Amish country. The grass and volunteer trees gave it the atmosphere of abandonment.

Abandoned. Like her. Nothing had changed. The furniture, Mom and Dad's clothing. Her stuff from her childhood and college. Her grandfather had taken care of the taxes every year, so it sat there, a time capsule of her life before the death of her mother.

When she'd walked into it the first day, she'd cried. She wanted to run screaming into the woods and truly disappear. The people she'd grown up with knew nothing about what had become of her. Had anyone noticed that she'd simply disappeared? Had anyone cared?

Had Del cared?

"Clyde, we need to get out of here." She stared straight ahead.

"You saw somebody you know?" He massaged her shoulders, and it felt good. She knew she was tied up in knots, and he'd been with her long enough to know the signs.

"I saw my best friend, Darcy." She looked up at him, tears poised on her lashes. "She runs the café."

"Oh." Understanding and then suspicion dawned on his face. "Did you know that when you came down here?"

She shook her head. "When I left, her mom was running it. She was a widow, so it didn't register. Then when they said it was a widow with two young kids, I never thought of Darcy until I saw her today. It never really hit me that someone from my past could have been hurt." She dipped her head, tears hovering. "They could have been killed."

He took a deep breath and sat next to her on the swing, joining her in looking out toward the random outbuildings and further into the woods. He finally turned toward her. "Did she see you?"

Becca nodded, tears beginning to spill as she continued staring into nothingness.

"Did she recognize you?" His eyes bored into hers when she looked back at him.

"I'm not sure. She may have." She shook her head violently and her voice dropped to a whisper. "Clyde, I don't think I can do this."

"Do what?" He took her hand. "Look at me, Becca."

He squeezed it until it almost hurt, and she looked up at him, a little afraid.

His eyes never left her. Didn't even seem to blink. "All you need to do is make sure there's nothing here that can tie Vic's organization to this place. All this other stuff was put in motion to speed things along."

"And I could have killed a man I once thought I was going to marry." Anger sent her tears away. She stared into his eyes, waiting for a reaction, getting no more than a flinch of his eyes. "I could have killed my best friend and her children, Clyde. *Her children.*" She emphasized the last sentence. The horror of what her grandfather did as a matter of course was coming home to roost in a big way. Now it was touching her. It wasn't another exciting, impersonal "job."

It was her life.

20

"One thing's for sure. I've got plenty of time to help you get ready for the wedding." Darcy frowned at the crooked bow on the tiny scrap of tulle and ribbon, which would only be untied and tossed away after the rice was thrown. She'd always wondered why weddings were such a major energy drain. Now she knew. It was the little things. Things you could buy ready-made but convinced yourself it would be "fun" to create on your own.

Lisa laughed. "Believe me. If it weren't too late to get them here, I'd be ordering these online and paying any amount of shipping they asked." She looked up from the task. "' Course, if I did that, we wouldn't be having this time together."

It was true. Darcy and Lisa had been friends before Darcy's mom married Lisa's dad, but the last few months had solidified both the friend and sister aspects of their relationship.

Darcy surveyed Lisa's well-appointed kitchen. "This kitchen is to die for."

Lisa grimaced. "Oooh, poor choice of words." Then she laughed.

Darcy joined in, shaking her head. "I forgot about the dead guy in the basement." She surveyed the marble-look quartz countertops, the continent-sized island where they sat, gleaming white cabinets and sparkling hardware, and the latest kitchen equipment you could buy. "This is a house for keeps, isn't it?"

Lisa sighed as she stopped what she was doing and nodded. "It is. I want to raise all my kids here."

"All?" Darcy blinked.

"Yep. ALL. As in multiple. I don't care how many sets of twins we have."

"Sis, you know not of what you speak." Darcy envied Lisa. Always had. Lisa was a couple of years older than her, so they hadn't run in the same circles in high school. She didn't know what happened in Texas, or the events surrounding Lisa's mother's death from cancer, but she could tell that for all the outward appearances of "a charmed life," she had known pain.

Settling back into creating the perfect bow with six inches of tiny ribbon, Darcy had to ask. "How did you do it?"

"Do what?" Lisa glanced up at her.

"Handle the death of your mother and still stay so positive all the time."

"I'm not positive ALL the time. Ask Del, Dad, or Nick. Nick wasn't around me in the aftermath, but I've told him some of it." She stopped and stared off, chin in hand, then seemed to come to a decision. "It wasn't just Mom's death. I was almost engaged to a guy I met working in Texas. I thought he was perfect—until he put his foot down and didn't want me to come home when Mom was dying."

"Red flag, much?" Darcy had never heard this. Maybe the princess had been through more than she thought.

"Serious red flag." She shook her head and turned toward Darcy. "Would you believe Nick's wife was killed about two weeks before Mom died?"

Her eyes widened in shock. "I didn't. How do you explain a coincidence like that?"

Lisa smiled. "You don't. You trust God and do the next right thing."

Darcy twisted her lips. She didn't want to appear callous. She'd been down that road and what had it gotten her? A dead father, a dead husband, fatherless children, a café with smoke damage.

And loneliness. So much loneliness.

"I'm glad you found comfort in your religion." Darcy picked up the tiny piece of fabric and tried to concentrate on the job in front of her. That was what she did when faced with something she didn't want to deal with. Find a job to do. Maybe it was laundry, cooking, picking up after the kids—which was a constant—or going over the café's books.

"Darcy, it's not religion. Surely you know that."

Darcy took a deep breath and stilled. "I'm not like you, Lisa. I know you were hurt, but for me, the hits just keep coming. Dad, Justin, the café. He didn't even let me finish school." She huffed a bit, knowing she sounded spoiled. "I decided God doesn't care so much about certain people, and I'm in that category. If He loves me, why do these things keep happening to me?" Darn it, she felt tears coming to the surface, and that was the LAST thing she wanted.

Lisa said nothing for a time. *Good. Maybe she'll drop it.*

"I think if you look back, God's been with you the whole time." Lisa held her hands up when Darcy tried to argue. "I know, you don't believe me, and the last thing I want is for you to be angry with me." She looked Darcy straight in the eye. "How do you feel about dares?"

Oh boy. Now she's got me. "I've rarely met a dare I wouldn't take." Darcy lifted her chin in defiance, then softened it with a faint smile. "What do you have in mind?"

"For the next week, I want you to write down every blessing you can think of in one column, and in another column, every bad thing that's happened to you. A week from today is my bachelorette party—me, you, Mel, and my cousins Cassie and Mandy—and I want to see your list, then."

"Write down good things that have happened? What time frame?"

"Good and bad. As far back as you can remember."

Darcy considered. She didn't have to take the dare. But she had something to prove. Lisa thought she would prove her wrong, but she'd surprise her.

It was amazing the things you counted on your right arm for. Balance notwithstanding, the act of putting on clothes was made twice as difficult. Del wanted to at least get to the office today. He'd been lounging around too long, and it was starting to get old. He could only watch so much television before his eyes threatened to stay crossed indefinitely.

He got into his truck and took a deep breath. *Step one: leave for work.* Or was that about step four? He'd lost track. Turning to look behind himself, he saw Darcy's van go by. Looked like she was in a hurry. She was heading toward the café. Maybe he'd just follow her and see what was up. Couldn't hurt.

Taking the scenic route—which meant one extra turn—he ended up at the stop sign near the café about the time Darcy was getting out of the van. Frank Stafford was standing next to the van, holding the door for her. Had Del missed something? There was Darcy, smiling up at the FBI agent like nothing was going on—about the case, anyway. To stop, or to drive on? He sat for a minute, thinking, only rousing when a horn honked behind him, bringing him out of his stupor.

———⁂———

Darcy knew there would be people there guarding the café, but she needed to stop in and pick up a few things from the apartment. She'd taken Lisa's dare, and was starting to compile a list of good things in her life, and there was a journal in her nightstand she wanted to use. This list might come in handy someday. She didn't want her children to think she was ungrateful for things that happened in her life—especially since Benji and Ali were tied for number one.

She had seen Del getting into his truck as she passed his house. Should she honk? No. Not this time. She felt funny about Del these days. Unsettled.

The black SUV and two rental cars in front of the café told her Agent Stafford—scratch that, Frank—was there, along with a few other forensic specialists. She was also unsure about her feelings toward Frank, who'd made no secret of his interest in her.

She pulled into a spot out of the way and saw Frank make a beeline for her car, smiling. Oh, boy.

Gentleman that he was, he opened the door for her as soon as she stopped.

"Thank you."

"You are most welcome, Darcy. To what do we owe the

pleasure this morning?" He was smiling broadly, hope written all over his features.

"I needed to pick up a few things from the apartment if that's okay?" She wasn't above a pleading tone in her question.

Frank looked at the men closer to the building, seeming to consider. "I think it'll be fine if I go up with you."

"No problem." She opened her lips slightly. Should she ask? "Any progress on the case?"

"I wish I could say yes. It's slow going." He lowered his voice. "We did find fingerprints, putting an interesting spin on it."

"How so?"

"Can't say, yet. Soon, hopefully. Forensics is doing comparisons to the evidence from Nick Woodward's basement and tunnels." He paused. "Out of curiosity, do you know anything about Nick's family?"

Unexpected. "No." Her head shaking, she frowned. "He didn't grow up here." She looked into his eyes. "I think he grew up in Elizabethtown. His dad grew up here, and his grandparents lived here."

"That's what I heard." He shifted his eyes away from hers, slightly. "Just wondered. It never hurts to learn about background stories."

Odd. "I suppose so." She raised her eyebrows expectantly. "Shall we?"

"Oh, yes, of course. Sorry. I'm sure you have more to do than stand around here talking to me all day."

"Not much. I just dropped the kids off at their preschool, and I'm meeting Lisa Reno to help with wedding stuff." She laughed. "I seem to be her right hand these days, and I'm glad. I would be going stir-crazy without the café."

"I can only imagine. We'll get you back in here soon."

"Promise?"

"As close as I can get to one."

"Gotcha."

They climbed the steps to the apartment and made their way in. The smoky smell curled her nostrils. Darcy was sure it would until a restoration service took care of it.

"Could we open a window so we can breathe in here?" She looked back at him before touching the windowsill. Hadn't she mentioned this to him before?

"I don't see why not." He lifted a few sashes, and a breeze came through, making it bearable.

Darcy went into the kids' room and pulled out a few toys they'd missed, and some books, before searching through her things for the journal. There it was, nearly at the bottom of the drawer. Right on top of her Bible. She sighed, pulling it out and looking at the inscription. "To Darcy Emerson upon her Baptism, June 8, 2002. Love, Mom and Dad." Tears came, unbidden, and she closed the cover. Why did it hurt? Dad had been so proud of her. She remembered the tears in his eyes when she'd made a profession of faith. She'd believed once.

She stuffed the Bible and journal into a bag and grabbed a couple of pairs of shorts and other clothes. "I think that's all I need for now." Finger to her chin, she paused. "Let me check the bathroom." She looked and picked up the kids' favorite bubble bath and tub toys. No reason for them to be without their creature comforts.

"Okay. I'm ready."

Frank chuckled. "Are you sure?"

She sent him a shaky smile, glad she'd had a chance to wipe the tears away. This wasn't the time to get into a personal conversation. She wasn't sure when would be a good time—but this wasn't it.

They made their way back downstairs and to the street.

Pausing by her van, she turned toward him. "You'll let me know as soon as I can get back to work?"

"I will." He narrowed his eyes. "Are you okay? Financially, I mean?"

That was sweet. And personal. "We are. Thank you for your concern." She tensed up, hoping that would be as personal as it got. She was thankful for the survivor's benefit she had received from the military.

"Glad to hear it." His eyes shifted as he cleared his throat. "Any more thoughts about going out with me?"

And there it was.

Taking in a deep breath, she observed him quietly. "Not really."

He seemed to understand it wasn't a good time and backed away. "That's okay. Just don't forget I asked."

"I won't." Darcy stowed the bag in the back seat and got into the van. "Thank you."

He raised a hand, saying nothing.

As she drove off, she could feel him watching her, unsure how she felt.

Unsure how she felt about him. Or Del.

Her blood pressure went up thinking about Del. She'd had a crush on him since she was fourteen, then she went off to college and fallen in love with Justin, relegating Del to a pleasant childhood memory. When she came back, there he was, and she was attracted to him, which made her angry at herself, and, to a certain extent, Del. She had softened toward Del since her mom had married his dad. It was different now, spending time with him as part of the family. She knew she could count on him for anything. Anything. But she felt there were strings attached.

Strings that told her if she wanted to be with him, she

would have to change. She'd have to give up her pride and walk by his side, living according to God's will, whatever that meant. She didn't think she could do it.

So if Del didn't make the cut, what about Frank Stafford?

Would this man make a good dad for Benji and Ali? The FBI was every bit as dangerous, in some ways, as being an Army Ranger. Maybe not every day, but it was a high-pressure job that put him in proximity with criminals on a regular basis. And those criminals usually had guns or knew people who did. Could she risk settling in with someone like him only to lose him?

Why didn't she feel more hurt at the thought of losing Frank?

She knew why. She was being practical. If you don't let yourself get too close, you won't be as devastated when you lose them.

And losing Del would be more than she could fathom.

———⟨∕∕⟩———

Maybe more meds were still in him than he thought. He drove on, praying as he drove toward his dad's house and the RenoVations office. Maybe Dad would be there.

God? What's next? Del looked heavenward, seeing only the ceiling of his truck with human eyes, but feeling a presence that comforted. That challenged.

Part of him wanted Darcy in his life to the exclusion of anyone else. But he didn't want any person to get in the way of his relationship with God. He'd experienced that, and he'd gotten a wake-up call this week that reminded him.

Becca.

He'd been transfixed by her in college. Why hadn't he noticed her when they were in high school? Sure, she was a few years younger than him, but they had gone to the same church, for crying out loud. When they got to college, she was different. More relaxed. Like she was experiencing freedom for the first time.

It had been intense.

They'd fought and made up. They'd laughed and loved. They hadn't gone as far as they could have, but they'd come close a few times.

By his senior year of college, he was willing to throw caution to the wind and marry the girl so he could say she was his. They didn't talk about spiritual things beyond their hopes, dreams, and fears. Mostly they just wanted to be together. All the time. He would have argued with God Himself to have her.

Del took in a deep breath and shook his head. God had been watching over them that last night he was with her. When he called to check on her the next morning to see if she was okay, she was gone, her roommate didn't know where she was, and he never heard from her again.

It was the worst time of his young life.

"When were you going to tell me there were documents hidden inside the café?" Becca's voice rose as she talked to Gabe, her grandfather's right-hand man.

"When it was time to tell you." He looked at her in disgust, as if she were a mere operative in this grand-scale business of theirs. "You didn't need to know, and now you do."

"I should have been given more details."

The cigar he held between his teeth made her feel sick. He was old-school. About the age her father was, she supposed. She hadn't seen her dad in eight years and hadn't wanted to. Why would she? He'd never tried to contact her. Her grandfather was still in contact with him—a fact that strained the confused relationship she had with her grandfather.

Becca faced him. "There have been...developments."

"That's what I hear." Gabe drew in the nicotine from the cigar.

She tilted her head and frowned. "From whom?"

Gabe took a long draw on his cigar, taking her in. It disgusted her, a little. He'd always had a look on his face as if he were about to pounce. "We have our sources."

"Clyde?" Surely not. Clyde was the only one she could talk to.

"Maybe." He blew smoke out, fortunately turning his head so it didn't go directly into her face. "We have other informants around."

She froze. It could be anyone. She racked her brain. Did anyone come to mind? Someone local? The FBI agents...one was from Kentucky, but the other one was from Chicago. Would he have allowed himself to be knocked out, potentially killed, if he were on the inside?

"You'll know when you need to know."

She wanted to scream. Truth be told, she'd wanted to ever since the day strangers appeared at her apartment on campus to take her to Chicago. She hadn't then because she'd simply been numb upon learning of her mother's death. Now she wouldn't because she was in too deep, and maybe her grandfather wanted it that way so he'd have something to hold over her. She knew how it worked.

Becca didn't trust Gabe, but she didn't think her grandfather would send her down here if there was any danger to her. Would he? Would Clyde keep information from her? *He would if those were his orders.*

The idea that she had no real ally was coming home to her. Before now, she hadn't considered it. Something about encountering, even from a distance, people who were important to her former life had touched her soul in a way she hadn't expected.

This was a job, plain and simple. Grandfather wanted to be done with the Kentucky branch of the operation, which had been dormant after Dad went to prison, until recently. And when the tunnels were discovered, it was unsafe to conduct business there.

Looking around the living room of the house she'd grown up in, memories crowded around her more and more. When she let them, anyway. Memories of a drunken, abusive father, and memories of better times when Dad was sober, celebrating Christmases and birthdays, tossing her in the air when he came home from work, laughing at some silly story she'd told him about her day at school. She thought about her mom, simply going about her day, humming a tune, smiling when she came into the room, sitting in her rocker by the window with her Bible. She wondered where it was. Wondered if, maybe, there was a message of some kind for her. Something that would help her make sense of what was happening around her.

There was nothing simple about this job or her life.

"Hey."

She jerked at Gabe's interruption to her thoughts. She glanced at the clock and was surprised to see that her mental meanderings had happened in about a minute's time. The brain was a complex organ.

"What's next?" She looked him in the eye.

He snorted. "Since Gerry couldn't seem to finish the job,

I'm counting on you to figure out a way to get those documents."

"And how do you propose I do that?" She narrowed her eyes at him.

"By finding the safe."

"Today is the first I've heard of a safe."

"Vic didn't want you to know too much in case you got caught or accidentally met up with someone here who knew you."

"I get that, but why now? Why didn't one of the guys tell me?"

"Wasn't in their instructions."

"And Clyde?" She stilled the roiling emotions running through her. If she couldn't count on Clyde, she may as well disappear now. The more she thought about it, the better it sounded.

21

Darcy was exhausted, and she needed to stop at the apartment for some more clothes. They'd have to be washed or dry-cleaned, she figured, to get the smoky smell out of them.

Oh well.

She yawned and turned her van toward the café instead of toward her mom's house. Her brain was in a fog. She wasn't fuzzy from drinking, but all the sugar they'd consumed had put the ladies in a sugar coma before the night was out. According to Melanie York, you couldn't have a bachelorette party without indulging in as much chocolate as you could eat. At twenty-seven, Darcy knew she was already too old for a slumber party.

Pulling into her usual spot around the corner of the café, she saw the usual traffic on a Saturday morning. The post office was busy, but since she was closed, it was the only thing going on. Earlier, when her hair hadn't wanted to cooperate, she'd pulled it into a messy bun. Now she couldn't resist checking herself in the mirror before getting out of the car.

She shook her head. Who was she primping for? *Stop it, Darcy. Lack of sleep is catching up with you.*

She slapped the visor back up, then grabbed her phone and keys. She got out of the van and stuffed the items into her pocket. She left her purse on the floorboard of the car, so she made sure to lock the doors.

Is it okay to just walk in?

The crime scene tape was still across the door. She looked around, part of her hoping to see an official of some sort in view. No such luck. She put her key in the lock and opened it carefully, then ducked under the plastic barrier. The smoky smell still assaulted her, bringing her to wonder when she could call the cleaning company to get rid of the smoke damage. She supposed she should be happy it wasn't fire damage. One of those "blessings" Lisa had talked about?

Everything was in order in the café kitchen and dining room. It was so quiet, it was almost spooky. Should she let someone know where she was? Mom would be wondering why she wasn't home yet.

Stop it, Darcy. You're a grown woman.

Still, it wouldn't hurt, would it? She opened up her phone and sent Mom a quick text. "Stopping at the apartment for clothes. Be home in ten." She grinned when she saw her answer, the 'thumbs up' emoji."

The building creaked and groaned as usual. It was well over a hundred years old and had once been a Masonic lodge before the Clementville chapter merged with the one in Marion. It had been a restaurant since the 1950s, and her mom had run it for over fifteen years before Darcy took it on under her supervision.

She heard a loud thump upstairs. It startled her, but she talked herself down. If she hadn't heard all those sounds before, she'd have thought there was someone in the building.

But it was normal. It wasn't like she'd never been here alone before. Huffing, she decided to head upstairs. She pulled out her keys and sorted through them to get to the one for the apartment. *I guess I'll have to get used to locking everything up tight, from now on.*

She shook her head in irritation, then opened the door at the bottom of the staircase and started up. The door at the top of the stairs, into the apartment, was open slightly. Odd. She'd been prepared to unlock that one, as well. Maybe since the bottom door was locked, the forensics team hadn't seen the need to lock this one.

The door creaked loudly as she pushed it open, being careful not to touch it any more than necessary. She had a fleeting thought that the door needed a squirt of WD-40 on the hinges.

Something was off. Nothing seemed out of place except for a broken glass in the sink. It hadn't been there the last time she'd come in with Frank. She frowned a little. Maybe one of the analysts had helped themselves to a drink of water. She might be imagining things, and she wasn't sure what it was.

She pulled out her phone and took a picture of the glass and for some reason sent it to Del. Why? He'd get a kick out of it, that's all. "What have these guys been DOING up here? LOL"

She chuckled to herself. Out of habit, she laid her phone on the cabinet next to the door, her usual out-of-the-way spot with the charger.

Then she stopped short.

Someone is here.

Her heart started pounding, her senses picking up on something that she couldn't quite put her finger on. A smell?

A difference in the air pressure of the room? She needed to get out of there. Quickly.

Turning back to the door, she felt her scream stifled as a hand clamped over her mouth. A faintly sickening smell came to her and she felt her legs give way and her eyes close.

And then, nothing.

———⌒———

Del heard his phone ding with a text as he was doing his best to shave with his left hand. He'd about decided to give up.

"What have these guys been DOING up here? LOL" Del frowned at the picture. Why was Darcy sending him a text on a Saturday morning? He knew this was the big "bachelorette weekend" and they'd had a slumber party.

He chuckled and answered her. "Having a party?"

Then, nothing. Odd. Darcy was seldom without her phone nearby, and he'd received the message in the last few minutes. She normally had to have the last word.

He tried again. "Darcy?"

Again, nothing. He pulled up her number and called. Straight to voice mail. He made another call. Same thing.

As soon as he ended the last unsuccessful call, his phone rang.

"Del?"

"Hi, Roxy. Yeah, it's me. Everything okay?"

Roxy paused. "Darcy sent me a text a half-hour ago that she was stopping at the apartment for some things, and that she'd be home in ten minutes. Have you seen her?"

It took less than five minutes to travel from the café to Dad's house. He raked his hand across his face. Something wasn't right. "She sent me a text about twenty minutes ago with a picture from the apartment. Roxy, I'll run over there and see if she's there. I'm sure she just ran into someone and got into a conversation."

Roxy's laugh was shaky. "I'm probably being silly. There's just been so much going on."

"I know. I'll let you know as soon as I find anything out."

They ended the conversation and Del wiped the shaving cream off his face. He wasn't going to waste any time. As he got in his truck, he tried to call her cell.

No answer.

Nothing.

He tried calling her again. Voice mail. Another time? Same result.

Maybe Darcy had told Lisa what she was doing. He knew the ladies had spent the night at the Tucker House, a grand old house-turned-B&B on Main Street in Marion, and Clementville was about ten miles away, fifteen or twenty minutes from there, barring farm implements or Amish buggies.

Forget texting, it took too long with one arm in a sling. He called her instead.

As soon as she answered, he dove in. "Lisa, did Darcy say anything to you about making a stop this morning before heading home?"

"And good morning to you, too." She sounded tired. "No, she left about forty-five minutes ago, heading to Dad's house, and hopefully, a nap. We're too old for this slumber-party lifestyle."

"Yeah. Roxy got a text from her saying she was stopping at the apartment and would be home in ten minutes. I got one from her right after that, and it's been over thirty minutes with no sign of her. Now she's not answering and her phone is going straight to voice mail."

"That's odd."

He thought so, too.

"Hey, let me know what you find out." Lisa sounded worried. He knew the feeling.

"I will. Talk later."

"Bye."

He grabbed his keys and wallet and headed to the truck. Unsure where he was going, he determined to find her. A fleeting thought led him to call Clay. Thank the Lord for hands-free linkup in the truck.

"Clay? Del." He turned to back out of his driveway.

"What's going on, Del?"

"I can't find Darcy."

"Isn't it a little early in the day to lose her?" He sounded amused.

That won't last long.

"She sent Roxy a text this morning, then she sent me one from her apartment. Now she's not answering. She's not at Dad's, and she's not with Lisa and the other ladies. I'm pulling up to the café now." He turned toward the café and stopped in front of it. Her van was around the corner, where she usually parked. For a moment, he was relieved. Maybe she'd turned her ringer off?

"Her van is at the café."

"Mystery solved."

"Maybe. I'll go check."

"Call me if you need me."

"Ten-four." Del turned off the truck and put the phone in the pocket of his jeans. He had to wait for a car to pass, then he sprinted across the road, wincing every time his feet hit the pavement. This wasn't doing his shoulder any good.

He looked in the locked van and saw her purse on the floorboard, passenger side. Odd, but not unheard of. When he got to the alleyway door, he saw the crime scene tape and paused. The door was locked. He pulled his keys back out of his pocket and selected the one for that door. He opened it and called out, "Darcy?" Nothing.

He walked into the café kitchen to find it empty, then into the dining room. She had to be in the apartment. He checked the door at the foot of the stairs, found it unlocked, and then made his way up the creaky staircase.

The door stood open. He pushed it further and called out, "Darcy?"

Still nothing. He walked through the rooms, thinking maybe she was checking the progress of the work they were doing. She wasn't there. When he got back to the apartment kitchen, which was the first room you came to upon entering, he looked around more closely. Neat as a pin, per Darcy, except for the broken glass in the sink and a piece of cloth on the floor.

Who carries handkerchiefs anymore?

He shrugged it off, and let his eyes rove across the counters, wondering how she felt about the fingerprinting dust everywhere. His eyes finally landed on a small, obscure cabinet right by the door. It was where she dumped keys, purse, mail, and anything else in her hands when she came in the door. He'd seen her do it. And this time something caught his eye that shouldn't be there.

Darcy's phone.

22

Darcy felt the pounding in her head before she got up the nerve to open her eyes. Had she fallen? Had there been an accident? Something had happened, and she couldn't put her finger on the last thing she remembered.

Del. Glass in the sink. She'd sent him a text. Why?

Questions rolled round and round in her head. Where was her phone? She tried to reach for it but couldn't move her arms. They were trapped, somehow, behind her. She was sitting on the ground. It was cold, and damp, which made her feel colder. That was when she opened her eyes and confusion set in. She was being restrained, somehow, and could see nothing. Darkness. Had she lost her sight? Panic threatened to rise up and overtake her.

Calm down, Darce. Get it under control.

She took slow, deep breaths, trying to get her bearings. Opening her eyes again, she began to see outlines of objects. It was damp and musty. She wasn't blind; she was, quite literally, in the dark.

Darcy must have passed out for a few moments because

208

suddenly duct tape was ripped from her mouth and there was a light in her face so bright she had to shut her eyes. A flashlight came toward her, blocking out anything and anyone behind it. She prided herself on being tough, on being able to take care of herself, but she'd never felt so helpless in her life. As hard as it had been to lose Justin, she hadn't been in danger herself.

This was different.

"Where is the safe?" The rough, gravel voice was unfamiliar.

"What safe?" Safe? She'd never seen a safe. Her voice was weak, and sounded strange, even to herself.

"There's a safe somewhere in your building, and I need to find it. I need you to tell me where it is."

"I don't know." When he didn't respond, fear began to rise. "I really don't. I've never seen a safe in the building, and I've lived there since I was twelve years old."

"We may have to tear the place up to find it." Another voice joined the original. "What do we do with her?"

"Hey." Another voice—female, this time—whispering loudly. "You can't hurt her."

Darcy saw the tip of a cigar glow as the smoker inhaled, then pulled it out to exhale, then turn toward the female voice. "Sweetheart, I'm tired of you thinking you can tell me what to do. If we have to hurt her, we will. If we have to tear the place to shreds, we will. We shoulda burned the place down and looked for the safe later. It would survive the fire. Her? Not so much. Here's the thing. I'm not leaving without the contents of that safe." He paused. "If I have to hurt *you*, I will."

Whoever this woman was, it seemed she was in as much danger as Darcy.

———————— ⟳ ————————

"Del!"

Del heard his name called as he was entering the tunnel. Clay. He'd hoped to get further in his search before he arrived. "Down here."

"Anything?"

Del looked up the stairs from the basement, Clay standing in the landing between the three doors. He shook his head, not trusting his voice, following the sheriff up the stairs to the apartment.

"Her phone is in the apartment?"

"Yes. Her purse is in the van, and the phone is upstairs. That's not like her. She keeps that phone on her when she's away from her kids." He swallowed thickly. "I checked the downstairs and the basement. Nothing."

Clay shook his head and pushed the button on his radio. "I need a sheriff's deputy at the café, stat." He turned back to Del. "We'll find her, Del."

Del's inner dialog with himself went on and on, berating himself for not making sure she was safe every minute. But how could he? He had no right to tell her what to do. She would have to give him the right, and she hadn't. He was angry. At himself and Darcy too. She'd walked right into danger.

"Let's go upstairs." Clay led the way, swinging his head back to ask another question. "Did you see anything out of place—besides the phone, that is?"

"There was a broken glass and a handkerchief on the floor."

They'd gotten to the top of the stairs and Clay turned to stare at him. "A what?"

"Yeah, that's what I thought, too."

Clay's face betrayed him. He was worried. "Did you touch anything?"

Del nodded. "I touched the outside door and the doorknob on the downstairs door to the apartment. The upper door was standing open. I also touched the kitchen and basement doors."

Clay looked around, as Del had done, earlier. He placed Darcy's phone in a plastic evidence bag. When he picked up the handkerchief with a pen and lifted it to his nose, he reared back and coughed a little. "Whoa."

"What is it?"

The grim look on Clay's face was not encouraging. "Ether." He looked up at Del and shook his head. "Time to call in the pros."

Was Gabe threatening her?

Becca clamped her mouth shut and went to the tunnel opening on the Ohio River, needing some fresh air. She hadn't known they'd grabbed Darcy until after the fact. She'd called her grandfather immediately, only to be told he couldn't take her call. Or wouldn't. Her grandmother was no help. "I love you, sweetie, but I can't help you with this one." For the first time in her life, she'd hung up on her grandmother.

When she came back, she felt helpless in the face of her friend in the dark tunnel-room in danger for something she had no part in.

Gabe was in Darcy's face. "We'll let you sit here for a while and think. Maybe you'll remember something." He turned off the glaring flashlight and followed Becca toward the light at the tunnel opening.

Becca squeezed her eyes shut and tried to contain her fury. She had been so wrong. Her grandfather hadn't put her in charge of this. He'd used her to slip in and out of the community, re-open her old house, and find people from a past life who had nothing to do with anything. Except for Nick Woodward, maybe. He was connected, but how?

Gabe took one long look at Becca before he started in on her. Probably thinking about what he was going to say to stay in Vic's good graces. "Listen, if you're going to be of no help, then you may as well go back to your pampered life as Vic's granddaughter." Gabe threw down the stub of the cigar and ground it out with his shoe.

"Did they have to take her?" She was torn between being livid at his insulting words and abashed at his leaving evidence behind in such a blatant way.

"What are you gonna do? Arrest me?" Gabe laughed in her face, the smell of his cigar smoke sickening. "The lady walked in on them searching the apartment. Didn't have any choice."

She heard footsteps coming. She looked up in time to see FBI Special Agent Frank Stafford. "You must be the famous granddaughter." He winked at her, leering as he scrutinized Becca up and down. "I've heard so much about you."

Had the world gone mad?

Becca felt sick. So this was their "inside man."

"You're a lot more attractive than what I'd expect any relation of Vic's to be." His phone sent out a soft "ding." He checked the caller ID and laughed. "Sheriff Lacey. Possible kidnapping. Wonder who they could mean?"

He jogged into the tunnel system as if he knew it well, probably looking for a better signal. The sheriff had found out Darcy was missing. Becca hadn't figured it would take long. Darcy had people. People who cared.

"You wouldn't happen to know Darcy's lock PIN, would you?" Del stood next to Clay on the sidewalk waiting for backup.

Del was about to lose his mind. Questions. All these questions. He had a few, too. "How would I? And when are we going to go down in those tunnels and search?" Del closed his eyes at the sick feeling in the pit of his stomach. He'd spent two nights watching the building, making sure nothing could happen to Darcy or her kids. The first night he'd been berated for his trouble, the second night he interrupted a sting operation, and last night? He'd slept like a baby, knowing she was with Lisa and the other ladies, and the kids were at Dad's. What made her come to the apartment alone, before going home to sleep after an all-night sleepover?

Clay's face was drawn. "We'll get there. I have a team coming. After your last excursion in the tunnels, I don't want anybody else getting shot, so we look at the evidence we have. Clay was staring at the lock screen of Darcy's iPhone. "Any ideas? If I try too many combinations, it'll lock us out."

"Can you get into it from the provider's end?"

Clay shook his head. "I'd need a warrant, and it takes too long. No judges in town on a Saturday."

"Maybe Roxy would know." Del almost didn't say it, because he didn't want to worry Roxy. Not yet, anyway.

"I'll wait until Stafford gets here before I call her. He may know some tricks I don't." For the second time, Clay punched in the agent's number only to get voice mail. "Stafford, Clay Lacey here. We have a situation at the café, possible kidnapping. Call me back ASAP." He looked back at Del. "He must still be out of range."

Deputy Ben Carson drove up in the Sheriff's Department vehicle. "Whatta we got, Sheriff?"

"Missing person."

Ben's eyes widened as he looked from Clay to Del. "No joke? Who?"

Del swallowed and spoke up. "Darcy."

He pushed his hat back unconsciously. "Good grief." He straightened his back and put his hands on his hips. "What do you want me to do, Sheriff?"

"Cordon off the area. I want to wait for FBI backup before we do any dusting for prints."

Del was impressed with Clay. He had been last year when Lisa and Nick were caught in the web of tunnels. He was a professional, and now a friend. If he would just speed this along. He wanted to be out there, looking for Darcy. Much longer and he would go back down there whether Clay approved or not.

Del heard a vehicle drive up. Maybe it was Darcy, having caught a ride with someone, and they were worried for nothing.

No such luck. It was Roxy.

Del walked toward her Ford Edge, away from the group of law-enforcement personnel.

She got out of the vehicle and met him halfway between the officers applying crime scene tape and Darcy's vehicle. "Del, what's going on?" Taking a deep breath, her voice shook. "This isn't like Darcy."

Darcy was a good mom. The best. "I know, Roxy." He looked up when Agent Stafford's SUV arrived, and the agent jogged over to the sheriff.

Roxy's attention was drawn to them, then to Del, her eyes begging him to tell her something good. "Why are Clay and the FBI here?" She swallowed. "I'm getting scared, Del."

He put his left hand on her shoulder. "Roxy, Darcy is missing." He glanced away briefly, unable to meet her eyes, knowing the last thing Roxy needed was to see tears in his eyes. The hitch in his voice was bad enough, and Roxy was pretty intuitive.

"Tell me what's going on, Del. Right now." Her voice was getting stern.

"We can't find her." He swallowed.

Her stunned demeanor tore at his heart.

She closed her eyes and seemed to come to herself. When she opened them, she faced him boldly, then at the law enforcement officials gathering next to Clay's vehicle. "What can I do to help?"

This was the Roxy he knew and loved. Suddenly, he was very proud of Dad for seeing her value.

"Can you get into Darcy's phone?"

"Her phone was here?" Her face drained of blood and the stuffing seemed to go out of her, and Del pulled her into a hug. "We'll find her, Roxy. I promise." He felt her head nodding as she pushed away after a moment of comfort.

"I know." She took a deep breath and wiped her eyes.

"Her phone was on the cabinet next to the door."

"That's where she tosses it when she comes home."

He'd seen her do it. "I know. Her purse is in the van. She told Lisa she was going straight to your house to sleep and hopefully get in an hour before the kids woke up. The question is, why did she come by the apartment instead of straight to your house?"

Roxy chewed her bottom lip in thought. "I don't know. She just said she was going to come by here for some more clothes." Looking up at Del, she tilted her head. "You said you got a strange text from her?"

He pulled out his phone and showed her. "There's the

last text we exchanged before this morning. See?" Darcy had apologized for yelling at him, and he had responded. This morning's exchange was short. A text and picture from Darcy, a response from Del, then nothing. Roxy frowned. "And you haven't deleted anything?"

"Nope." He shook his head. "I pretty much keep all my text threads."

She was a mom on a mission, and her next order was meant to be obeyed. "Get me her phone and I'll see if I can get into it. She's gotten a new phone since I knew her password. Chances are, she used the same one."

"I think I've had the same passcode for the last ten phones I've owned."

"Me, too." She slipped her arm around his waist. "Thank you, Del, for being here."

If only she knew. Thinking about it, feeling the responsibility of her faith in him, maybe she did. "There's nowhere else I could be right now."

She pressed her lips together, gathering herself. "Let's see that phone."

Darcy was so drowsy, in and out of consciousness, reality mixed with a long, disjointed dream.

Probably from the drug they'd used to knock her out. As the sounds of her surroundings grew clearer, she saw nothing but darkness. She wished, not for the first time, that she, Del, and Clay had done a little more exploring of the tunnels around the café. When they shone the light in her face earlier, she could see around the edges and knew she was underground somewhere. She could feel damp earth underneath her as she sat there on the ground—her hands and feet bound—and smell the dirt-laden moisture in the air. There were no sounds. It was what she would imagine it would be like to be buried alive. Peaceful, yet horrifying.

No, I won't think of that. Think of Ali and Benji. Think of Mom. Think of...

She refused to think of Del.

And here I am, thinking about him.

Was she just yards away from her own basement, or had they carried her, unconscious, farther into the system of caverns and tunnels?

She began going over what she knew. The pudgy man with the florid face and the putrid cigar was the only one she'd seen up close and personal. There was a woman. She'd heard her voice but hadn't recognized it. The woman was in the shadows, just out of her line of vision. There were some other men, and then there was another...

Frank Stafford. That voice she recognized. The memory made her want to be sick. She'd trusted him. He was a federal agent, after all. Then it started coming back to her in larger chunks. He'd gotten a call. From Clay. He probably thought she was still out of it when he spoke in front of her.

She shut her eyes and allowed the tears to squeeze between her aching eyelids. The FBI was the first to be contacted upon report of a kidnapping. Could they trust the FBI?

She'd left her phone in the apartment. Had Del gone there? Had anyone found it?

Oh, Del, Del...where are you?

Resolve opened her eyes. Okay, what would Mom do in this situation?

First, she'd pray.

Right. Like that's going to happen.

Her heart pounded. Memories of Sunday school,

vacation Bible school came in waves. She wondered why those particular images kept running through her mind. Some of the memories were of before Dad died. There was the Sunday she'd come forward, offering her heart and life to Jesus.

I'm just thinking of that because I found my Bible.

No, it had happened. She was still angry with God for all the trouble she'd gone through. But there was a tiny spark inside of her that knew God was there, waiting for her to invite Him back in. He was always there.

Earthly daddies may die. Your Heavenly Father never will.

Where did that come from? She shook her head furiously. Now wasn't the time to get maudlin. It was time to get her brain in gear and get herself out of this predicament.

The tape on her mouth had a loose edge from being ripped off and replaced so many times. Her captors probably thought she couldn't get out of it without her hands available, but they didn't know her. She rubbed her cheek against her aching shoulders on each side, trying to get the tape to roll, or come off. That would be optimal. She couldn't see well enough to determine what her hands and feet were bound with. Wriggling her hands, she could feel a plastic strap of some kind. She couldn't wear it down because it was so tight. Zip-ties? Probably.

A wave of tiredness came over her again after fighting against the bindings. She had to close her eyes and relax. Maybe something would come to her.

Count it all joy...

Her eyes flew open again. Joy? The snippet of a Bible verse stirred within her. From somewhere back in time, she remembered one of the older teens reciting the first chapter of the book of James in the New Testament. She'd been so impressed, she claimed that passage as her "life verse." And then life happened.

From deep inside of her, the first verses she'd memorized came to her. She'd learned it using the Living Bible translation. *Dear Brothers, is your life full of difficulties and temptations? Then be happy, for when the way is rough, your patience has a chance to grow.*

She couldn't keep struggling with her bindings. It was wearing her down and making her feel hopeless. The verse coming to mind didn't exactly comfort her. Be happy about difficulties and temptations?

What a crock.

Hard to be happy, God, when I think you've been punishing me for something I never knew I did.

23

The minutes ticked by. Darcy was in and out of consciousness and had no idea how long she'd been down there. She hadn't seen anyone since the encounter with Frank and the others who had been responsible for her being taken. She was hungry, thirsty, and more than a little bit in pain. Her shoulder felt like it had been wrenched, probably when they tied her hands behind her back while unconscious. She'd gone in and out of sleep, crying, railing against her bindings, squinting to try to see more of her surroundings, talking to God both in the positive and the negative.

She thought of the list of "blessings" Lisa had dared her to write down. It had been eye-opening. She'd done it because she'd been dared and because she liked to think of herself as a grateful person, even if it wasn't to God that she was grateful. She was grateful to her mom, to her customers, for her babies and their abundant health, and for the work she'd been able to do. Friends and family were listed, although when she thought about it, her list was rather short.

She had lots and lots of acquaintances due to her work, but her family, until Mom married Steve Reno, anyway, had been dismally small. When she came back to Clementville, she'd built a wall around herself to keep people out.

There was a vague recollection of her grandmother, Mom's mother, who'd died when she was ten years old. She'd loved her intensely and liked to think that, as the one and only grandchild, she was extra-special. Grandma would fuss at her thought process now. She'd say, "Darcy-girl, you're cuttin' off your nose to spite your face."

At the time Grandma said it, Darcy had laughed and hadn't a clue what she meant.

Well, Gran, I know what you mean, now.

All this time she'd considered herself "alone," she'd had a Heavenly Father and a multitude of people around her ready to love her and care for her. And now? Now she was truly alone, physically. If only she could get a message to someone that Frank Stafford could not be trusted.

In her mind, she called out to Del, knowing she was being foolish.

But I can pray.

And she did.

———— ⌒ ————

Sling or not, Del wasn't going to leave the scene of the kidnapping until someone told him they knew where Darcy had been taken. This was the last place there was evidence of her presence.

Clay had dusted Darcy's phone for prints before letting Roxy try to get into it. Once she had it in her hand, it had only taken minutes to get past the lock code.

"Darcy fussed when they gave her the option to use six

digits. Said it was hard enough to remember four." She tried a few combinations, and finally pressed in the numbers 9-1-17 and looked at them through tears when it opened. "The twins' birth date." She handed it to Del. "You check. My hands are shaking too badly."

He took it and looked for the familiar Messenger icon and pressed it, bringing up her text messages. The top two conversations were with himself and Roxy.

Questions about the apartment, touching base with her about keeping the kids the other night, and then, at the end, it didn't make sense. She'd sent the message he'd received this morning, to which he'd replied, "Having a party?" Then, "Darcy?" And no response. Her Missed Calls showed his calls, Roxy's, and Lisa's. No outbound calls.

Del looked around at the street. The few cars parked on Broadway were official vehicles for the most part. With the café closed, there wasn't much reason for folks to come in unless they needed something at the post office, which was only open a half day on Saturdays.

The sun had risen high. It was noon, and Darcy had officially been missing about two hours. Why were they wasting so much time? Were they waiting for Stafford to coordinate the search? He seemed to be dragging his feet.

Del was surprised that the guy who'd been trying to get Darcy's attention seemed to be stalling.

Lisa flopped down on the sofa at Dad and Roxy's house. The twins, having awakened early, had played themselves out and had crashed as soon as they'd had lunch. She'd tried to show no signs of worry or nervousness, but Ali, ever intuitive like her grandmother, she thought, kept an eye on Lisa every time she checked her phone or it made a sound. Ali was one smart little girl.

Lisa had planned a restful day of checking things off her wedding to-do list, napping, and making a few more lists. It hadn't worked out that way. Her bachelorette party seemed so long ago, considering it was just last night.

Nick came and sat next to her, dishes done.

"Thank you for cleaning up after lunch." She turned her head, then changed direction and laid it on his shoulder instead.

"Glad to help."

"Have you heard anything?" She knew Nick had talked to Del earlier.

"Not since the last time you asked." His twisted smile was worried. "God's got this."

"I know." She sighed loudly, free of preschoolers with prying eyes. "Fear is a very real thing."

"It is, but remember, 'perfect love casts out all fear'?"

"I remember."

She cut her eyes up to his, and he bent to kiss her lips tenderly, then gently pushed her head back on his shoulder as she curled up next to him. If she weren't so worried about Darcy, she could seriously enjoy a quiet afternoon snuggling with her fiancé.

If only she could get her mind to rest.

Nick suddenly spoke. "Did you hear if Agent Rossi went home from the hospital?"

"I don't think so. The last I heard, her blood pressure had bottomed out, and she was in ICU for a few days."

"I heard." He was pensive.

She looked up at him. "Why?"

He shrugged. "I don't know. It seems strange. She was there for minor smoke inhalation."

They were quiet for a few moments, each in their thoughts. Nick's hadn't moved on from Agent Rossi. "Is it me, or does it seem odd that the moment the tunnel was found at the café, and Agent Rossi was injured, our tunnel was pushed to the side?" When she smirked at his turn of phrase, he shook his head. "You know what I mean."

"I get it. I was prepared for a whole ordeal again."

Nick's phone buzzed and he sat forward, answering. "Del."

Lisa whispered, "Did they find her?" as he shook his head, put his finger to his lips, and stood up.

"I'll be there in ten minutes." He ended the call and turned to Lisa.

"They're sending teams into the tunnels to look for Darcy."

"Finally. I'll be here with the kids. What about Dad and Roxy?"

"Roxy won't leave, so she's staying there, and your dad is going with us."

Lisa got up. "Let me fix you a tumbler of water."

"Fix one for Del and your dad, too."

"Gotcha."

Nick looked in what he knew was the "junk drawer" in the Reno household. There it was. "I'm taking the extra flashlight. Don't let me forget to put it back."

"I won't." She screwed the lids on the three insulated tumblers and reached up to kiss his lips briefly. "Be careful down there, okay?"

"I will." He pulled her close for a few seconds. "I don't want a repeat of the last time I was down there."

"Exactly. And make sure Del's careful. He probably shouldn't be involved."

Nick snorted lightly. "At this point, I think it would be impossible to keep him out of it."

———— ⌒ ————

Rebecca paced the floor of her former home. The thought of Gabe Torrio being in charge of her future turned her stomach, but not as much as the fear that Darcy would be hurt, or worse. Up to now, she hadn't been involved with an operation that included kidnapping. Extortion, running numbers, a little terroristic threatening? Yes. But not kidnapping, and certainly not murder. She should probably be thankful her grandfather had kept her out of those areas. Maybe, instead, she should be thankful to her grandmother for that small blessing.

Somehow, she didn't think "thankful" was the word to use for any of this. Her grandfather had used her connection to this place to confuse her. To trick her into thinking she could be in charge of anything. Not while he was alive, and not while his minions were higher on the food chain than she.

Agent Frank Stafford. So he was the inside man. He'd come across as your normal, run-of-the-mill Boy Scout FBI agent when she'd surveilled him. His comments earlier were anything but.

Had Darcy recognized her voice? Had she been able to see her at all? Oh, she hoped against hope she had not. The tears Becca had banked for years were threatening to surface, and the last thing she needed was for Clyde to see her crying. See her weakness.

She couldn't trust anyone, could she?

Oh, Mom, why did you have to die?

Mom thought she'd gotten out of the mob life when they

left Chicago. She'd been so wrong. Looking through things in the house, Becca knew when the FBI arrested her father, they'd taken any evidence of his continued mob ties. There had to be something. Once when she went into their bedroom to put away laundry, she remembered seeing her dad crouched on the floor next to the far side of the bed, with a floorboard up. He'd shouted at her to knock when she came into his room, and she threw the clothes on the bed and ran out the door.

How old was she then? Ten? Twelve?

Old enough to know something wasn't right, and old enough to realize she couldn't trust him to do what was best for her, like other girls' fathers she knew.

She hadn't thought about that day in years. When she went to college, she tried to keep from going home on weekends and holidays and mostly succeeded. She'd talk to Mom on the phone, and they were constantly messaging back and forth. She finally gave up asking Mom why she didn't leave.

They'd talked every day. Until they didn't.

Becca had seen him slap her mother across the face so many times. The memory of it made her flinch. Why was he still alive and Mom dead?

Clyde was outside, sitting on the porch, keeping watch. She hadn't been very talkative, and when she had gone to her bedroom and closed the door upon her return, he had gone outside to give her space. There were moments when he was so kind to her. And then there were moments when she wasn't sure she could trust him. Anybody, for that matter.

While he was out would be the perfect time to see if what she remembered was right. She went into her parents' bedroom, trying not to notice the bedclothes thrown all over the place. He'd killed her here. Thank goodness they'd taken the mattress and anything with blood evidence away. But it had been there.

She crept around the foot of the bed, listening as if her father was going to come in and catch her. There was a rug askew, and she pulled it away from the edge of the bed, feeling around underneath. When she found a slightly raised section of the hardwood floor, she stopped to listen for movement outside the room. Nothing.

When she quietly scooted the bed over, wincing at a loud scraping sound on the floor, she saw what appeared to be a loose floorboard.

24

The maze of tunnels was enough to blow Nick's mind. Judging from the different methods used to clear the underground paths, it had been done over time. Over many years, in fact. What were the original tunnels for? And how did the others get dug without the people who dug them getting caught?

He shook his head. For the same reason nobody had found the tunnels. They weren't looking for them. The tunnel leading off his basement had been discovered accidentally, and now they knew of an entire system.

The search party had been broken down into three teams, three men each. He and Del had been put on Clay's team, and he was glad. He knew he could trust them. The others? Not so sure.

"Watch that section over there." Del pointed out the ledge he'd fallen off of when he'd been shot. "It doesn't look like much, but it packs a punch."

"Getting shot probably made it worse." Clay, in front, flashlight trained ahead with his service revolver.

"Possibly." Del turned to look back at Nick. "How did you guys find me so quickly?"

"You can thank Clay for that. He followed your instructions to the letter, came in quiet, and I was there to meet him and show the way." Nick didn't speak for a few seconds. "You thought it was quick? It seemed like an eternity until we got to you."

"I hear you." Del took in a deep breath, then expelled it slowly in the cool, damp corridor. "Darcy went missing this morning, and it feels like she's been gone for a week."

Clay held his hand up. "Smell that?"

Nick took a whiff. "Tobacco." He thought a moment. "Cigar smoke."

"I agree." Clay began walking, slowly and stealthily. "The smell can last a long time down here. There's no reason to broadcast our location. Watch where you step. No talking."

Nick was entering an unfamiliar section. Was this a leg of the tunnel connecting "his" tunnel to the one going toward town?

Clay looked back and spoke intensely, his voice low. "Cut your lights. Watch my beam, and be extra-careful. The fewer random beams of light, the better."

Was it even safe for him and Lisa to live in his house? Would there be a way to ensure that nobody could get into their house from the tunnels? That was a topic for another day. Today was about finding Darcy, and he prayed as he walked as stealthily as possible.

Help us find her, God. Keep her safe.

How long had she been here? After her bona fide "come to Jesus moment," she'd fallen asleep, worn out from nerves and the relief that comes from utterly trusting God. She'd thought for so long she had to be superwoman, keep her guard up, and protect herself and her babies at all cost, but that wasn't what was required of her.

In the darkness, her clenched jaw relaxed as another Bible verse, this time in Micah, came to her as soon as she thought of the phrase "what was required of her."

He has shown you, O man, what is good; And what does the Lord require of you but to do justly, to love mercy, and to walk humbly with your God?

Silent tears ran down her face, her running nose affecting her breathing with the tape across her mouth. She tried, once again, to loosen the tape.

If you're ready for me, Lord, I'm willing.

She swallowed, unsure of the truthfulness of her statement.

But please, oh please, take care of my babies.

Working the covering over her mouth, her heart leaped when she felt it give in one spot, and then another.

Please, Lord, Please...

Hearing sounds coming from somewhere, she tensed, her arms and legs nearly numb from sitting there so long. Echoes rang around her, keeping her from getting a fix on her location or anyone else's. Friend or foe? If she called out, would it be her rescuers, or would it be the people who took her?

What do I do?

If it was the man with the cigar, the woman in the shadows, or Frank Stafford, she wouldn't be any worse off. It might end more quickly for her. If it was someone else, maybe someone looking for her, it could be her only chance of being found.

She tried desperately to stand, her limbs screaming. About the time she would give up, she was able to hoist herself up, using the rough wall of the tunnel for leverage. Once she was on her feet, she scraped her face against the jagged surface, trying to remove the tape, cringing as she felt the rocks and dirt scraping the tender skin. But it worked. She'd loosened the tape to where she could call for help.

"Help me!" She shouted, repeating it several times, tensing to listen as hurried footsteps came closer.

Let it be Del. Please Lord, let it be Del.

A flashlight beam caught her face as three men walked into the cavern where she was being held. She couldn't see faces, just spots where the flashlight had blinded her temporarily. Who was it?

"Darcy?" She recognized the voice. It wasn't Del, but she'd take Deputy Ben Carson any day. "Are you all right?"

"I'm fine. You'll need a knife to get these bindings off."

"I'll take care of it." She looked behind Ben to see who she thought was one of the FBI analysts from Louisville. Behind him, she recognized a familiar face. She stilled as she saw the knife in his hand. Frank Stafford. His eyes bored into hers. Ben got up to get out of his way, and Frank knelt beside her, cutting her bindings.

She knew she'd tipped her hand. It had been his voice she'd heard in the tunnel. His face said it all. He helped her up. Shaking from more than the experience of being kidnapped, bound, and left in an underground tunnel, she reached past Frank for Ben. There was no way she was giving Frank another opportunity to threaten her. She knew that if she outed him, he would, somehow, get to the people she loved.

Ben led her out, filling her in on what had happened. The late-afternoon sunshine blinded her when she climbed out of the trap door on a hill overlooking the Ohio River.

"Where are we?" She was confused, expecting to come out at the café.

Ben scanned the area around them. "The old Woodward homestead. We think it's where the original tunnel started, going out to the river."

She'd never been here. After the excitement last summer, she had thought about asking Lisa to bring her up here to see it, but it had been forgotten.

Ben called Clay on his radio, reporting that Darcy had been found. She didn't let Frank out of her sight. There had to be a way to let the authorities know Frank Stafford was dirty.

She sat, shivering, on what had once been a front stoop in front of a house. Now the former residence was nothing more than a chimney and foundation. Frank stood a little to the side, within earshot of anything she could say, ostensibly reporting in. To whom? The man with the cigar? She startled when a blanket came around her shoulders. "Thanks, Ben." One of the analysts brought her a bottle of water and left her with the deputy.

"What can you tell us, Darcy?" Ben looked at her gently. He'd always been a sweet man. They had graduated together. Started school together.

She shook her head. "Not much. I was unconscious a lot of the time." She looked past Ben, seeing Frank walking up to them. "They just scared me, mainly." So much for a chance to warn Ben about him.

"Clay said to bring you back to the café if you feel like it. He'll have an ambulance there to check you out." He eyed her closely. "Or I can take you to the hospital if you need to go."

She gave him a sad smile. "Café sounds good."

Del would admit that he'd wanted to be the one to find Darcy, but he was more than relieved when Clay got the call. She was safe and on her way back to town.

He, Nick, and Clay made an about-face and found their way back into Nick's basement, then Clay took his vehicle while Del rode with Nick.

"Relieved?" Nick gave his friend the once-over.

"You have no idea." Del couldn't explain his feelings. Relief. Anger. Gratitude. An overwhelming desire to put whoever was behind this away for a long time. And then there was the physical pain. That would heal. Anger? The desire to take revenge on whoever was responsible? Not sure.

"Oh, I might have some idea." Nick chuckled. "You don't have the market cornered on being in love, you know."

"Who said I was in love?" Del stared at his friend. "I haven't said a word."

"Nope, you haven't said anything. I have to tell you, though, it's written all over you every time Darcy comes within range."

"So you're an expert, now?" Del shook his head and stared out the windshield.

"On love? No way. I have a feeling I'll be a lifelong learner on that one." Nick chuckled. "We're too much alike. I can read you like a book."

"Great." He hated being so transparent. First, he was predictable, now he wore his heart on his sleeve. It felt like weakness, somehow. He shifted his shoulder in the sling. "Is it me, or does something feel 'off'?"

Nick was quiet, thinking. "I didn't want to say anything, but I know what you mean. It seemed almost..."

"Too easy?" Del's voice was grim. "Yeah."

They rode in silence, passing the familiar countryside and not seeing it. Nick unconsciously lifted his hand to wave at an Amish buggy they met. Conversation was nil. Del kept replaying the day in his mind. When they stopped in front of the café, he was surprised.

"We're here." Nick sat there a minute after turning off the vehicle, waiting.

"Somebody wanted access to the café."

Nick nodded in agreement. "Apparently."

Del was trying to work it out in his head. "They tried to smoke Darcy out. All that did was bring in the cops, as it was a crime scene."

"Yeah, that kind of backfired on them."

Del thought a minute. "Maybe." He paused. "Maybe not."

"What do you mean?"

"Stafford and Rossi were both on the scene for the sting operation, right?" Del looked over at Nick. "Julia was injured, and pretty badly, it seems, since she's still in the hospital."

"Still mostly unconscious, from what I hear." Nick frowned. "What are you thinking?"

Del twisted his lips in thought, brows furrowed. "Probably the same thing you are."

"Something they want in that building. She interrupted them, and law enforcement was put to work searching the tunnels."

"Did anybody stay at the café to make sure nobody got in?" Was he reaching? He had to talk it through, and Nick and he were usually on the same wavelength. "If nobody was watching the café, it was left wide open."

"We need to talk to Clay. What about Stafford?"

Nick hesitated, and Del picked up on it. They didn't trust the man. They looked at each other grimly, and Del answered the unspoken comment.

"Me, neither."

Yep, Nick was his best brainstorming partner.

25

"It was hard to see. I was mostly in the dark or with a flashlight in my face."

Darcy was going to go crazy. Since they'd been back, except for a much-needed bathroom break, Frank Stafford had not left her side. If she'd thought about it, and had anything to write with, she'd have written a note on toilet paper, warning the authorities about him. She didn't, so it was a moot point.

She had finally warmed up, no longer in shock, but still shaky. It was May, after all, so the warm spell they'd had the last few days was welcome to her after a day in a cold, damp, underground prison.

Mom had come straight to her when they drove up, tears streaming down her face. "Oh, my baby."

"I'm fine, Mom." She cried with her as she hugged her mother as tightly as Mom hugged her. She wouldn't mind spending a long time in her mother's arms. But she wanted to see her babies. When she had thought she might never see them again, it was both devastating and enlightening. Her time alone had forced her to face her own demons. "God was there, Mom."

Both women clung to each other through a fresh spate of tears, mingled with laughter. "He sure was, baby girl."

The EMTs checked her over and told her she might have a headache for a few days from the remnants of the chemicals in her system. They cleansed and put ointment on her face where she'd scraped the tape off her mouth, and the same with her wrists and ankles where she'd been bound. Other than that, she was good to go.

Go where? Home, she hoped. She had to make sure they were safe.

Where was Del?

She'd kept watch of the comings and goings of the people around her. Sitting outside the ambulance, resting with Mom, she couldn't seem to shake Frank Stafford. He hovered. Eventually, he would have to leave her side, and she could get a message out. Even then, would she be safe? Her children? Del? She closed her eyes briefly, emotions coming and going.

When Clay's SUV and then Nick's truck arrived, she breathed a sigh of relief. Seeing Del get out of Nick's truck, she wanted to run to him, make sure he was all right, rest in him. She couldn't. Her legs wouldn't let her, plus their relationship was not at that point. There were times when she wondered if he had feelings for her, and yet she'd tried very hard to block herself from them. Maybe she'd done too good a job.

Maybe not. When he saw her, he walked quickly to where she was sitting, not taking his eyes off of her. It was as if the crowd knew they needed to "make a hole" to let him through because if it had been choreographed, it wouldn't have seemed this smooth. Or maybe it was all in her head because when she stood, their eyes meeting, the only things she could hear, other than her heart beating in her ears, were indistinct background noises.

When he got to her, she could see all his feelings written on his face. He glanced behind her. She was sure he saw Frank there because his eyes narrowed ever so slightly. She may have been the only one to notice. He opened his good arm and she went right into his embrace. It might have been more satisfying had he not been limited by his injury and the sling protecting it, but it was Del, and she was close to him.

A few minutes before, she'd thought nothing could compare with her mother's embrace. When she walked into Del's arms?

She was home.

—————⚬—————

Becca tiptoed into the living room to see if Clyde still sat on the front porch. He was there, cell phone in hand. This might be her only chance to see what was hidden under the floorboards.

She crept back into the bedroom and began taking loose boards out, revealing a deep space underneath. It wouldn't be easy to get whatever was down there. Her father had probably created it for his reach, and even with her height, her arms were shorter. Besides, she couldn't see clearly. She needed a flashlight.

There it was. A flashlight was tucked into the nightstand next to where she knelt. Of course, the batteries were dead and corroded. She closed her eyes to think. Cell phone. She felt in her back jeans pocket and pulled out her phone and found the flashlight app.

Shining the light into the cache, the only thing the light caught even slightly was the burnished metallic handle of a box. It was dull, and unless you were looking for it, you might not find it. She listened for any movement, and, hearing none, she lay flat on her stomach to reach down to bring up the box. It was heavier than she thought, but she was up to it. She pulled it up, careful not to bang it against the sides of the opening. As she set it down and began putting the boards back into place, she heard the front door open.

"Becca?"

Clyde was looking for her.

She carefully put the box under the bed, wincing when she hit the rail of the bed with the metal handle. Did he hear that? When she was satisfied he hadn't, she quietly slipped into the bathroom next door. She ran water and sniffed loudly. Maybe if he thought she'd been crying, he would leave her alone. "Be out in a minute."

"Gabe called."

That obnoxious, evil little man. He scared her. Even more, he disgusted her.

She took the opportunity to wash her hands. There was rust on them from the box. She had been crying, so her eyes were slightly puffy, mitigated by holding a cold washcloth to her face. The action also gave her a boost of energy.

"What did he say?" She walked out and faced him, hands on her hips.

"The woman's been found, so she's okay."

"How?" She narrowed her eyes slightly. Would Clyde be honest with her?

He shifted his jaw and looked out the window. As if he couldn't meet her eyes. "Stafford."

A feeling of utter dread wafted through her. To get the authorities out of the way of the café, they'd taken Darcy and threatened to kill her, her kids. For an antique safe with documents that would threaten her grandfather's organization.

She and Clyde stood there, looking at one another. How she wished she could trust him. Tell him about the hiding place in the bedroom. Of course, she wasn't sure what it was.

Hesitating, she bit her lips, mashing them between her teeth. "What about the safe in the café?"

"Gerry found it while everyone was out searching. Files connecting Vic with crimes dating back to the sixties." He smiled, seeming to be proud of their little ruse.

"So that's the only reason she was taken? To pull the cops away from the crime scene?"

Clyde shook his head. "No, she got in the way, caught them searching the apartment." He frowned, then looked at her curiously. "I thought you'd be happy this was almost over."

"We're not clear yet." She looked around the room where she'd spent her formative years. She'd been forced to leave. Forced to live a lie. Forced to obey a grandfather who only cared about what she could do for him. If she'd been killed along with her mother, would he have even cared? And if he'd told Grandma not to care, would she have given her another thought?

Becca walked away from Clyde to the picture window overlooking a field with a pond and a small stable behind it. She covered her face with her hands and raked her fingers through her long, black tresses, digging her nails into her scalp. Part of her wanted to get caught. Wanted to bring down the operation. No, bring down the "family" she was a part of.

An unexpected, unexplained calm came over her. She'd keep it together until she saw what was in the box. She had a fleeting thought of the drawer where she'd found the useless flashlight. Her mother's Bible was in there. Did it have a word for her, as it had for her mother? Her soul felt a little lighter. Is this how it feels when you think you're going to die or want to die?

"Would you believe Mama loved it here?" She looked over her shoulder at Clyde, who stood there with his hands in his pockets. "She would sit on the porch during a rainstorm and be happy as a clam." Her southern accent was showing. She didn't care anymore. "She learned to plant a garden, cook southern, you know." She shook her head in disgust. "It wasn't enough for Daddy, though. It never tasted the same as his mama's cooking." She shrugged. "I didn't know his family. They were dead and gone by the time my parents lived here."

Clyde walked over and stood next to her, looking out the window. "I can see why she would like it here. It's beautiful. No people around. Peaceful."

"As long as Daddy wasn't here. When he came home, it was anything but." She took a deep breath and glanced at him. She felt detached as if she weren't a part of this life she'd come to hate so deeply. "I'd like to see it peaceful again."

"Maybe someday you will."

He turned to face her, then stared at her a moment. He put his hands on her arms and squeezed slightly. "Becca." His eyes narrowed on her, his face carved granite. "You need to get out. Now. Before something happens that you won't survive."

―――――∽―――――

Del had her in his arms. Well...*arm*. The sling couldn't be gone soon enough. It was distracting, and he wanted to focus on one thing. Darcy. He felt her begin to move, and he knew he had to let go. He didn't want to. He could easily have lost her today, and he didn't want to ever let her out of his sight again. He gave her an extra squeeze that she returned, then pushed away, looking at her closely.

He gently touched the bandage on her face, wanting to kill whoever dared touch her. "Who did this?" He was going to get to the bottom of this. "Did they hurt you?"

She shook her head, her eyes filling with tears. "No. They scared me, and they threatened me and everyone I love, but they didn't hurt me." Her eyes were luminous as she looked up at him and whispered. "Talk later?"

When he nodded, Darcy laid her forehead on Del's chest, and he pulled her to him again. It was as much as he could stand not to whisk her away there and then. Her breath was soft. Wait. Was she whispering?

He put his head down, ostensibly to be closer to her, maybe to kiss her—which he put in the back of his mind for another time—but hopefully to hear her.

"It was him." She was trembling all over, looking at him with resolve.

As he suspected, she was cutting her eyes toward Frank Stafford.

"Darcy, we need to debrief you. We can sit in the café." Stafford had been directly behind her and stepped up to put a hand on her arm.

Del noticed Darcy flinch when Stafford touched her. When she looked at the agent, then back at him, there was fear in her eyes.

"Does this have to be done now?" He needed to get her alone. Besides, she was in no shape to be under scrutiny. "She'd probably like a shower and a change of clothes."

"Sorry, we've found if we don't question victims immediately, they tend to forget little details that could help us catch their kidnappers. I'm sure you understand." It was a statement, not a question. And as far as Del was concerned, a crock. For a guy who for the last few weeks seemed to be wooing her, Stafford was stone-cold now.

Del clenched his jaw and then turned to Darcy. "You'll be okay." He reassured her as much as possible.

"Go with me?" Both her voice and her eyes begged him, and there was no way he could say no.

"If it's okay with Agent Stafford." Del looked at him, daring him to refuse.

Stafford paused, looking at Darcy with narrowed eyes, then at Del. "Sure. Whatever makes you comfortable."

Del couldn't figure out who Stafford was trying to intimidate, Darcy or him. It was for sure he hadn't let Darcy out of his sight since he had been here, and, he thought, not for reasons of protection or comfort. The agent was afraid of what Darcy would say. Had he threatened her? Anger welled up in Del, but he kept it under wraps. Anyone who was vile enough to threaten a young mother was dangerous enough to kill.

At this point, Darcy's safety was Del's main objective.

26

Becca looked up, startled. "Clyde? What do you mean?" He'd told her to get out. Why would a trusted foot soldier of her grandfather's criminal organization advise her to get out? She'd felt they were getting closer, but this? This was insanity.

"You can turn state's evidence and be free of all this." Clyde put his hands back in his pockets and looked away.

She stared. "The only way I can get out is to die. I know that now." The resignation in her voice caught his attention.

He wheeled around and shook his head furiously, walking back to face her. With his hands on both her arms, he shook her. "You. Don't. Get. It." His frustration was growing, she could tell. He paced the floor, hands on his hips. "I won't see you die."

"Then maybe you should explain." A strange calmness came over her. Suddenly, she felt she didn't have anything to fear from Clyde, and she wasn't sure why. Was she being protected? Clyde was her bodyguard, but who was protecting her from Clyde?

"Sit down."

"I'd rather stand if it's all the same to you." She crossed her arms and stared at him.

"Sit down." He growled at her, and she obeyed, feeling the upholstered chair behind her legs. He was serious.

"All right, I'm sitting." She held out a hand. "Now tell me."

He pulled a dining chair in front of her, leaning forward, giving her nothing to look at but his face. "I've been with you for a long time."

Becca thought about the first time she met Clyde. She cracked a smile. Once she'd gotten over Del, nineteen-year-old Becca thought Clyde was so good-looking. Twenty-seven-year-old Becca did, too. "Eight years."

He nodded, and took her hands, looking down.

"Sorry, I didn't mean to distract you."

He faced her, shaking his head. "You've been distracting me for a long time, even before I met you."

Now she was confused. Had her grandfather told him about her, even before she'd arrived in Chicago? "I don't understand."

"I know."

"Clyde, you're scaring me."

"I'm sorry. I wish it were different." He pulled her hands up and kissed them softly. "I really do."

"What's going on? Why are you doing this?"

"Because the people I work for want me to pull you out of your grandfather's organization and use you to bring it down."

Her eyes flew open. "You're kidding me?"

He shook his head.

"Are you with another organization?" There were always turf wars, and she knew of other, smaller organizations that had their eyes on her elderly grandfather's assets, and she was one of them. But if that were the case, how had he been a part of Grandpa's organization for so long? "Are you a mole?"

One side of his mouth curved up in a half-smile. "You might say that."

She stood up and began pacing the same trail he'd walked a few minutes earlier. When she looked back, he was checking his watch. He was the only guy she knew that still wore a watch.

"Who do you work for?"

He took a deep breath and peered up at her through thick lashes. "FBI."

"You're a Fed? Seriously?" Becca couldn't have been more surprised if he'd said he had two heads. Which, it would seem, he did. Bodyguard Clyde and Federal Agent Clyde. Which one was she attracted to? Was he a criminal, or was he a hero, and could she trust either?

"Seriously."

She sat back down, her legs betraying her. "So, when you said I could turn state's evidence on Vic, you were speaking in an official capacity?"

"Yes and no."

"I don't follow." She narrowed her eyes. "How do I know I can trust you?"

"I'm still the same person you've trusted for eight years."

"You said you'd known me longer than eight years."

"I infiltrated your grandfather's operation about ten years ago." He shrugged.

Amazing. Ten years of being someone he wasn't. In her life, people who spent that long doing something eventually became what they were doing. "You've been undercover for ten years? What about your family? Do they know?"

"It worked out okay. I wasn't married, didn't have any family."

"Jason Bourne, huh?" Her gaze was focused on him.

He sighed. "Something like that, but without the amnesia. I gained favor with your grandfather, doing small jobs for him...and I'd done enough research to know about you. What you were doing, where you were, seeing pictures of you in the house."

Her mother had mailed them the graduation picture on her grandfather's desk, even though she never met her grandparents until after her mother's death. Mom had tried so hard to protect her from her family, and as a child, she'd begged to meet them.

He'd noticed her? "What's your name?"

"I can't tell you that. Not yet."

"Did you ever kill anyone?" She'd wondered.

Clyde stared her down. "No. Your grandfather thought I did, but I was able to cover up several operations that appeared successful, but in reality, added fuel to the fire we wanted to use to bring down the operation."

She liked knowing his hands were clean in that respect. "How do you spend ten years with the mob and not become tainted by them?" She had to ask, but she couldn't look into his eyes while she did it, so she looked down at her hands, then up at him through a curtain of dark hair when he answered.

"Same way you have."

She twisted her lips. "You had a good mama?"

He smiled proudly. "I did."

"How do you know I won't tell my grandfather all this?" She stilled, waiting for his answer.

"I know because I know you better than your grandfather does."

He seemed so sure. Was that wise? "That's probably true. But still, what about 'blood's thicker than water'? Maybe I want to inherit the business?"

He contemplated her, and she felt as if he were looking straight into her soul. "Somehow, I don't think so. I want to help you, Becca."

"Witness protection?"

"Definitely."

"If I do that, I may never see you again." Her voice shook a little. Unacceptable. In her circles, if you go into witness protection, you put a target on your back.

"Maybe not." He clenched his teeth, the muscles in his jaw tightening. "Once you've testified, it may be safe to live in the open. If not, I'll go with you and protect you."

The possibilities before her were overwhelming. She'd resigned herself to either going along with her grandfather and his cronies or dying. Her preference, oddly enough, was to die. The idea of marriage and children wasn't in her plan. She knew she didn't want to continue the lineage of the crimes her mother, father, and grandfather—and who knew how far back—had been involved in. So far, she'd not met anyone she was related to with clean hands.

"You'd do that? Leave the FBI to protect me?"

"In a heartbeat."

Darcy sat at one of the tables in the dining room of the café with Del next to her and Frank across the table. If Del weren't there, she'd be afraid for her life—and his. Was she being wise, involving him? She wasn't sure. God had put Del in her life for a reason. It wasn't only a physical attraction. She looked up to him in a way she'd never considered before.

After so many years of going it alone, even while she was married to Justin, she was tired of it.

Honestly? She was just tired.

Frank hadn't left her side since the rescue. He knew she knew he was involved. Was he giving the rest of his gang time to get out of the county? Why take her, though?

She folded her arms across her chest and leaned toward Del. She needed to feel him next to her. His warmth was addictive.

Frank pulled out his notepad and pen and began questioning her. Before she could answer the first question, his phone buzzed, and when he looked at it, he seemed confused. "I've got to take this. Excuse me."

About then, a car drove up, catching their attention. He wheeled out of the chair and into the kitchen before he said any more than "Stafford."

Del pulled her to his side with his good arm, wishing he had the use of both so he could hold her even closer.

"Del, he's in on it." She looked up at him, fear and more than a little resolve on her face. "I was terrified that if I told anyone, they would kill me, my kids...you." She shook her head, her eyes wide with residual fear. "I'm sorry to involve you in this." Tears began to leak out of her eyes no matter how hard she tried to hold them in.

"Nick and I had about figured he was involved." He leaned back to get a better look at her face. "Did he, or anyone else, hurt you in any way?"

"No, they just scared me, mainly. I wasn't sure how long it would take to be found, and then when Stafford's group found me, I knew it was a setup. They want something inside this building. They kept asking me about a safe, and I know nothing about any safe."

"He's coming back." Del looked steadily at Frank as he

sat back down. "Hope there aren't any more kinks in the investigation?"

"No, no problems. I'm being recalled to Chicago tonight." The agent seemed nervous. In a hurry. Something had changed in his demeanor.

I'll bet you are.

Darcy wanted to confront him, but this was a man who carried a gun.

He cleared his throat and began again. "Darcy, I know this has been a trying day, but is there anything else you can tell me about your kidnappers? What did they want from you, or were you simply leverage?"

Darcy stared at him long enough to make him nervous. How dare he think she would shield him from this? How dare he threaten her and her family? He dared because of the handgun tucked into his holster, and probably other lethal weapons on his person.

"They kept asking me where the safe was." She took a deep breath. "I tried to convince them I knew nothing about a safe—which I still don't." Rubbing her forehead, she continued. "I wonder if rather than wanting information from me, they were trying to distract law enforcement so they could search the building more thoroughly?"

He closed his notebook and tucked it into his inside jacket pocket. "It's possible." He answered, avoiding her eyes. "You'd make a good investigator."

"Maybe, but I'm an even better cook." She smiled sweetly as she felt Del reach for her hand underneath the table, pulling it over to him. "At this point, I hope they found what they were looking for and will leave us alone."

"Thank you, Darcy. Del." He kept looking at the clock on the wall. Was he in a hurry? "We'll be in touch with you in the next few days." He strode out of the building and into his official vehicle.

Clay came in as Frank drove away. "What did he ask you?"

Darcy looked from Frank, speeding off, to Clay, an anxious look on her face. "He's getting away."

"No, he's not." Clay laughed. "There are roadblocks on every road out of Clementville." He sobered. "The FBI stepped up to take down one of their own." He shook his head. "I didn't want to take the chance of gunfire with so many civilians around."

She had to move. As much as she wanted to stay seated next to Del, she had to do something. Anything. Finally, she got up to make a pot of coffee, only to discover the pot was full.

"Clay, he was there. He was one of the people questioning me in the tunnel." She busied herself pouring coffee. Mom had been busy while everything was going on, and, like her, she had to keep moving. "It was like he was a different person."

Clay nodded. "In a way, he was."

"I don't follow you." Del frowned. "Was Darcy in danger unnecessarily?"

Clay turned away from Del and addressed Darcy directly. "Darcy, you were in danger. You were kidnapped, and we weren't sure who it was behind it." He looked triumphant. "Until a few minutes ago."

Del tilted his head, looking at Clay. "Who drove up just now?"

"Agent Julia Rossi."

Darcy's eyes went wide. "Julia Rossi? I thought she was still in the hospital?"

"Seems she'd been dosed with sodium pentothal. The

person who did it has turned informant and is in protective custody at this moment. They were able to counteract the effects of the drug they'd given her, and when they did, she made the right contacts." Clay nodded his thanks as he accepted the steaming cup of coffee.

"But...who...?" Darcy brought two more cups over and sat back down. She was so tired, and so turned around, she couldn't verbalize. Was it really over? "So..."

"Yes, you're safe." Clay leaned forward, hands around the warm cup. "I can't tell you much, but I can assure you the people behind all this have been arrested, and those tunnels can be sealed off as soon as they get all the evidence they need to put away one of the major crime bosses in Chicago." He shook his head. "This goes way back and is far-reaching. I'm talking pre-prohibition liquor-running to the current methamphetamine operation."

"The missing bleach?" Darcy sat down, staring.

"Yes, and ether." Clay was grim. "We won't know the full story for a while."

"Sheriff?" Deputy Carson called him from the doorway.

"Yeah." Clay looked at Del and Darcy as he got up from the table. "I wanted to let you know what was happening."

"I have one question. No, make it two." Darcy looked at both men, weary to the bone. "When can I see my kids, and when can I take a shower?"

Del took a deep breath. "As soon as we can get you to Steve and Roxy's house."

She nodded, then the tears she'd been holding back while in the presence of Stafford came to the fore, and she found herself sobbing into Del's shirt. It was all too much.

The comfort she found as he held her was more than she could fathom, and yet the tears continued.

Nick watched Del. As soon as he got out the door of the cafe, the sling came off. It had to hurt, but he was sure Del was sick of not having use of his arm. Darcy had gone with Steve and Roxy to see the kids, shower, and rest, and it was starting to get dark.

"You to ride with me?" Nick had waited, watching for Del to come out with Clay and Darcy.

"No, but I probably should." He sighed, watching Steve's taillights in the distance. "Can you get me to Dad's?"

"That's where I was headed." They walked to Nick's truck, parked across the street from Del's.

"Imagine that?" Del gave him a tired grin. Not much he could hide from Del. Besides, Lisa was there.

"I got a little more info you might be interested in. I'll wait and tell everybody at the same time." Nick had started the truck and was backing out of the parking space. "Your truck will be okay here, won't it?"

"It's Clementville, Nick."

"Yeah. And today it's been full of local law enforcement, KSP, and FBI." He laughed, and Del finally joined in. It had been a long day, and it was good to hear him laugh.

"It's been different, all right." Del sat, motionless, staring out the front. "Do you think she likes me, Nick?"

A laugh bubbled up and out of Nick. He'd watched when they'd met back up with the search party after Darcy was found.

"I don't think she practically ran into your arms because she considers you a good friend." Nick shook his head and turned to look at him. "Which you are, but I think there's more to it."

"There is on my part." Del kept his eyes straight ahead.

"Ever since she moved back when the twins were babies, I've wondered what would have happened if I'd noticed her in high school, or if she'd gone to college with us. As it was, she got married." He paused. "Becca was there, and we got together."

"Hindsight is twenty-twenty, and it usually doesn't do any good to rehash old times."

"You're right, as usual." Del looked over at him.

"God had it under control. We can have faith in Him." Nick paused, wondering if he could say what he was thinking. His instinct said yes. "Losing Kristi was hard." He swallowed. As happy as he was, about to marry Lisa, it still stung when he thought about it.

"I know, bud."

"But you know what? God had more for me. He led me to Lisa, and He even solved some issues in my own family."

"How's that?"

"Ah, that's part of what I'll tell you once Darcy's cleaned up and the kids are tucked in." He looked over at Del as they pulled into the driveway and past the RenoVations small office building. He put it in Park and opened the door.

"Not even a hint?"

"Nope." He paused, waiting for Del to climb down, careful of his shoulder.

"Okay, one hint. Let's just say my family tree has a few branches on it I didn't know about."

———— ✿ ————

Del sat there, dumbfounded, his family around him in his dad's living room. Benji and Ali were safe in bed, and he sat on the love seat next to Darcy. Somehow they had ended up there after they ate the dinner of lasagna Lisa had put together while waiting for word.

Del took off his cap and threw it down on the table next to him. He leaned forward. "Let me get this straight. This 'Trip Durbin' fella is related to you, is Becca's father, and he's in prison for murdering Becca's mom?" He sat there a minute. "And it was Becca in the hospital." It wasn't a question. It was a statement. He'd felt it all along.

Nick nodded. "It was. She confessed to drugging Agent Rossi and to being a party to Darcy's kidnapping. She also said she saw you in the hospital but didn't identify herself, and she was in the tunnel when Darcy was being held."

Darcy was still in shock. Her hair, damp from her long, hot shower, was beginning to curl as it dried. "Becca was my best friend from elementary school on." She looked at Del, a question in her eyes until she glanced away. "Lisa said you two dated in college." It wasn't a question, but an accusation.

"Yeah." He was reticent to go into detail.

"How did I not know?" She was hurt, he could tell. "She was my friend, but once we both started college, I hardly heard from her. She'd send me a text occasionally, but after I called her and told her about Justin, I don't think I ever heard from her again." She paused, looking down at her hands.

Roxy frowned. "Darcy, I think Lydia's—Becca's mom's—murder happened right after you and Justin married. You weren't here, and your mind was on everything but the folks at home. The funeral was in Chicago, where Lydia's parents lived. I remember thinking that was strange, but then they had no other family here that we knew of. She was dead, and then it was over. Very odd."

"And Becca dropped off the face of the earth." Del kept glancing at Darcy, wanting to reassure her that his relationship with Becca was firmly in the past. It was the future he was concerned with, now. She kept her eyes averted.

"How are you related to Trip Durbin?" Lisa turned in Nick's arms, looking him in the eye. "And are there any other criminals in your family I should know about?"

Nick chuckled. "Trip Durbin's mother was a cousin to my grandfather..."

"The skeleton they found in the tunnel?" Lisa was trying to get it straight.

"Yes. Her family was involved in the rum-running along the Ohio River, and Trip's dad met her on a courier trip and started working for my great-grandfather, who, in turn, worked for Vic Pennington's father. Trip grew up and began working for Vic. After a while, he got too hot up in Chicago, and Vic sent him down here. Vic's daughter was married to him, and she came with him." Nick shrugged. "I come from the fringe of a long line of gangsters and general all-purpose crooks."

"So Becca is a cousin of sorts." Del was incredulous. How much more information could there be? "And did she know?"

"I doubt it. She told Clay she didn't know any of her dad's family."

"Where is she now?" Darcy asked the question that Del had been thinking.

"At a safe house. Her bodyguard was an undercover FBI agent who infiltrated Vic's organization ten years ago. Now, with Becca's help, he's bringing it all down." Nick shook his head. "She'll be in witness protection until they get it all sorted out."

"She told the men not to hurt me." Darcy's voice shook. She was struggling with tears, Del could tell. She shook her head. "Will she serve time?"

"Hard to tell. Agent Rossi had just been briefed when

she had one of the analysts drive her out here. They're still talking about a deal. I'm sure she'll get probation at the very least."

He still had his sling off. It was sore, but he didn't care. He pulled her into his arms, wishing he had the right to keep her safe from now on. When she relaxed and put her arm around his waist, he felt hope. When Becca had disappeared, he'd been pretty torn up. He'd been infatuated with her, and she with him. They probably could've made it. But this? This was something to build on.

He whispered into her hair. "God was watching out for you." As soon as it came out of his mouth, he wondered if he'd said the wrong thing, and he wanted to take it back. Too late.

"I know." She sniffed loudly and pulled her head up to face him, smiling through her tears. "I know I've been stubborn..."

"What? You? Stubborn?" Roxy laughed, wiping the tears from her face, as well. "Sweetie, if the Lord can be patient with us, who are we to be impatient with anybody? I knew He would wiggle His way back into your heart."

"Because you prayed."

"I did." Roxy looked at her family gathered around her. "We all did."

Del wondered how hurdlers felt when they jumped over the last, most difficult obstacle on the track. He felt the tension in his forehead ease.

Probably a lot like this.

27

JUNE

Nick stood in front of the bathroom mirror at Del's house, frowning at his tie. The charcoal-gray suit fit perfectly, but that tie. It wasn't that he didn't like the vintage ties they'd found for himself and the groomsmen. It all started when he found an old tie of his dad's that Lisa decided he wanted to wear. It was a different width and material than he was used to. He couldn't seem to get it right.

Since Del's place was close to the church, they'd opted to get dressed there. Del was his best man, his cousin Jake—Melanie's husband—and Clay Lacey were the groomsmen.

"Bro, your tie is perfect."

"Doesn't it seem a little off, that way?" He pointed in the mirror to his left.

Del held up his hands. "You're asking the wrong guy. I made sure to choose a profession requiring minimal necktie wearing."

"I just want it to be perfect." Since he was marrying the

perfect girl, he wanted the day to be as near perfect as possible.

"I don't think you have to worry about that."

"I know." From time to time, his thoughts went back to his first wedding day when he married Kristi. He'd been excited, on top of the world. Today, he was all that, and more, but he was marrying Lisa, and God had given him a second chance to love someone more than himself.

His eyes met Del's in the mirror. "Do you ever wonder what our lives would have been like if I'd gotten together with Lisa first, instead of Kristi?"

"Sometimes. I'm not sure how I would have felt about it, to be truthful."

Nick could count on Del to be brutally honest. "I get it. We were young back then, weren't we?"

"Yeah. If you'd married Lisa, she wouldn't have gone to Texas. Then again, if I'd married Becca, so many things would be different.

"Wow." Nick shook his head. "Have you heard from her since they caught her grandfather?"

"I got a blank postcard, unsigned, about a week after she disappeared for the second time." He chuckled. "I wasn't sure what to make of it until I thought about it for a while. I recognized her writing, thank goodness."

"What did it say?"

"It said, 'Two ships passing in the night—again. I'll always be sorry I lost you and our mutual friend. Thank you both for showing me what happiness is.'"

"I'm assuming 'our mutual friend' is Darcy?" Nick's thoughts finally moved from himself and his past to Del and his future.

"Pretty sure." Del looked happier than he had in a long time. "Tonight, I'm going to ask her if she'll go out with me."

"Doesn't it seem weird, at thirty, to be asking a girl out on a date?" Nick chuckled. "Most guys our age are married with kids by now."

"If I play my cards right, by this time next year maybe I'll fall in that category."

"Thank goodness you'd have a head start on the 'with kids' part of the equation." Nick pointed to Del in the mirror, and they both laughed.

Mom and Dad came down the hall, Dad looking at his watch. "Boys, don't you think it's time we made our way to the church?"

Nick was finally relaxing and looking forward to what was to come. "Yeah, Dad, I think it is. I'm ready to get this show on the road."

He left the mirror and stood in front of his father, who put both hands on his shoulders. "Son, I'm proud of you." He looked away for a moment and sniffed loudly. "I wish I'd been a better father. You've turned into a good man despite me."

Nick hugged him. "The past is in the past, and all is forgiven. Time for a new start." He pulled back and shook his dad's shoulders. "Hey, you're gaining a daughter today."

"Yeah. I wish I'd taken the time to get closer to Kristi. I'll always regret that."

"I know. No regrets. Today is a fresh start. We've both got a fresh start with Lisa, and she knows Kristi will always be with us."

Mom hugged him, tears in her eyes. "Your dad's tie looks good on you."

Nick grinned at her. The tie, straight out of the 1970s, had been a challenge. "Is it straight?"

"It's perfect." She straightened it a bit, anyway, which made him laugh. "Now, we'd better get to the church so your dad can walk me down that aisle, and I can watch my handsome son and beautiful daughter-in-law get hitched." She winked at him as he laughed.

"I'm more than ready."

Nick gave himself one more check in the mirror, smoothed his unruly dark hair one last time, and when it insisted on falling back down in his face, he shrugged and left, turning off the light.

He might not be perfect, but he knew Who was, and he knew this day was going to be remembered for years to come.

"Hold still."

In the basement dressing room at the church, Darcy was helping Melanie and Mandy close the more than forty buttons up the back of Lisa's dress. It was beautiful, but didn't the designer know they made zippers?

Where did Mom go?

She'd no more than had the thought when Roxy came through the door, handing her a tiny crochet hook. "Here you go."

"Mom, what is this for?" Darcy frowned, first at the hook, and then at her mom, who chuckled. "Let me."

Darcy handed her the small hook and Mandy stepped back. Lisa strained to look over her shoulder.

"I saw this on a YouTube video." Roxy adjusted her bifocals and began. "See, you pull the elastic hook out and over the button, then unhook it and go to the next one." She glanced up at the younger women over the top of her reading glasses.

"Gotta hand it to the Internet. You can find anything and everything." Lisa, the beautiful bride, chuckled. "I'll tuck this idea away for future reference." She glanced back at Darcy.

Oh no she didn't.

She did. All Darcy could do was blush and ignore the comment. "If I ever get married again ..."

"Yadda, yadda, yadda." Mandy arched a brow at her.

"As I was saying," She put Mandy in her place with a look. "If I ever get married again, I will have a zipper."

"I wish I'd known about this when you got married the first time." Roxy was finishing up the row of buttons much quicker than three sets of hands could have. She looked at the other ladies. "She had buttons from what seemed like neck to hemline."

"You're exaggerating a bit." Darcy rolled her eyes and shook her head. "It had a low back."

"Oh yes, all right, it was from mid-back to thigh."

"I remember trying to get out of the dress later in the evening." Darcy laughed out loud when she thought about poor Justin, and his all-military, he-man thumbs trying to undo the buttons and claiming it was a conspiracy to keep a groom away from his bride. She laughed and looked down, surprised. This time, she didn't have the urge to cry when she thought about him. She had good memories.

"Poor Justin." Melanie, the only married bridesmaid, shook her head in sympathy, and they all laughed. Lisa may have turned even pinker than she had been earlier

"Girls!" Roxy was finishing up. "Don't embarrass the bride."

"Too late." Darcy giggled at her mom mischievously. "You're the most recent bride, so what are your thoughts on wedding gown buttons?"

"My suit didn't have this feature. People my age have arthritis, you know." She looked around, smirking at the laughing women. "Where'd my cane go?" She winked as she grabbed the edge of a chair to pull herself up.

Lisa twisted around to see the completely buttoned dress in the mirror. Her eyes filled with happy tears. "Thanks, ladies. I don't know what I'd do without all of you."

Darcy saw the tears in her friend and stepsister's eyes and her heart went out to her. To get married without a mom was right up there with getting married without a dad, and she knew how that felt. She stood next to her and hugged her gently. "That's what we're here for. To do all the stuff you can't do."

"Like button my own dress?" Lisa laughed, grabbing the tissue Mandy handed her. "The last thing I need is to get tears on my dress." She stood in front of the full-view mirror, fanning her face.

"They'll be there eventually."

"I wonder what Nick's doing right now?" Lisa had a dreamy, bridal look that made Darcy want to laugh.

"Probably the same as us, but in comparison, dealing with a very small number of buttons and needing no help." She shook her head. "Men, right?"

Mandy sat in one of the chairs scattered around the room and picked up her bottle of water. "I'm glad Nick asked Clay to be a groomsman. He was rather touched by the gesture."

Lisa's mouth curved into a grin. "Clay is practically part of the family by now, no thanks to me."

Mandy blushed. "Yeah." Her smile broadened. "Did I ever thank you for dumping him at the cemetery?"

"No, but you're welcome."

⟡

Lisa took a deep breath and looked into her dad's swimming eyes. "Dad, if you cry, I will lose it, big-time."

He chuckled, pulling out his handkerchief and mopping up before the big march down the aisle. "I hear ya, sweetie." He cleared his throat and held out his arm, which she took with gladness. "Mel's up, then the kids."

A sudden thought came to her. "Wait. Help me get the veil fixed."

He turned to face her, then pulled the front part from the back and helped her put it in place, as they'd practiced. Usually, it was the mom who did this, but her dad was willing to do her bidding.

"There. Looks good."

"I'm going for perfect, Dad." She twisted her lips.

"Perfect, it is." He shook his head and turned back to his place beside her, sticking his arm out once more.

Lisa looked past her matron-of-honor to Darcy, watching with her heart in her eyes for her two preschoolers who had important jobs in today's festivities, almost afraid to hope today would go as planned. When the kids got halfway up the aisle, Darcy seemed to relax.

"Look at those two. Could flower petals be any more evenly spaced? And Benji is doing great, walking in front of Ali." She marveled at her step-niece and step-nephew, Darcy's two urchins. The four-year-olds were in fine form, for now. Who knew what would happen with an extended time on the platform during the ceremony?

"Little Ali is a perfectionist, all right." He winked at Lisa. "Must take after her grandma."

She had to laugh. From humor or nervousness? She wasn't sure. When Dad married Roxy, it had been a happy day for the family in so many ways. Roxy hadn't tried to take

Mom's place, but she had filled an empty spot they hadn't realized they'd had.

"We're up." Lisa gazed at her dad, and when he turned to her, she smiled. "I feel Mom here, you know."

"I know. She wouldn't miss today for anything." He squeezed her hand, resting on his arm. "You ready?"

"I've been ready for a year, Dad." She took a deep breath, raised her eyebrows, and then focused on the head of the aisle, at Nick. She'd avoided seeing him, and he, her, but now? She was ready, and her bridegroom was waiting. "Let's go. And none of that slow walking, you hear?"

"Better be careful, Lisa-girl. You don't want to trip on that gown." He winked at her and laughed.

A giggle bubbled up. She hoped it would subside before it turned into nervous laughter. She thought about her first reacquaintance with Nick last year when she fell through the rotted porch floor as they went in to tour his house. Not her finest hour and one nobody in her family would let her forget.

She gathered her wits about her and looked up the aisle at Nick, who was smiling broadly. Was he reading her mind? Probably. He was smart like that. "I'll be careful."

Ali was in place next to her mom, and Benji next to Del. It was happening. And now. Wait a minute...did Del just wink at her bridesmaid?

'Bout time.

The music changed, and the congregation stood. If Mom had been here, her rising from her seat would have been the signal. Today, Roxy took the honor, along with her Grandmother Reno, who sat between her stepmom and Grandpa.

Lisa's heart was full, and while she'd shaken with laughter a few minutes ago, she felt the tears begin to form before she was halfway down the aisle. This was happening. She was going to be Mrs. Nicholas Grant Woodward.

———— ◦ ————

Benji and Ali had followed their instructions to the letter. They'd practiced the night before, and Del, who had cut his wedding-teeth on being a ring bearer—or "ring bear," as Benji put it, because it was more fun than a "bearer"—had tutored him until he got it right.

Ali did it right the first time, and today, watching from the front, Del was amazed at the look of intense concentration she had as she very slowly made her way down the aisle. She paused once, frowning when she noticed her flower petals were getting uneven, but she didn't come to a complete stop. She corrected and moved forward. He wanted so badly to laugh, but instead, he glanced at their mother, who seemed very relieved when they found their spots, marked with a couple of small pieces of tape on the carpet, one on the ladies' side, and one on the men's.

Del watched as his little sister came down the aisle with their dad. He felt a little misty, which was unexpected. He hadn't thought about the fact that Lisa was, seriously, marrying his best friend. His best friend would now be HER best friend, and they would be a separate entity from him and the rest of the family. They were starting their own family.

He glanced over at Darcy, who had tears poised on her lashes. The golden yellow gown, almost a duplicate of the ones worn by the other attendants, was the only one he saw, and it made him smile. She caught his eye and tilted her head slightly. She nodded as if answering an unspoken question.

Usually, at weddings, Del allowed himself to get lost in his thoughts. This time? This time he was paying attention.

Not only did he have to sign on the dotted line that he had witnessed this marriage, but he wanted to understand what was happening. The last time he'd thought seriously about marriage was nearly ten years ago, when he was dating Becca.

Now, all his focus was on Darcy. Could he possibly measure up to be the man she needed not only as a husband but as a father to her two children? He looked down at Benji and saw him push his finger up his nose and dig. Peeking at Darcy, he saw her go pale and close her eyes, so he bent slightly and put his hand firmly on the boy's little shoulder. "No picking, bud."

The little boy looked up, mid-exploration, and pulled his finger out, then wiped it on the tissue Del had retrieved from his pocket. He'd thought he might need a tissue, but he didn't think about this particular use. He wanted badly to hoist Benji up and laugh, but he didn't dare. His sister and Benji's mother were both watching.

Darcy closed her eyes in relief and mouthed a quick, "Thank you."

Benji wasn't the only one garnering attention. When the ceremony seemed to be taking a little longer than she thought it should, Ali started stretching and yawning, holding her basket up in her outstretched arms and dumping the remaining flower petals on the floor. Darcy quickly grabbed her hand and pushed her arm down, while sending her daughter a glare only a mom could give.

Del almost lost it when he saw an identical glare on young Ali's face as she looked up at her mother and then crossed her arms across her chest. Mothers and daughters, right? He winked at Darcy when he finally caught her eye, and she shook her head and smiled, appearing to relax a bit.

28

Darcy made herself relax. Kids were going to be kids, and in all probability, the crowd in the church was enjoying watching her children as much as the bride and groom. Easy for them—Benji and Ali weren't their kids.

Del being in her line of sight was a comfort. They hadn't had much time to talk since her rescue and the subsequent round-up of a methamphetamine ring.

The mystery nurse was Becca Durbin, her best friend from childhood. Darcy had known it, yet when she'd seen her in the parking lot of the hospital, she'd almost talked herself out of it being her. The eyes were wrong. She read later that brown contacts can alter a blue-eyed person's appearance tremendously. She found a letter from Becca tucked under the door of the café a few days after they'd released the building back into her "custody," telling her as much of the story as she could, legally, and thanking her for giving her good memories to look back on. She'd almost forgotten, she said, what it was like to be around people who were honest, stable, and willing to sacrifice for others.

She would treasure the letter.

But now, here they were, at the wedding of Lisa Reno and Nick Woodward. They'd been planning for this event for nearly a year, and she was so happy to be a part of it. She glanced out at the congregation and caught the eye of her friend, Ellie Rogers, from California. She and her husband had moved to Clementville three weeks ago and were already finding their place among newfound family and friends.

Why was God suddenly blessing Darcy in such big, meaningful ways? Was it because she had finally let go of her pride and let Him in? Thinking back, He had been blessing her even when she pushed Him away, while she thought she was being persecuted unmercifully because of the trials of her life. Sure, hers had been rough, but when she thought about what Jesus had done for her? It was a walk in the park. Thinking about Becca and the lifetime of horror she'd lived through, Darcy knew she'd been blessed.

Benji stood there, straight and proud, beside Del. He'd stepped forward when Del had prompted him to present the rings to the pastor. She wanted to cry. She'd known Ali would do a good job, but Benji was a wild card.

Today, "The Wild Card Award" went to Ali. It never failed that the one you thought would be unruly wasn't, and the one you counted on for being on-task was woefully not.

The rings were exchanged. Darcy couldn't see Lisa's face, but she could see Nick's as the pastor prayed over them. She saw his tears and was envious of the love for Lisa shining in them. She should have her eyes closed, but she knew if she did, her tears would come, and with them closed, they would only multiply, big-time. She glanced over at Del, who had his head bowed. As if on cue, he opened his eyes to look at her. He gave her a grin, and somehow she felt warm all over.

The pastor pronounced them man and wife and told

Nick to kiss his bride, which he did without hesitation. After the introduction of Mr. and Mrs. Nicolas Woodward, the recessional began.

Behind Lisa and Nick, Benji and Ali skipped up the aisle, Benji holding tightly to his sister's hand. Hmmm. He probably realized he was responsible for his sister. When she looked up at her partner, she startled a bit seeing Del, who was smiling from ear to ear.

He whispered in her ear. "I traded with Jake so he could walk with Mel." His smile, if possible, grew even wider. "Or maybe I just wanted to walk with you."

Darcy knew her color was high when she passed her mother and Steve—Mom laughing and shaking her head, and Steve smiling as broadly as his son. She was relieved when she saw Mandy's friend, Caryn, corralling the children. She was their favorite babysitter, outside of family.

When they found their places in the receiving line, Darcy leaned toward Del and whispered. "It was nice of you to escort your stepsister." Her smile was coy.

He shook his head. "If I never again hear anything about you being my stepsister, it won't bother me a bit."

"So you're ashamed of me?"

"Not hardly." He straightened his tie, getting ready to shake around two hundred hands. "I've already got a sister. I'd rather have a wife."

She swung around to stare at him. "Excuse me?"

He didn't look at her, but continued to laugh, speak, and shake hands with the guests as they came through. At one point, he gritted through his smile, "Darce, you're not paying attention to the guests."

She shook it off and held out her hand, knowing anything she said would be gibberish at this point. As long as she kept a smile on her face, no one knew her head was spinning. There were a few lulls as people bottlenecked at the bride and groom, making her extremely happy they'd decided to put Lisa and Nick at the beginning of the line. At least she wasn't stuck here, having to make conversation with people when her mind was anywhere but with the job at hand.

During one such lull, she turned to Del. "What did you mean?"

"About not needing another sister?"

She could tell he wanted to laugh it off, but there was a serious glint in his eyes she hadn't seen before, and she wasn't quite sure how to answer his question.

"Well, yeah." Who was she fooling?

A few stragglers, including the musicians and the pastor, came through, signaling the end of the line.

"Dance with me later, and we can talk about it."

Del looked up at the facade of the one-hundred-year-old building in downtown Marion. Fohs Hall was an auditorium built by a wealthy fluorspar miner when business was booming, and he'd gifted it to the community. It had been used as a school and a theater, and for proms, dances, and many, many wedding receptions.

Del was annoyed at himself. What was he thinking? "I'd rather have a wife."

Stupid, stupid, stupid.

Darcy wasn't ready for that, and he knew it. It wasn't his plan to rush things, but when it came out of his mouth, he realized he meant it. He one hundred percent meant it. He wanted to marry Darcy and adopt Ali and Benji for his own. He wanted them to know about Justin, their biological father. He'd died for his country, and he'd loved their mother and loved them. But Del wanted them to know the stability of having a dad that was going to be there for them. Something even Darcy had missed out on in her formative years after her dad died.

Del had it all planned out.

He stepped aside, watching as the guests arrived. Somehow Darcy had managed to become separated from him as they divided up to drive to Marion from Clementville Church. He had been pretty sure she was behind him, but when she didn't appear, he decided to go into the foyer and see if she'd somehow gotten past him.

Sure enough, there she was. The din of silverware against china from inside the reception hall was a good sign that food was being served.

Thank goodness.

He stopped just inside the doorway on one side of the foyer to gaze at her before approaching. She was standing by the wall on the other side of the room, not talking, quietly taking in the foyer full of people and smiling when she was spoken to. He leaned against the wall on the opposite side, watching her. The bridal party was waiting for the master of ceremonies to introduce the bride and groom once the guests were seated. The parents of the happy couple were already in the reception hall, and Benji and Ali were with them at the large round table with their grandmother, Roxy.

Del couldn't take his eyes off of Darcy. Finally, she glanced around and caught his gaze, then quickly looked away from him as they were instructed to get with their bridal-party partners.

Clay and Mandy, then Jake and Darcy, then he and Melanie went in before the stars of the show, Lisa and Nick. As soon as they were in and proceeding to the buffet, Del made his way to Darcy's side and stood there, looking out over the crowd. "Darcy."

"Del." Darcy was looking anywhere but at him. She was focused on the coming announcement signaling the beginning of the dancing portion of the reception

"Hungry?"

"Nope." She still maintained her stoic stance. Did he notice a slight elevation in her coloration? Yep. She was blushing. "I got the kids' plates and nibbled off theirs."

"Perks of parenthood?"

She cracked a smile and looked up at him. "One of them." Her eyes were sparkling. "You haven't eaten, have you?"

"No, not yet. I'll get to it."

"You have to be starving." Darcy laughed softly. "You're always hungry."

Applause swelled as Nick twirled Lisa onto the dance floor. All Del could think was they had to have taken dancing lessons because he hadn't seen his sister this coordinated in her life. The thought made him laugh, which seemed to break the tension.

"What's so funny?" Darcy finally looked up at him. He smiled down at her. She was nearly a full foot shorter than him, and yet, he couldn't imagine a taller woman being nearly as beautiful or desirable as Darcy.

"Wondering if Lisa took dancing lessons."

Darcy huffed, then grinned. "Maybe it just takes the right dance partner."

He considered. "Maybe."

They stood, not saying much, through the first dance, the father-daughter dance, and the mother-son dance before the dance floor was open to anyone.

When he thought surely the dance floor was fair game,

Del looked at the beautiful woman beside him and held out his hand. "Would you care to dance?"

She gazed up at him, biting her lip, which threatened to drive him out of his mind. She'd had plenty of time to think about what he'd said, and what he'd hinted at. What did she think about it? Was he the farthest thing she would consider?

"I think I'd like that, Del."

His heart pounding, he took her hand and led her to the center of the dance floor, surrounded by couples of all ages. He pulled her closer, and she didn't resist. They swayed along to the music. It was a romantic tune, and after they were already out there, close to the end of the song, the announcer mentioned it had been a couples' dance. He'd missed it the first time. Darcy had, too, because she looked up at him, surprised.

"Did you know this was the couples' dance?" She looked around them, then back at Del, suspicious.

It was all married, engaged, or at least dating couples on the dance floor. Roxy and Steve. Mel and Jake. Mandy and Clay. So. Many. Couples.

"I did not. I must have been too busy thinking about the lady I wanted to dance with. Do you mind terribly?" His eyes narrowed on her, holding her there. They slowed as the music shifted to an even more romantic tune.

She shook her head, keeping her eyes on him.

A fleeting thought came to Del that there weren't any other people there except him and Darcy. Strange. This was a wedding reception, after all. The music and the girl in his arms were all he could think of at this moment. He tucked her closer into his arms as the slow dance continued, talking not necessary.

He could have danced with her all night until he felt a tug on his pants leg. He loosened his grip on Darcy and looked down at two blond-haired kids who were looking at them strangely.

Ali, ever the spokesperson, spoke first. "Mommy, we want to dance, too."

Benji nodded. He'd go along with whatever sister wanted. Del knew how he felt. It was easier that way.

Del knelt in front of them, Darcy's hand still in his. "Tell you what. How about Benji, you dance with Mommy, and Ali, you dance with me?"

Ali jumped up and down with alacrity, and Benji threw his arms around his mom.

They parted, a longing glance between them. Del held Ali's hands and let her put her little feet on top of his. She squealed in delight, gaining the attention of the crowd. Darcy looked over at them as she danced with her handsome son.

Nick and Lisa sat at the head table after their dance, catching their breath and nibbling on their dinner. Nick had his arm along the back of his wife's chair, satisfied in the notion that he could now touch her any time he wanted, and for now, was content with stroking her exposed shoulder. She shivered occasionally, which made him extraordinarily happy.

Lisa leaned into him to whisper. "Look out there, Nick." She pointed to Del, Darcy, and Darcy's twins, Benji and Ali.

"Yeah, I've been watching." He kissed the side of her head. "I'd rather be watching my beautiful wife."

Her eyes sparkled. "Honey, you'll be watching me for the next fifty years or so. It's not often you get to be in on the beginning of a love story." She chuckled. "Well, except for your own."

He pulled her closer, looking forward to getting her

alone. They'd had so little time alone in the last weeks leading up to the wedding, and between kidnappings, intruders, and sting operations... Maybe it was a good thing they'd had lots of distractions.

He leaned in and kissed her neck, just below her ear, then whispered. "So, to the house from here?" He liked to plan ahead.

She looked into his eyes. He probably could have talked her into running out of the room right then, but he didn't. "Yes, husband. To our house."

"I'm glad we're not leaving for a couple of days." He sighed with contentment. With this lady by his side, why wouldn't he be content?

"Me, too." She looked at him with a question. "You didn't tell anybody, did you?"

He shook his head. "Just Del. I figured somebody needed to know to keep people away."

"Very true." She paused, thinking. "At least the shivaree has gone out of style."

Nick laughed. "Can you imagine being rousted out of bed on your wedding night to the whole community banging on pots and pans outside your bedroom window?"

"Which is why you don't tell people where you're honeymooning." She nodded emphatically. "Del knows I would kill him if he tried something like that."

"Noted." He watched as Del and Darcy left the hall, heading to the door. "So we can't do it to Del?"

Lisa gave him a sly smile. "I didn't say that."

29

When Darcy heard Ali's delighted squeal, she turned to see a very patient Del with Ali standing on his brand-new shoes so she could keep up with him. She had a sudden vision of the future. Del and Ali dancing the father-daughter dance at Ali's wedding. Tears blurred her vision as she looked down at Benji. They were holding hands and swaying with the music. The look of adoration she saw on the little upturned face was her undoing. Someday, she would dance the mother-son dance with him.

Someday. She was in no hurry. She wanted more time. Needed more time with her son and daughter.

Life was short.

She was tired of being alone, but she wasn't desperate for companionship. She'd resigned herself to the fact that Justin was dead. Things happen, and life goes on. She didn't have to keep herself sequestered, refusing to let anyone else in. Starting with her mom, right after her rescue from the tunnels, she'd begun breaking down walls.

Walls between herself and God, walls between herself and whatever would happen in the future.

When the song ended, they made their way back to the table she and the kids shared with Mom, Steve, and Del. The "family table." When Ali and Benji were situated with a large piece of wedding cake, Del touched her elbow. "Walk outside with me?"

"Did you eat?" She was surprised. Del was usually hard to fill up, and tonight was totally out of character for him.

He coughed quietly. "Yeah."

"When?" She shook her head and was distracted when Steve laughed out loud.

"He ate a full plate of food while you were getting the kids' wedding cake." Steve shook his head at his son. "I used to suspect he had a hollow leg."

A laugh bubbled up from inside her. She liked being a part of this family. They'd taken her in as if she'd been there from the start. Everyone but Del, that was. She thought he hadn't treated her any differently than he had before Mom and Steve married, but looking back, there was a difference she couldn't quite put her finger on.

"Well?" Del still stood there, waiting.

When her eyes met his, she remembered his question. "I'd love to take a stroll outside. It's getting warm in here."

His lips twitched and he held out his arm, which she took.

As before, walking out the door with Del, she lost track of everyone and everything around them. She felt like she was in an old movie. The heroine in a flowing gown suitable for a romantic dance sequence, and the hero in a suit and tie...and a haircut.

"You got your hair cut for the wedding." She tilted her head. "It looks so good."

"I know Nick is better-looking than me..."

"I wouldn't say that."

"Oh?" Del's half-lidded eyes did something to her when she turned on the sidewalk to face him.

"Don't get the big head." It came out much softer than she'd intended.

Del's face was, as he would put it, serious as a heart attack, which she wondered if she wasn't experiencing.

"How can I not, when I have the prettiest girl in the county standing here in front of me?"

Nervous butterflies had been fluttering inside her all day, but now? With the sun setting in the west behind the historic building, the golden glow around them feeling magical? Those butterflies were threatening, big-time, to escape into the atmosphere when she flew apart piece by piece if Del didn't do something, and quick.

———————

Del put his hands on her cheeks, feeling the soft skin beneath his fingers. How could such a contrary, bossy woman, be so tender at the same time? The thought made his heart soar. Yeah, she was bossy, and she would argue with a stump, but he could handle it. After all, he'd had his sister, Lisa, around from his first memory.

He leaned down, his eyes smiling into hers, and touched her lips with his. When her hands went instinctively to his chest, his arms drew her closer even than when they'd been dancing. That had been torture.

This? This was bliss.

She was standing on her tiptoes, he knew, and he pulled her up until he was sure her feet weren't touching the ground. After a time of exploring, giving, receiving, relaxing in one another's touch, he moved his head back but didn't let go.

Her eyes were shining, her lips were full, and he'd won the lottery and gained entrance to Heaven all at the same time. He shook his head, trying to clear the cobwebs. "I love you, you know."

Darcy stared into his eyes, searching his face, not letting go as he was afraid she would when he declared himself. Maybe it was too soon, but when she'd been taken, he knew he didn't want to waste any time. He couldn't. He watched. Watched as realization dawned on her face, as a tinge of doubt clouded her expression only to have it clear and turn into wonder.

"I should pull a Han Solo on you and say 'I know,' but I won't." Her laugh was carefree. She lifted herself even closer, if possible, to the point they were almost eye-to-eye. "I love you, too, Del."

Her voice was so soft, it was almost a whisper. Or was it the blood pounding in his ears keeping him from hearing properly? Either way, he'd heard it, and he'd seen it on her face, and he was going to do something about it.

Grabbing her lips with his, he deepened his kiss immediately, she following along without question.

Between kisses, reality began to invade. The proper order of things. "Is this where I ask you out on a date?"

"Could we count this as our first date?" Her voice was gentle as she slid down until her feet touched the ground, her hands grasping the lapels of his jacket.

"I can go along with that." He grabbed a kiss before he spoke. "Gets that whole 'first date' thing out of the way."

"Yes, and we were well-chaperoned."

Del looked around. There wasn't a soul in sight.

Everyone was still inside, dancing, visiting, and enjoying the party. "This is my kind of chaperone."

She shook her head. "You are incorrigible."

"I know, right?" Del gave a low chuckle and tilted her chin up. "Are we done with pictures?"

"I...don't know." She frowned slightly. "Why?"

"Because your beautiful up-do is fixing to come down. I'm sorry, the only good thing about a woman wearing her hair up is access to her neck and shoulders." On which he nibbled while he had a chance. "Other than that, a guy is afraid of messing it up and getting yelled at." He had to be honest.

She took her hands from his jacket and shook her head as she pulled a few pins out of the back and Del pulled a few from his viewpoint on top of her head. She started to rake her fingers through it to loosen up the hairspray holding it in place when he stopped her.

"Let me."

She pulled herself up by his shoulders to reach his lips. "Go for it, cowboy."

And he did.

It was time. Time to start her life as Mrs. Nick Woodward. She beamed as young ladies of the single persuasion gathered for the customary "tossing of the bouquet." She looked down at the small version of her bridal arrangement, then at the ladies in front of her. Where was Darcy? Mandy? She searched again. She saw Mandy, but no Darcy.

Darcy, where are you?

Darcy was standing next to Del. Was she trying to put her hair back in a bun of some sort? Lisa laughed. If what she figured had happened to Darcy's hair had happened, she didn't need a bouquet. Lisa had faith Del had this buttoned up.

She turned her back to the group, thinking about where each person was, and knowing she was a terrible pitcher. Closing her eyes, she made a few practice lifts, then let go to applause and cheers.

When she opened her eyes, they fell on Clay Lacey, and he was smiling to beat the band. She turned to see Mandy Reno, her cousin, holding up the bouquet triumphantly.

Another Reno wedding in the future?

She hugged Mandy and then turned to Nick, right behind her. "Are we ready?"

He whispered in her ear, and it tickled deliciously. "I'm more than ready."

Her pulse went up a notch, but she wouldn't leave without saying goodbye. "Daddy, thank you for giving me the happiest day of my life."

He pulled her into a bear hug. "You deserve all this and more."

When she pulled back, a tear was running down his cheek, but he was smiling. Roxy stood next to him, and Lisa hugged her tightly. "Roxy, Mom would love that you've been here for me."

"I love you, Lisa, and I'm proud to help you in any way I can."

"I love you, too." Lisa wiped the tears from her own eyes. If Mom couldn't be here, having Roxy was more than she could have hoped for. She hugged her again, trying to imagine it was her Mom hugging her.

Del walked up to her. "I'm proud of you, little sis." He pulled her into a hug. "I'll save all the paperwork for you at the office."

"I'm sure you will." She swatted his shoulder and put her hand to her mouth when she saw him wince. "Oh, Del, I'm so sorry! Was that your bad arm?"

He winked at her. "Nope. Just wanted to see you squirm."

"You are impossible."

"Isn't he, though?" Darcy pushed Del aside and enveloped Lisa in a hug. "Thank you for being such a great sister."

Lisa squeezed her. "I'm glad you're here." She smiled broadly, looking from Darcy to her brother. "Anything I should know?"

Darcy snorted. "Nothing you don't already know, by the look on your face."

Lisa laughed and looked at Darcy conspiratorially. "I'll need details when we get back from the honeymoon." She poked Del in the chest. "Don't you go getting married without me."

When Del looked down at Darcy, Lisa felt a slight shiver. Oh, they had it bad, all right. And it was so, so good.

30

SEPTEMBER

It was a whirlwind, and Becca wasn't sure if she could keep up.

She walked into the Kentucky State Penitentiary in Eddyville, Kentucky, unsure what her role was. She was there to visit Trip Durbin, her dad, for the first time since her mother had been killed. She hadn't been in Kentucky for her father's trial, and she hadn't been encouraged to communicate with him.

Becca hadn't seen her dad since she was nineteen years old. Eight years. In prison-terms, a drop in the bucket compared to the life sentence he'd been given. If she'd known what was in the box he'd protected for so long, and that she'd recently found, she might have acted differently. No "might" about it. She would have.

All the evidence checked out.

"You'll be okay." Clyde had come with her, and two Federal Marshalls had escorted them this far and would be waiting outside when the visit was over. She was still under house arrest, as much for her protection as punishment for the crimes she'd been involved in.

Clyde had been with her every step of the way. No more undercover work for him. Because of the hazardous nature of the last ten years of his service, he'd been given a year-long leave, paid, but he requested that be put on hold so he could watch after her. He'd helped her through the process of informing on her grandfather and beginning the tear-down of one of the biggest illegal drug operations in the country.

She trusted him, but part of her didn't trust that it was almost over and that she would be safe. He'd told her his legal name, but he was still Clyde to her. He told her he was used to it after ten years. For the last five months, she'd been in hiding, and it was only after her grandfather was arrested that she felt safe to come back down to Kentucky for closure.

Before she and Clyde left her former home on that terrible, amazing, wonderful day, he'd called his FBI contact, who in turn had called Agent Julia Rossi, who was being released from the hospital. Following Clyde's instructions, Julia called Stafford, telling him they had the information and he had been made. This sent him into a tailspin that led to his capture and revealed his confederates and their part in the operation. What Stafford didn't know was that before Julia called Stafford, she'd called the sheriff, who, in cooperation with FBI agents from a three-state area, cleared the area and set up roadblocks on every road out of Clementville—and there weren't many. Roads, that was.

Becca stood, waiting to be searched, more confident than she'd been in a long time. It was amazing what telling the truth did for a person. She looked up at Clyde, and he nodded, unobtrusively reaching for her hand, linking them together. A buzzer sounded, and a wall of metal bars slid open, giving them access to a dingy room with a row of cubicles. Each one had a reinforced-glass window and a telephone mirroring the one on the other side of the glass. No physical contact. For that she was glad.

She was shown to the one on the far right. There were two chairs, and the gray walls seemed to close in on her as she sat. If Clyde had not come with her, she wouldn't have had the courage to come. He ignored the other chair and decided to stand, resting his hand on her shoulder, and it calmed her.

Another heavy clank of metal and her father was sitting in a chair across from her. She wasn't sure what she'd expected. For her, eight years was a third of her life. For him? It was just a few years ago. He didn't look so much different from the man who drove her to college when she was eighteen. A little grayer, bearded now, looking as scared as she felt.

"Hi, Dad." She couldn't pull her eyes away from his.

"Hi, Becca." He looked down, breaking the gaze. "I'm glad you came to see me."

"My grandfather wouldn't let me. Until now, I didn't want to." A rush of feelings came to her. This was the man she'd been told had murdered her mother in a drunken rage.

His eyes met hers. "I didn't kill her, Becca. You've got to believe me."

The orange jumpsuit didn't do his complexion any favors. Or maybe he was pale from emotion. She figured she was too.

Becca looked at the counter in front of her, at her perfectly manicured hand. She noticed a slight roughness in one cuticle. Her mind was doing its thing—pulling her out of thoughts of trauma and into the everyday. To what she could control. All this other stuff would go away if she didn't think about it.

She pulled herself back into the present and paused,

wondering what she could say. To be honest with him would be cruel, wouldn't it? But to gloss it over would compound the hurt. Facing it was the only way out.

She looked up with hurt and more than a little resolve. "I was scared of you, Dad. When I was old enough to know it was the alcohol, I couldn't understand why Mom didn't leave you. I begged her to. She would just smile and say, 'But I love him, sweetie,' and it made me furious at her."

He closed his eyes, and she saw a tear trail down his cheek. "I will pay for it every day for the rest of my life."

Enough with the feelings. She had to regain control. "Have you talked to your lawyer lately?" She wanted to change the subject, and fast. No more emotions. Not now, anyway.

"I got a letter from him saying you were working with the FBI to bring Vic down, and that I might get out of here." He searched her face. "Is it true?"

"I don't know how long it would have taken if Vic hadn't sent me to Clementville."

"He didn't know I'd hidden evidence." He rubbed his jaw. "Clementville is a nice place. At least it was when I was a kid." He eyed her. "Our family has had its ups and downs."

"Mostly downs." She smirked a little. "We come from a long line of crooks and ne'er-do-wells, don't we, Dad?"

"Afraid so. I used to wish we'd stayed in contact with the good side of the family."

She frowned. "I understand we're related to the Woodwards?"

"Yeah. I didn't have anything to do with them when I came back to Clementville as an adult." He shrugged a little. "I tried to stay under the radar as much as possible."

"Nick Woodward owns some of the property where the

tunnel system is. I remember him from college. Didn't know he was a relative."

Dad's lip curved up on one side. "His grandfather and my mother were cousins. I guess it would make him a cousin of some sort." There was a faraway look in his eyes. "All of them worked for Zeb Woodward and my grandfather Trip. Talk about hard old men."

"You were named after your grandfather? How did I not know this?"

He shook his head sadly. "Not something I was real proud of. I guess the times made them that way." His brow wrinkled. "My grandfather's name was William Thomas Durbin III, hence 'Trip' for triple. My mother decided to name me just plain 'Trip,' rather than saddle me with a 'fourth.'"

She grinned, then the serious nature of the visit sobered her. "Why didn't you tell me about the box? I would have gone to find it earlier." The idea that they'd wasted so much time hurt. It hurt deeply.

"I couldn't." His eyes were rimmed with red as if he were close to tears. She sympathized. She was close too. "When I was arrested for the murder..." He swallowed thickly and rubbed his face with his free hand. "When I was in jail, Vic came to see me." He smiled when she looked surprised. "Yes, Vic, himself."

The surprise on her face was nothing compared to what she was feeling. For the past eight years, she'd been deceived into thinking that her father had murdered her mother in a drunken rage.

"He told me that if I didn't take the fall for the murder, he'd make sure you and anyone connected to us would die. The goons that killed her were after Vic and had enough on him to take over his empire. He wasn't worried about his daughter's death. Just himself." He looked longingly into her eyes. "I couldn't take the chance. This was a man willing to sacrifice his daughter and granddaughter for his gain."

Her mouth went dry. "What if I'd never gone back?"

He shrugged. "Then I would have spent the rest of my days in here. It's still not enough for what I put your mother through."

Becca couldn't say anything. She agreed on some level, and on another, she felt the weight of responsibility.

"I'm not the same man I was when you were still at home." He looked down. "When I walked in on them in the act of killing my wife, I begged them to kill me, too. Instead, they beat me up and left me there with the corpse of my wife and two bottles of whiskey. Enough to kill me, they thought." He shook his head. "They didn't know I had a tolerance. I drank them until I was blind, passed-out drunk, but not dead."

"That's when they found you and assumed you'd done it."

When he looked up to meet her eyes, his were clear. "Before I started the first bottle, I wrote it all down. Names, dates—everything."

"If you hadn't, I'd be in Chicago working for Vic. Or dead." She would have welcomed death rather than continue on the course she had found herself on.

"After that, I was forced into sobriety." He twisted his lips ruefully. "With the folks I'd been involved in, I knew that I had to keep my wits about me if I was going to survive. I went through detox in prison, and it wasn't pretty. At the time, I didn't care whether or not I lived or died, but I couldn't take the chance on you getting hurt. Or other people in the family who didn't have a clue they were in danger. Like I said, it's been a small price to pay."

"Dad..." Her voice cracked and Clyde's strong presence was made known by the squeeze on her shoulder.

"I was able to get in touch with the FBI through my lawyer. He found some back-channels that wouldn't get back to Vic."

"Enter Clyde?" She looked up at him. "He's protected me for eight years, Dad."

Her dad smiled. "That was the idea. I couldn't take a chance that Vic would find out, and thankfully, he didn't. He's in prison, right?" There was still fear, uncertainty, in his eyes.

"Prison nursing facility. He had a stroke about a month before his sentencing in September, but he was convicted, anyway. He'll be there for the rest of his life."

Dad closed his eyes for a moment, color coming back into his face. "That's what my lawyer said, but I wanted to hear it from you." He paused, taking it in. "What about your grandmother?"

"She'll serve some time for aiding and abetting." It hurt, knowing her sweet-tempered grandmother was so knowledgeable about her husband's activities. She'd hoped that she was oblivious, but she should have known better.

He swallowed hard. "She helped your mom and me get away from Chicago, you know."

"I didn't." Maybe she'd misjudged her.

"I was in trouble, and your mom and I begged Vic to let us leave town. He refused, said he wanted me where he could keep an eye on me. She distracted Vic until we could get out of town. Lydia missed her so much." Sadness was etched in his features. "I'm not sure what your grandmother said to him, but he left us alone for the most part."

"She's okay. I saw her a few days ago." She had promised herself that no longer would she forsake her family for a mistaken notion of superiority. God had mercy on her, so she was bound to have mercy on her grandmother, her dad, and even, to a certain extent, Vic. "You'll be out of here soon, Dad."

"I like the sound of that." He took a deep breath. "I have a lot of things to make up for, and a grown daughter to know."

The tears threatened again. "I look forward to it." She gazed up at Clyde, threading her fingers through his as they rested on her shoulder. "Clyde wants to get to know you, too."

"Does he, now?" Dad eyed the younger man with narrowed eyes. "Is he worthy of you?"

"All that and more."

Dad's face cleared, his countenance as happy as a man's could be in federal prison. "The tunnels are interesting. It wasn't all crime and violence. Some good things happened down there, too." An expression of hope came across his features. "I've had time to do some research since I've been in here."

"Good things? Like what?" This was taking a turn she hadn't expected. Her dad was interested in history?

"You've heard of the Trail of Tears?" There was a sparkle in his eyes.

"Of course I have."

"The winters were brutal, and the groups of Cherokee on their trek through there to Oklahoma late in the season would have been in trouble had they not found the natural ledges at Mantle Rock and caverns along the Ohio River." He warmed to the subject. "There were a few references of it being used in the Underground Railroad, too."

"That's amazing. I knew about Mantle Rock, but not the caverns." She looked over at Clyde, who hadn't said a word because all he could hear was her side of the conversation. Next time there wouldn't be a wall of glass.

The guard signaled her as another came up behind her dad. "Time's up."

She nodded at the guard and then gazed at Dad. "I have to go."

"I know." He paused. "Becca, thank you."

She looked at him with compassion. "I'll come back when they release you." She meant it. The bitterness of a lifetime was in the process of sliding off her shoulders.

He smiled and ducked his head. Did the light she saw in his eyes make all that had gone before worthwhile?

She'd already decided if her Heavenly Father could forgive her, she could at least try to forgive her earthly father. Becca mourned her childhood while thanking God for a future that included her dad, Trip Durbin.

31

OCTOBER

Darcy finished adding up receipts as Del went around turning off lights in the dining room, and checking to see everything was locked securely. She wrote down the last number on the deposit slip and paused to watch him for a minute, chin in hand. He'd been so adamant about making sure they were safe and secure since she and the twins moved back to the apartment.

Nick's friend, the historian from Murray State, had partnered with one of the geology professors and they'd put together a team of graduate students to explore and map the tunnel system.

The entrance from her basement was still there, but it had been locked, double-locked, and triple-locked by the time Del was finished with it. The same went for the entrance from Nick and Lisa's house.

Needless to say, she felt very safe and much loved.

She went back to her task and wasn't paying attention

when he seemed to appear at her side. "Need me to take the deposit to the bank?" Del had finished what he'd set out to do.

"No, I'll put it in the safe and take it to town tomorrow." Fortunately, they'd found the safe during the investigation, and between what was in there and what had been found in the metal box on the Durbin farm, there was enough evidence to put Vic Pennington away for longer than he was likely to live anyway. They'd had the combination changed, and now they had a secure place to put the deposits overnight without having to make the trek into Marion.

"I don't mind." He leaned his elbows on the counter, putting himself eye-to-eye with her.

"I know you don't." She looked around. Jimmy had gone, and Mom had left before the supper rush, so they were alone, except for the kids asleep upstairs. She smiled when she heard a slight snore through the monitor sitting next to her. "I'd rather take this party upstairs and relax for a little while before I kick you out."

He leaned forward and took her lips with his, obliterating the part about kicking him out. Almost—but not quite.

He stopped kissing her and whispered in her ear. "Sounds good to me."

She shook her head, smiling. She honestly didn't remember when she had ever been more content than she was right now, at this moment in her life. "Do you want to take pie upstairs with us?"

"I'm always up for pie."

She pulled two pieces of plated pecan pie from the cooler and set them on the counter. "Don't let me forget them."

Del kissed the top of her head. "If you're done, go ahead upstairs and I'll get the rest of the lights."

"Sounds wonderful."

"You're being very agreeable tonight." He gave her a roguish grin.

"And that's a problem, how?" Her teasing smile was his undoing, and she knew it. He loved to tease, and when she gave it right back? It only enticed him further.

Which may, or may not, have been her aim.

She walked up the stairs carrying the plates of pie, then set them on the coffee table before making a fresh pot of coffee. Sure, she could have poured up the leftover coffee from the kitchen downstairs, but fresh was better. She went back to retrieve the pie slices and put them in the microwave for about twenty seconds.

Darcy looked around the well-appointed apartment. Del and Nick had done a fabulous job. The electrical service had been updated so she no longer had to worry about having a hairdryer and oven going at the same time, and blowing a fuse in the ancient fuse box. The extra bathroom in her bedroom was pure luxury, and she knew for a fact they hadn't charged nearly enough for the care they'd taken to make it perfect.

She brought the warmed pie into the living room area and, after putting away a few toys, sat on the sofa, facing away from the door and toward the almost floor-to-ceiling windows that were dark, now. It was heavenly. Seeing the plush blanket next to her, she draped it around herself and snuggled in. She thought a minute, then grabbed the remote for the gas fireplace, which was nestled between the two windows. It might be her favorite feature of the new and improved suite of rooms. Sure, it was only October, and it had been up to seventy-five degrees today, but it had cooled off when the sun went down.

When Del walked in, she rested her head on the back of the sofa and looked at him, upside-down. "Fresh coffee in the kitchen."

He laughed and tweaked her nose before kissing her in her awkward position. "I'll get it."

"Pie's already in here."

She turned her gaze back to the flickering fire, content. When Del came in, he set the cups on coasters in front of them and sat next to her, pulling her legs across his lap so she'd be closer, and arranging the over-sized throw over both of them.

"Who needs pie when I have all the sweetness I can handle, right here?" He proceeded to kiss her until she'd almost forgotten about the coffee and pie in front of her.

"Del, Del, Del." She ran her fingers through his hair that hadn't been cut, she was sure, since Lisa and Nick's wedding. "You must have it bad if you'll take me over food."

"That goes without saying." He waggled his eyebrows at her. "There are all kinds of nourishment, you know."

"True." She twisted her lips, thinking. "But right now, would you please hand me my piece of pie? I've been saving up."

"I thought you'd never ask."

She laughed and untangled herself from him to get a sip of her coffee and a bite of pie. She didn't want to leave his arms, and yet, sadly, she had to in order to eat her dessert.

"This apartment turned out great." Del looked around as he ate, appraising his workmanship. "I can see why you and Roxy love it so much."

Darcy pointed at him with her fork. "Plus, there is no commute to work." She popped the bite in her mouth and closed her eyes happily. "This is good if I do say so, myself."

"You make the best pies in town."

She shrugged, forking another bite of sweet, sweet pecan pie. "I may be tied with Mom for pie-baking, but I'll take it." She smiled and took another bite.

"I think I could live here." Del spoke, his mouth full of his last bite of pie, and cut a glance at her.

"Whoa, there, mister, that's quite a topic change, don't you think?"

"I didn't mean now." He put his empty plate on the coffee table and took a swig of coffee before putting it down. He leaned back on the sofa, hands linked behind his neck, relaxing.

Darcy had stopped, mid-bite, not knowing what to say. How dare he drop a bomb like that and then simply relax?

Since Lisa and Nick's wedding in June, Darcy and Del had been inseparable, except at night and when they were working their separate jobs. She and Mom traded off doing the evening shift, keeping the twins until time to tuck them in when Darcy was in charge. As soon as Del cleaned up after his work, he pitched in at the café, and she didn't mind at all. It was hard, at first, to let him in. She still had her moments of extreme self-sufficiency, but once she let God back into her life, those times came less often. She'd learned that to experience a joyful life, she had to include her Savior and the people around her.

She placed her plate carefully on the table next to Del's. When she turned sideways to face him on the sofa, cross-legged, she simply stared at him, and he stared back.

"I love you, Darcy."

"I love you, too, Del, but weren't we going to take it slow?"

"I think we've done a pretty good job, don't you?" He reached a hand, threading his fingers through her silky hair.

She wanted desperately to simply crawl into his arms and stay. He loved her. He made it abundantly clear every time he looked at her. He loved her children. They had begun going to him as much as to her. At first, it bothered her a little.

After all, she'd been their only parent their whole lives. Another part of her watched him with Ali and Benji and marveled at his wisdom and care with her babies.

She loved him. Without question.

Consider it pure joy.

Not long after the siege of trouble that brought her back to Jesus, she'd printed James, chapter one, verses two and three onto an index card and taped it to her bathroom mirror. She'd been determined to rebuild joy in her life. With Del's help, she had.

Her life had been a series of "various trials," and her faith had been tested. Had it produced endurance? Patience? She thought a minute. She was certainly not finished learning, but yes, it had produced good things for her.

And now, what brought her joy? Her faith in God's love was first and foremost, even if it had only become real to her after the next things on her list. Without God's love, she wouldn't have joy. She would still be trying to claw her way forward, pushing everyone in her life into a corner where she could control her interaction.

Del was the very picture of patience. They'd talked about her experience losing Justin, but not just *losing* him. Being married to him. Del had told her about his infatuation with Becca in college, and it had floored her that her best friend had dated the boy Darcy had a crush on in high school. She was almost sorry she told him about her crush. He liked to hold it over her head from time to time.

She didn't mind. Much. They'd had their share of missteps, but God was there at every turn, even when she didn't see it.

"Marry me, Darce."

She'd become lost in her thoughts when his words filtered through. "What?"

He took her hands, facing her on the sofa. "Marry me."

His eyes, his words, were soft. Gentle. They comforted as much as they excited. The thought of living the rest of her life in the embrace of his love was almost more than she could bear. When she'd realized God loved her so much he'd sent his Son to die for her, it was overwhelming.

This was, too. She'd thought about it. A lot. She'd hoped that someday...

"Darcy."

"Yes, Del."

"Yes, acknowledging my presence, or yes, I'll marry you?"

"Yes, I want to marry you."

Watching the smile bloom on his face, she knew hers matched.

She put on her serious face. "I have a few ground rules, though. You're going to have to be more careful. No more broken bones, no more gunshot wounds." She went quiet for a moment. "I can't lose another husband."

He looked deep into her eyes, a muscle in his jaw twitching with desire. He nodded and gave her a salute, then narrowed his eyes at her. "Got it. And you... No more calling your customers 'Honey' or 'Sweetie.'"

She gave him a dirty look. "I don't do that anyway, on principle."

He winked at her. "I know. I had to come up with something."

She shook her head, laughing, loving him so much she could burst. "You are somethin' else, Del Reno."

Del pulled her further down with him on the sofa, brushing her hair back from her face. "I don't know about that. What I do know is I'm all yours—yours, Ali's and Benji's —and I want us to be a family. Who knows? Maybe even make it bigger?" He waggled his brows at her, but then he got serious. "And that's a promise."

Darcy gazed at him, completely aware of his closeness. "For better or worse?"

"Um-hmm," he nodded. "In joy and in sorrow."

Sorrow, she'd had. "I'll concentrate on the joy part if it's all the same to you."

"I'll be glad to help you out with that." Del gave her a tender smile and brushed her lips with his.

Her lips tingled, wanting more.

"You bring me joy by being you, my love."

THE END

<<<<>>>>

A NOTE FROM THE AUTHOR

Dear Reader,

It has been a joy to once again share a little bit of my community with you through this story.

In 1991, my husband, 2-year-old daughter, and I moved sixty miles from our hometown of Symsonia, Kentucky to Marion, Kentucky, little knowing, thirty years later, that it would be the place where we would raise our children and create a life. In 1995, we added our second daughter, and now it is home. Crittenden County has a population of 9,200, and the county seat, Marion, mentioned in the story, has a population of approximately 3,000.

I've tried to be as accurate as possible about Marion and the geography of the county. Some of the businesses (like my favorite hair salon!), in Marion are mentioned (the names were changed), as well as our community hospital, Crittenden Community Hospital. Some characters are fictionalized versions or compilations of real people that I love. When I think about the "Clementville Café," I think of "The Red Onion," a restaurant across the Ohio River in Equality, Illinois!

What is fictional, once again, is Clementville – but not completely! In the early 1800's there was a Clement family in which the patriarch dreamed of creating a town on the river called "Clementburg." Sadly, this man died in a sawmill accident, but I was inspired to create my own town of "Clementville" upon hearing the story.

The area I have placed Clementville is in the area between the Cave-In-Rock ferry landing on the Crittenden County side of Kentucky, east to Riverfront Park, which is where the old "Dam 50" was located.

I hope you've enjoyed another glimpse into my home county, and into the lives of the Reno family. Stay tuned!

Thank you for reading,
    Regina Rudd Merrick
    Psalm 37:4

ACKNOWLEDGMENTS

It's been an insane year, and I can't stop writing until I thank the people in my life that help me get this done!

First, I want to thank my husband, Todd. He's proud of me when I'm not sure of myself, and loves me even when I'm a crazy deadline-crazed woman. I have been so blessed. In this time of COVID-19, it's been a roller-coaster ride, but we've survived!

My children – Ellen, Emily and Ben – it's been an unreal year for us all, lots of ups and downs, joy and sorrow, and I need more of you! You have my heart.

To my parents and in-laws – it's been a challenging year for us all, health-wise, and quarantine-wise, but you've never stopped encouraging me. I love you.

My Mosaic family – you continue to bless me and surprise me with your love and willingness to help with advice and simple faith that I can get this done!

My writing groups – KenTen and CCPL – I love you all so much. It's been a hard year of not meeting, Zoom meeting, etc., and you're still so important to my writing life.

My community – I'm so proud to have lived in Crittenden County longer than anywhere else in my life!

And finally, to my Lord and Savior, Jesus Christ. Joy is a hard commodity to come by these days, but He's taught me that joy is a decision we make every day. We can choose to have joy, or choose to wallow. It's much easier to wallow, but oh, how much more rewarding to choose joy!

ABOUT THE AUTHOR

Regina Rudd Merrick began reading romance and thinking of book ideas as early as her teenage years when she attempted a happily-ever-after sequel to *Gone With the Wind*. That love of fiction parlayed into a career as a librarian, and ultimately as a full-time writer. She began attending local writing workshops and continued to hone her craft by writing several short and novel-length fan-fiction pieces published online, where she met other authors with a similar love for story, a Christian worldview, and happily-ever-after.

Married for 35+ years and active in their church, Regina and her husband have two beautiful grown daughters and a handsome son-in-law who share her love of music, writing, and the arts. The children have flown the coop, but Regina and her husband live in a 100-year-old house in Marion, Kentucky.

Connect with Regina at www.reginaruddmerrick.com, Facebook, Instagram, Goodreads, BookBub, and Amazon.

TITLES BY REGINA RUDD MERRICK

SOUTHERN BREEZE SERIES

Carolina Dream

Carolina Mercy

Carolina Grace

Coastal Promises

(novella collection that includes "Pawley's Aisle," a Southern
Breeze Story)

THE MOSAIC COLLECTION

Hope is Born: A Mosaic Christmas Anthology

A Star Will Rise: A Mosaic Christmas Anthology II

(Novella collections that include "RenoVating Christmas" and
"The Twelve Days of Mandy Reno," both RenoVations Stories)

RenoVations Book 1: *Heart Restoration*

RenoVations Book 2: *Rebuilding Joy*

COMING SOON

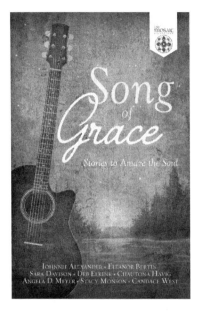

Available July 2021

How amazing is grace? Eight short stories trace the path of grace through the lines of a well-known hymn that was birthed in tragedy.

These characters each desperately seek a variety of prizes: relationships, hope, fame and fortune, security, eternal youth. All of them struggle through trials and troubles to stumble upon the same amazing answer.

THANK YOU FOR READING!

We hope you enjoyed reading *Rebuilding Joy* by Regina Rudd Merrick. If you did, please consider leaving a short review on Amazon, Goodreads, or BookBub. Positive reviews and word-of-mouth recommendations honor an author and help other readers to find quality Christian fiction to read.

Thank you so much!

If you'd like to receive information about The Mosaic Collection's new releases and writing news, please subscribe to *Grace & Glory*, Mosaic's monthly newsletter.

Made in the USA
Columbia, SC
28 May 2021